PRESS
PLAY

ALSO BY ERIC DEVINE

Dare Me
Tap Out

RUNNING PRESS TEENS

PRESS PLAY

BY ERIC DEVINE

RP|TEENS
PHILADELPHIA • LONDON

Books published by Running Press are available at special discounts for
bulk purchases in the United States by corporations, institutions, and other
organizations. For more information, please contact the Special Markets
Department at the Perseus Books Group, 2300 Chestnut Street, Suite 200,
Philadelphia, PA 19103, or call (800) 810-4145, ext. 5000, or e-mail
special.markets@perseusbooks.com.

ISBN 978-0-7624-5512-6
Library of Congress Control Number: 2014937889
E-book ISBN 978-0-7624-5553-9

9 8 7 6 5 4 3 2 1
Digit on the right indicates the number of this printing

Designed by Sarah Pierson
Edited by Lisa Cheng
Typography: Berthold City, Big Noodle Titling, Helvetica, Sabon, and Tahoma

Published by Running Press Teens
An Imprint of Running Press Book Publishers
A Member of the Perseus Books Group
2300 Chestnut Street
Philadelphia, PA 19103–4371

Visit us on the web!
www.runningpress.com/kids

*For those who believe that
change is not the only constant,
so is truth.*

CHAPTER 1

THE FOOTAGE OF ME SQUATTING is horrific. Not my form so much, but my body. It's like a baker's piping bag, overloaded with frosting and about to burst.

Quinn slides weight onto the bar. "We'll review later. Relax."

"Yeah. All right." What else can I say? Quinn's been right so far, and I don't want to screw this up.

If I can create a badass film portfolio using this transformation as a crucial element, then by this time next year, I'll be accepted into a good school, and on my way. Possibly, if all goes well, I'll be a skinny-jeans wearing beast, too.

But first, the workout.

Quinn slides the last of the weight on and then reaches to me. "Hand it over."

I give him my phone and he steadies it to record. "You ready?" he asks.

I nod and get myself under the bar. "Set up?"

"Good man. Two steps back. No more. Remember to send your butt back first."

I take a deep breath, brace my belly, and step back, one-two. This is a burnout set, max reps, and my ass already feels twitchy. I squat.

"Good, Greg. Keep that chest up."

I stand and feel all right and I'm right back into the next. Sweat's dripping and I think of it as fractions of pounds I'm shedding. I squat another handful of reps.

"Easy, Greg. That last one looked like dick."

"Your dick, maybe," I manage to say around the pressure. The bar feels wobbly, but shit, I just want to finish. I was hoping for at least twenty.

Q grabs himself and laughs.

I try to take a deep breath, but I'm tired and can't and the laugh trickles out. It feels like I'm pinned to the floor and resisting a tickle torture. "Damn." I rack the bar, slide out, and lean on it.

Quinn stops recording and slaps my back. "You needed to cut that. Your form was for shit."

I nod and sweat flies off my nose. "Felt that way."

"It's good you're feeling the difference." Q starts stripping off the weights.

I join him, but moving makes my legs feel like Jell-O.

"A little hustle, G. I need to get *my* workout in, and no one's saving me."

"That's because you like to kill yourself."

He ignores me because I'm right, and we slide the weights onto the tree stand.

"So, two weeks in, ten pounds gone. That has to make you feel good."

"It does. But the long haul, that's the hardest. I have no stamina."

I expect him to crack a joke because I realize I've left the door wide open, but he doesn't laugh, just tilts his head.

"You hear that?"

"What?"

Q raises a finger. "There it is again. Chanting?"

"Or some weird-ass music."

We look at each other and it feels as if we have the same realization simultaneously. Quinn hands over my phone and we make our way to the practice gym doors.

I grab the handle, but the giant Warrior logo on the door doesn't split in two.

Quinn tries, too. Same result. "That makes no sense. The bros are practicing now," he says.

"Unless they locked it."

Quinn looks past me. The noise from the bros has grown louder. "There's an access door for the bleacher crank through that closet."

I ask how he knows this, but Q ignores me, and in a moment,

we're passing through a supply closet and through another door that opens up beneath the bleachers.

It's dark and dusty and tough to tell which way to go. The lights are dimmed.

"This one must be perfect. In unison, you shits." Andrew Alva's voice is instantly recognizable. We move toward it, stepping over the bleachers' tracks and litter.

We emerge near the middle of the gym, thirty feet from ten guys on their knees in nothing but shorts. Another ten players stand behind them, holding their lacrosse sticks. Alva is in front of them all. He raises his hand. "Remember. Perfect."

I hit RECORD and ZOOM and can see the boys on their knees shaking. One has blood dripping down his side. Another looks like he might cry. What is this?

Alva drops his hand and the boys start chanting: *Our allegiance is to the Warriors, our bodies are weapons, ready for sacrifice. We will dominate at whatever cost to our opponent or to ourselves.*

Some of the boys stutter through the ending and Alva flexes his thick biceps and shakes his head. Then he goes still. "Not. Good. Enough."

I pan back to get the entire room.

Alva raises his hand again and the players raise their sticks. Alva drops his hand and the sticks fly, cracking into the backs of the kids in front of them. Some drop to the floor, others cry out. Some try to fight the pain.

"Get up! Get up, you stupid fucks! You want part of this team? You want to be a man? Get the fuck up!"

Alva's words frighten me, and I'm thirty feet away. I cannot imagine how those boys must feel. I look at Quinn and he's ready to run out there. But he can't. They'll kill him.

I grab his arm and he whips around. "No, Q!" I check to see if they've heard me, but they're too busy screaming and bleeding. I point at my phone and Q nods. I motion to head back, but Quinn stays rooted in his spot. We have to go. The bros on a regular basis aren't safe to be around. If we interrupt this moment, I honestly think everyone will find our bodies in the woods. And would look the other way.

Finally, Q turns and we pick our way back. Some kid's voice asks them to stop, and Alva's laughter echoes around us. I shut off my phone.

We pack our gear without speaking and head to Quinn's car. I climb into the passenger seat and Quinn gets behind the wheel. We just stare out the windshield at the Warriors' stadium, and say nothing. I shiver from the sweat now gone cold, or something else all together.

I find the thumbnail on my phone and press PLAY. Alva's screaming, the kids are being hit, and everything is so damn dark.

"The hell, man?" Q says and holds a hand to his mouth.

I hit PAUSE and stare at Alva's contorted face. The kid's an animal. Always has been. Him being captain was the most logical event that I've ever seen happen around here. Which is one of the reasons I want out of this town. But, now, I feel safe with him on my phone, because he's there, and not real in a way.

"I figured they did this kind of shit, but damn . . ."

"Yeah. We've got to let someone know."

My response wriggles though my mind, and I feel like such an asshole for it. "No."

"What do you mean, *no*?"

"Think about it. Who am I going to bring it to? Callaghan?"

"He's our principal, *first*, their coach second."

"You think that's how it works? Besides, what did we really see?"

"I don't know, but he *has* to do something, regardless of whatever *that* was. Let him make the call."

I love how naive Quinn is, and I also hate him for it. He's a good-looking guy, has an easygoing attitude, gets along with everyone, so he has no clue how the world works for the majority of us. The ugly, the nerdy, the obese. Especially the fat. We can't hide under goth makeup or just be in with the nerd herd. Nope, it's best we're by ourselves.

The amount of shit that's happened to me, that I've had to listen to and endure because principals up and down the line haven't done shit, could be its own documentary.

I look at Quinn. "In theory he has to do something. That doesn't mean he will."

Quinn squints. "What are you saying?"

"Do you trust Callaghan?"

Q scrunches his face some more. "Not really, but . . ."

"But what?"

"But with that evidence, come on, he has to."

The gym door opens and the lax bros file out, Alva taking up the rear. It's March and still cold, snow on the ground, but the boys are all wearing shorts and T-shirts. Through the zoom on my phone, trickles of blood stain their shirts and shine red. Alva barks something and the boys take off running, pounding up the hill, through the snow. He turns back, as if sensing us, but only pauses for a moment and then is on their heels. The last thing I want is for him to be on my ass. Well, any more than usual.

"You see that? They're still bleeding."

"I saw."

"And?"

The shock of that scene from the gym has worn off, and I fully understand who we're dealing with. That changes things. "Why do you care? The lax bros are assholes."

Quinn looks at me like I've just shit on his mom. "So we just let that go because they're dicks?"

"That's not what I'm saying."

"No. That's exactly what you're saying."

I take a deep breath. "Fine. I am. But it's not so simple."

"Bullshit!" Quinn shakes his head. "You don't want to help them because you're afraid of the heat."

"Maybe." I don't look at him when I answer. "Or maybe they don't deserve the help."

Quinn starts the car. "I'm going to pretend you didn't say that. We know the truth. You're scared to put your neck out there."

He's right. I am. But I have good reason. "We working out tomorrow?"

"Of course. But don't change the subject."

"I'm not. Let me get *more* of that on film. Not because I want to see them suffer, I just know one piece is never enough. But two. Maybe? Then we can take it to Callaghan, or someone else. All right?"

Quinn grunts. "I feel ya. A stronger case makes sense." He looks back at the field. "Promise you won't let them all hang just 'cause Alva's psycho and you hate everything around here."

"I promise," I mutter. "Shit, why you gotta always do the right thing?"

"Unlike you, I'm not afraid of the truth." Quinn starts the car and we roll out of the parking lot. The lax bros are running hill sprints, and their skin is already that cold color pink.

CHAPTER 2

MOM'S AT THE STOVE WHEN I COME IN, humming to herself, chicken frying in the pan. "Hey, honey, how was your day?" she asks in her singsong, teacher voice. It takes her a while to come down from her "preschool high," as my dad likes to call it, to her mother/wife self.

"Fine." I sniff the air. "Chicken and bacon?"

"The bacon's for the double-stuffed potatoes. Good nose."

I've had a good nose all my life. And a good tongue. And the combo has given me a not-so-good body. Mom still kind of thinks of me as her taste-tester for all the cookies and cakes and casserole dishes. I feel heavier as I picture the meal. All that work today with Q reduced to nothing.

I head up to my room and climb out of my sweaty clothes. Really, my more than regular sweaty clothes. I am one swampy fuck. So much so that I'll wear an undershirt under my T-shirt just so it acts like a sponge. I usually put deodorant on before I go to bed, regular roll-on shit, and then a full body spray with more roll-on in the morning. After my showers. One in the afternoon and one in the morning.

I toss my clothes in the hamper, turn on the water, and step on the scale. When Q and I started this shit I was 352. The digits pop: 337. That's a five-pound loss since the workout, which I know is mostly water weight, but still, it's moving in the right direction.

I reach in to test the water and catch myself in the mirror. I've got moobs and folds and shit sagging every which way, so I turn away and stand under the water and don't give a shit how hot it is. Maybe the scalding will shed a pound or two?

After I dry off and dress, I crack open my MacBook and log onto my iCloud account. I find the day's films and click on the first one, the hallway at school this morning:

"Hey, *check her. Over there.*"

"*Which one?*"

"*That slut with the ponytail.*"

"*Which one?*"

"*The one in the boots with that long-ass face. Watch this.*"

"*Hey, sweetie? You want to go horseback riding? Yeah? What size saddle do you wear? No, no. I meant wear. Imma ride you.*"

The kid neighs and the girl flashes red. She bolts down the hall, and the kid returns to his friend. They both crack up, can barely breathe they're laughing so hard. I think they're football players, but could be just regular douches. I file the clip in the "Everyday BS" folder. I've got a few hundred clips like that I keep meaning to do something with, but don't, because I get hung up on the ones like the next.

"Hey, Dun the Ton, how's it hanging today?"

"Hey, Todd."

My voice sounds like a girl's.

"No, for real, Moby."

"Funny."

"You should do porn with Tracey whatever. That real fat chick. I'd pay to watch that shit. Or I'd, like, dare people to eat a bunch and try not to puke when they see your bumping and grinding."

The asshole clings to me and laughs and pats my shoulder like we're good friends and then he's on his way. It's amazing he's not one of the bros. Then again, after what I saw today, maybe they handpick who they can abuse?

I file the encounter under: "Me, myself, and I." This is the kind of evidence I tried to use back in middle school but got nowhere with. There was my first film, the one about the cafeteria food and how it wasn't healthy. Principal Nelson pointed out how I ate the meals every day, sometimes two helpings. He felt

I'd "failed to present all the facts." Basically he thought I provoked kids into calling me "Dough Boy" and "Fattie Toucan" and the one name that's stuck, "Dun the Ton."

Inspiration came in the form of documentaries. I was searching for answers that relieved me of responsibility and found *Super Size Me* and *Food, Inc.* The answer was as obvious as the grease stain on my favorite shirt. It wasn't how much I was eating, but *what* I was eating that'd turned me into the largest kid in class.

I started by investigating after school, checking the trash for the boxes the food had come in. Most of it was this generic label, and the first ingredient for everything was high fructose corn syrup. I recorded this, as well as the meals that were created from that crap for an entire week. I spliced footage together from the documentaries discussing the problems with processed foods alongside what we were served. And then I made a mistake.

Interviewing should be left to the professionals. Somehow the head lunch lady agreed to meet with me—I think she thought I was creating an homage to her cooking. After we sat down, I just ripped into the details I'd found and explained what the documentaries had taught me. She started to answer, all flustered and confused, and then she realized I was recording.

I'd placed my phone off to the side, like no big deal, but she shut right up and told me to leave. Next day I'm sitting with Principal Nelson and he demands to see what I did. I said no, not because I was trying to be a piece of shit, the film just wasn't ready.

He shut his door and sat across from me and said the kind of line I've come to expect whenever dealing with administrators. "If you ever let this film see the light of day, I will make sure you regret ever coming up with the idea."

Fuck that. What was he going to do? Suspend me? That would have been a welcome vacation from all the shitheads at school. I went ahead with the film, tied it up with some vomit gifs, and created my YouTube account.

A week later, after thousands of views and a lot of questions about the school in the comments, I sat across from Nelson, with my parents this time, and that's when he suspended me for violating the school's code of conduct regarding electronic devices. My parents didn't even argue.

While I was out, he let it be known that the film was a giant lie, that I'd made up the facts because I was sick of being overweight. He asked kids to be nicer to me. When I returned, of course they did just the opposite, and that's when Nelson told me I'd brought this on myself.

He was partially right, but back then I couldn't pinpoint which part and what that meant. The picture is much clearer now.

My workout's next and the thumbnail for the incident is after. I have a folder labeled "Workouts" and put today's in with the rest. Even though I'm filming them for the documentary, Q said it's good I have them, so I can see the change and check my form. I don't think I could be tortured into watching these, though. Me on a screen just isn't pretty.

I create another folder, "Lax Bros," and move the file from the practice gym into it. I don't want to watch it again. Once is enough. But will there really be more tomorrow?

I'd put my money on it. If there's anything I'm sure of, it's that weight is hard to lose, and kids are ruthless. Especially the bros, with their tournament less than two months away. The one that turns the town into a weeklong pep rally, everyone into even more fanatical douches, and the bros into demigods. All because of the money.

Teams travel with their families from all over the state to play. They rent all the hotel rooms, eat all the restaurant food, and buy tickets, for the day or for the weekend. And then there's the merch. Shirts and bumper stickers and lanyards, even phone cases, all with the list of teams, the year, and team logos. It's all gone by the end, and we have cash coming out of our ears. At least Coach Mallory, the assistant coach, who also runs the booster club, spreads the wealth. The "Mallory Media Center," aka the tech wing, is a testament to that. Or possibly that's because of his son, Max, the war hero. Either way, after what I've seen, I don't know if it's worth the cost.

I check Facebook and Twitter. Not much is happening, but I tweet about my results for my workout today. That's something else Q told me to do. That way it's not just the two of us who know. Others can chime in. But since I don't follow kids from school, just famous filmmakers and reviewers, no one responds.

"Greg! Dinner!"

Mom's voice cuts through me. I used to love that call, but now I feel as nervous as I do walking into the locker room. Food was always my friend, until it became my enemy.

I head downstairs and Dad's home, filling drinks. "Hey, buddy. Water? Milk? What's the diet these days?"

It's an innocent question, but I feel like telling him to fuck off. "Water. Thanks."

"You got it." He fills my glass from the pitcher and sits. I follow his lead.

"So how was school?"

There's not even a moment's hesitation where I think that I could possibly talk to him about what I witnessed today. "Fine. Same old. You know?"

"Do I?" Dad rubs his eyes. "I'm telling you, there's not much difference between school and work. Sit down for eight hours and hope you don't pass out from boredom."

Which is exactly why I want to go to film school, leave this town, and never look back.

Mom walks in with the platters of food. I eye them. Dad eyes them and asks, "How was your workout today? Quinn still cracking the whip?"

I wince at his choice of words. "Yeah. I'll be sore tomorrow, that's for sure."

"Well, take a day off if you need to. How many potatoes?" Mom holds out the platter and her eyes glitter. If I were casting her in a movie, she'd always be wearing an apron.

"One's fine," I say, and sip my water.

"One? You're a growing boy. At least two." She plunks one down and spears another with her fork.

"He said one." Dad's voice is steady, but the tone is challenging.

"Frank, I heard him, but really? He's working out like a mad-man; he'll get sick."

"He won't, and you know why he's busting his ass in the gym. It's not so he can eat more of your potatoes."

Mom's face flushes red, and I see the tears beginning to well. This is how it goes.

"Excuse me for wanting to be a good mother." She sets the platter down and retreats to the kitchen.

Dad sighs. "Sorry, bud. She doesn't get it."

"I know. Thanks."

He stands and goes to her and starts his soothing talk. I stare at the potato on my plate. I could easily eat three of these. With butter. And sour cream. And bacon. And cheese. My stomach growls so hard I put my hands to it. The squish of my flab reminds me why one is enough.

I tried my first diet when I was ten. My doctor couldn't believe my BMI: 43. Now it's 50. Back then I just stared at the multicol-ored chart with Mom and was as clueless as she. Dad read the plan my pediatrician provided and set forth with it. I did well, eating shit like carrot sticks and mayo-less turkey sandwiches on multigrain bread for lunch and tiny servings of vegetables and meat for dinner. But I was always hungry. And Mom would make me rewards every Friday, chocolate chip cookies or muffins or whatever I wanted. We'd eat them together before Dad got home from work. When the diet stalled, Dad was confused. When I started gaining weight, Dad gave up on that one, but asked for another.

And so it's been on again, off again like that for the past six years. Mom ends up in tears when I won't eat, and Dad has to remind her that it's not about *her*, and I feel so damn gross and guilty. Why can't I just eat like normal people? You know, regular sizes, not second and third helpings? It's not because I hate myself, as one of the therapists I've seen suggested. I'm just hungry. Or food just tastes so good. Or something like that.

Mom returns with a tissue to her eye. "I'm sorry, sweetie. You know how it is for me. Eat whatever you like. Okay?"

I nod and shoot Dad a look. "All right. Thanks."

I eat my dinner of chicken—skinless—and potato—just one, bacon picked out—and try not to stare at the platters. When I'm finished, I want more, but just drink water. It helps, but nothing can take the place of food, not even my films.

I head back to my room, do some math, and spend the rest of my night online reading movie critique blogs and watching previews of indie films and some YouTube suggestions.

I feel like texting Q because the Internet just isn't taking my mind off this afternoon. But we don't really have that kind of relationship. I don't see much of him during the day because he's off all over the place. Even though he's in ridiculous shape, he's not a jock, doesn't play any sports. And he's not a nerd or artsy or any of that shit. He sure as hell isn't a stoner or goth or gay. He's really a drifter, just bouncing around groups. But for some reason he always connects with me. It's weird, I guess, but we've been friends forever. From before I was fat, even. And that, right there, is enough for me.

I'm sore all over and know I should stretch. But first, because I have to, because I won't be able to sleep if I don't, I pull up the scene from today. I watch it again. In slow-mo. I zoom in on the boys, trying to recognize any of them. I don't, only Alva and his little peon, Gilbey.

I lose count of how many times I watch it. Each time is as bad. In fact, I feel worse. I get Quinn's point. I bet these kids just want to play lacrosse, have fun, fit in, not get abused. But what do I know? It's not like I ever played a sport. Maybe this is just part of the deal?

Then I remember the other scene. I didn't file that. I pull it up, and the zoom on their backs is the most revealing. The blood. I let the film roll and the car is moving and the boys are sprinting. Alva is at the bottom of the hill, watching the boys run up, and that's when he looks over. But it's not toward the parking lot. No, he's looking back at the gym.

I rewind and slow it down and zoom in even more. In the doorway, standing just outside watching the lax bros, is Callaghan, our principal, their coach. Alva looks at him and Callaghan nods. Then Alva takes off up the hill.

I rewind and play again and zoom even closer. Callaghan's face is more clear, the lines deeper, more accurate. He is smiling a weird, twisted smile. Or maybe I feel that way because I never see him show his teeth.

But there's more. There was something else in the doorway. I pan down. It's white and red, and it takes me a moment to realize what I'm staring at. It's a bloody towel.

I click the scene back a notch and now the image takes on a meaningful picture. Callaghan is holding a bloody towel and smiling and nodding his approval to Alva.

He knows.

CHAPTER 3

I PACE IN THE LIVING ROOM the next morning until I see Quinn's car roll up. I yell "good-bye," to my parents and fly out the front door. Seated next to Q, I launch. "Callaghan knows. He fucking knows what the lax bros are doing."

"What the hell are you talking about? Did you have some weird-ass dream or something?" Quinn shoots me a glance but then concentrates on the road. He hasn't had his license that long, and because of his workouts he's always so damn out of it in the morning. I've suggested coffee but he told me his dad won't allow it. Not natural or some shit.

"No. I have it on film. Yesterday when we were leaving and the bros were sprinting, Callaghan was there. He had a bloody towel and was doing this whole thing with Alva. . . ."

"Slow down. What was he doing?"

"Just pull over."

Q slides against a curb and I take out my phone. I show him the recording, even though it's more difficult to see than it was on my computer. He nods after the second time. "I don't know, Dun. I mean, yeah, it's a bloody towel, but that doesn't mean anything."

"Bullshit! You know it does."

"Easy, G. Just chill for a second. Take a deep breath."

I do. Q's good, and like with our workouts, I listen.

"All right. Now I know Callaghan's an evil son of a bitch, and it would be awesome to pin all this shit on him, but that there," he says, pointing at my phone, "doesn't prove shit. That towel *could* have come from anywhere. You follow?"

"But," I say, even though I know where he's coming from.

"No. Don't. Let me finish." He waits for me to breathe again. "I know I was all about jumping the gun yesterday and you talked me out of it. Well, here we are in reverse. Like you said, one piece isn't anything. More? Hell, yeah. And I'm all for getting it. We're on the same page. But this isn't it."

He's right. I know he is. I thought the same thing while I stewed all night. In spite of how many times I failed with Principal Nelson and then again with Callaghan, this urge takes over me. This desire to share what I've found, what I captured on film. I can't help it.

"All right. I hear you. Maybe we'll catch them after school again?"

"That's the plan," Q says, but he's busy reading a text, not really paying attention.

"Who's that?" I ask, trying to remain just curious, nothing more.

Quinn smiles. "Nobody. Just this girl."

"Who?"

"You don't know her."

I sneer at him, even though he's probably right. I most likely don't know her. But still, would it kill him to pretend it's possible? "Right, right," I mumble.

Quinn signals and pulls away from the curb. I just stay quiet and stare out the window, imagining how different the picture looks through Quinn's eyes.

•   •   •

"How could you like that? It's so fucking gay."

"The book?"

"Yeah, the book. What did you think I was talking about?"

The kid doesn't answer, just stares at the book in his hand and tosses it into his locker, slamming it shut and saying, "Whatever."

"Not 'whatever.' What did you think I was talking about?"

I stop filming and move down the hall toward Mr. Blint's. I guess I like the class, the Mechanics of Film, but it's filled with a bunch of burnouts who really don't give a shit and just want an A. Blint's not one of our regular teachers. He's here through some grant or something. Him and all the awesome technology that came along with it. The one Mallory found, I guess. Which is why everything is covered with our stupid Warrior mascot: a jacked-up, comic book–like Native American. Is that even PC? But without that cash, our school would suck. Blint has the only good computer lab, and I think the other teachers envy him. He keeps a low profile, but does provide good feedback for the handful of us who truly care.

"Dun the Ton. Dun the Ton. Dun the Ton," I hear off to my side. It's a group of bros, older ones. They probably were the ones beating the underclassmen yesterday. "That's right, fat ass, keep moving." I swallow it. More fuel for my workout, for my motivation to get out, no problem.

I head to the back. Kids are talking, clustered here and there. Taleana, by far the hottest girl in here, stops midsentence when I approach, and dramatically holds her breath until I'm past.

"I cannot stand the smell of fat," she says, and her friend Gretchen laughs and laughs. More fuel.

The bell rings and Blint closes the door. He claps twice to get attention but does nothing more, even though a number of kids are still talking. "Today we are going to spend some time on trailers."

"Like mobile homes?" some girl asks.

The room laughs.

"Not quite. As in for movies."

"Previews?" someone else asks.

"Exactly!" Blint points with a touch of enthusiasm.

"Why didn't you just say that?" the first girl asks.

Blint's energy leaks out of him. "Because the technical term is *trailer*. You've had the term and its definition since the first day."

It's true. Blint gave us a long sheet of terms we're supposed to know at any time. But it's not like he quizzes us on them or anything. He just tosses them into his lectures. They're not difficult though. I read much more challenging terminology online.

"Whatever," the girl says.

Blint lets it pass and carries on. "Part of the requirement of your portfolio is a trailer. You all have the outline and due dates, so please do review them."

Blint rambles on about trailers and their purpose and how they've changed in recent years. I zone out and think about how I'm going to tell Blint that my portfolio is going to be a documentary on my weight loss. He knows all about my past film mishaps—the ones from middle and high school—even uses them in other classes as examples. So I'm not sure how he'll respond to what I have in mind. Because it's not as if getting into trouble with Principal Nelson or Callaghan has slowed me down.

I've slipped some of my hallway footage onto the school's website, once hijacked another kid's presentation by changing the link in his PowerPoint to a video from my YouTube channel, and even slipped a looped clip of the cheerleaders puking in unison after a party onto the squad's Facebook page. I pulled that last clip from Twitter, so it's not as if I broke anyone's privacy.

Finally he shuts up and passes out a worksheet to guide us through note-taking while we watch the three trailers he has cued up. We take notes and then form a giant circle to discuss. This and lectures are basically all the "teaching" we can expect from Blint. I don't mind the lectures, but I hate the circle because I'm so exposed.

"So let's discuss." Blint perches on a stool just outside the circle.

No one says a word. Some kids text. Those with their backs to Blint close their eyes. Most don't have anything written down on the handouts.

Blint taps a pen on his clipboard. "Adriana, your thoughts?"

Adriana Jones always acts surprised when Blint calls on her, which he does every single class. She's a cheerleader, super popular and pretty damn smart, but in that teacher's pet way, just regurgitating whatever has been said or the teacher wants to hear. I doubt she's recently had a unique thought.

She spits her ideas and, again, I zone out.

Blint thanks her and calls on a few more pets and looks at the clock. He's about to tell us to "pack it up," but Ella Jenner speaks up.

"You know, Mr. Blint, I've been sitting here thinking about trailers and, well, they're a bunch of bullshit."

The room gasps. The stoners wake up. Texting halts, and even Taleana sits up.

Ella Jenner. Transferred here at the end of eighth grade. I don't know much about her except that she's quirky, just doing her own thing. I never see her hanging with any clique, but what do I know? She could be übercool, more awesome than any of us. Or just on the fringe.

"Let's refrain from such language, please." Blint ruffles a bit but that's all.

"Sorry." Ella just stares at her desk. "Here's the thing. Trailers are like candy. They're all exciting and interesting but ultimately empty."

I take note. She's just combined my two favorite subjects, candy and film. Ella's done this a few times now, been so spot on I feel as if I could talk to her because she'd actually know what the hell I'm talking about. But there's more to talking than just exchanging words, and that makes me nervous.

"How so?" Blint asks.

Ella is now thrumming her leg and picking at her nail. "There's no context. Really, we have no idea where these one liners or bits of action are coming from. It's complete shi . . . I mean ridiculousness. I could take the worst movie imaginable and find thirty seconds of good material and make you think it's awesome. It's lying. That's all trailers do."

Blint nods and we all follow him. "Are you suggesting there should be no trailers?"

"No, just ones that are honest and genuine. That's all I want."

The room's attention tracks between these two and then Blint says, "Well, let us apply what Ella has said to *your* trailers. Don't fake out the audience; be straightforward."

I can't help but stare at Ella. She catches me and I turn away. When I peek back, she's still watching, and I'm afraid of what she's thinking.

The bell rings and I head to lunch. It is my least favorite part of school next to PE. Fat kids can't eat. At least we're not supposed to. It's perfectly fine for the stocky football or lacrosse player or freakishly tall basketball player to gorge on three lunches, but heaven forbid if a fat kid has a cookie. The insults. I stopped filming those. It's enough to live them once; I don't need to see them a second time.

I get in line and my phone buzzes with a text. I know it's Quinn, he's the only friend I have.

> Get the chicken salad. Ask for the dressing
> on the side. Water and an apple.
>
> K.

I follow his instructions and scurry to my table. Too much time out in the open is no good.

I sit alone because Quinn's . . . somewhere. Freshman year, a couple of guys sat with me for about a week. We talked and shit and I thought I'd made some friends, but then one by one they drifted to other tables. I came up with reasons for why it was okay that I ate alone: *I had time to study. I didn't really need company. Other people sat alone.*

I bite into my salad and drink my water and pray for the half hour to be over.

"Hey, mind if I join you?"

I don't recognize the voice, but wait for the insult, something like, *Of course you don't, fat ass!*

It doesn't come. I look up. The beaming face is familiar—Oliver Leonard, resident fat kid, like me. I shrug.

"Thanks, Greg. Man, am I hungry."

He sits and I look at his tray. It's covered. Not an inch of plastic remains. He's taken one of everything it seems, except for the salad. Burgers, fries, pudding, three chocolate milks.

Oliver dives in with abandon. I shake away from my stare and notice kids pointing and laughing. A lot of them are bros, and I think to say something to Oliver, but I know how happy he is right now and I don't want to spoil that. Not for him, not for me.

I eat my salad and ignore the squeals.

•   •   •

The late buses have all gone home and I'm headed toward the locker room. I have to wait until now, biding my time at Blint's computer lab, because I can't work out with other people around. It's too embarrassing. Not that anyone uses the shitty gym reserved for nonathletes. But still.

Quinn's already changed. We slap hands and he reviews the workout while I get my gear on. I so appreciate that he keeps his head to his notebook/workout log/food journal/whatever, and he never looks at me when I change. My belly sags and my shirt is drenched and the cuts from earlier, from the hall and from Taleana, come back. I swallow them again.

"We're gonna hit some body-weight stuff today, step-ups, push-ups, sit-ups. Then I'm thinking some light dumbbell and kettlebell work. I've got a real nice finisher for you."

He's talking an entirely different language, but I'm slowly catching on. He kills me with heavy weights one day, and the next some body work and conditioning and then back to the weights.

"And we'll keep an ear out. You know?"

I've finished changing and am panting less than I usually do. "Absolutely." I grab my water bottle and phone and we head off to the gym.

We go through the ritual. Q gets me on film, indicates what day we're at, and then he gets the number from between my feet: 340. When he talks about our goals for the day and beyond, I feel like it's someone else he's describing, because imagining me at 225 pounds is impossible. I haven't been that small since eighth grade.

"Ready, G?"

I smile but don't mean it. "Of course."

"Let's do it!"

An hour later I'm on the floor writhing around like a clubbed baby seal. Well, maybe an adult-size seal. Holy shit, Quinn wasn't kidding me with the finisher being a killer. I don't think I can get up, and whoever this "Tabata" motherfucker is, he better pray I never meet his ass. He literally invented four minutes of hell.

"You all right, Dun?"

I wave and nod.

"Damn. Let me know when you feel right again. I'll record that so we have a benchmark for next time. See if you improved."

Next time? Oh hell no.

Whap!

"Fuck!"

Whap!

"Ahh, shit!"

Whap!

I open my eyes and Q's already handing me the phone. His eyes dance, but he bends over and helps me up. Shit, I forgot all about the lax bros, that's how bad this workout was.

Whap!

Another scream.

Quinn looks at me and I know his question. "Yeah, sounds like it." As much as I want to move, I can't. I sit.

"What are you doing?"

"Give me a second."

Whap!

"Get your fat ass up, Dun! We have to record this."

Quinn typically doesn't make any fat comments to me. I'm a little pissed. "*We* don't have to do anything. *I'll* take care of it."

"Not sitting there you won't." Quinn's jaw is tight and he's bouncing on his toes. I get that he doesn't like what's going on, but it feels like there's more to it.

I use his energy to get up, but hold onto the "fat ass" comment.

We creep into the gym just like yesterday, because, again, the main door is locked. No way that's an accident.

Whap!

I record. Alva has his upperclassmen under the light, armed with lacrosse balls on one side of the gym. The underclassmen stand in a line on the other, in the shadows. Alva turns to the row of juniors and seniors and raises five fingers.

The selected marksman fires his ball. It wails an underclassman, who lets out a muffled scream. But I'm confused, because the sound of the ball striking him was loud, metallic. I squint and notice he's wearing a helmet and shoulder pads.

"This drill is perfect for game-time contact. You never know where that elbow or stick is going to come from. That's why you're in the dark. You need to be prepared, and be able to take the hit." Alva addresses the younger group and another kid rotates into the center.

Quinn and I both step back. "Shit, that was just a drill."

"Looks that way." Quinn seems as disappointed as me. Which is kind of messed up. We should be happy the kids aren't getting hurt.

"Maybe it was just yesterday, a one-time thing?"

Quinn shakes his head. "Maybe, but I doubt it."

Whap!

"Yeah. Looks like we're going to have to keep up the detective work. And in the meantime, you'll just keep whooping my ass down here." I laugh. So does Quinn.

"It's really you kicking your own ass. I'm just watching."

I think about that and his fat-ass comment. He's right, I guess, I'm doing all of the work. But what does he see?

* * *

Mom prepares another awesome meal that I only eat a small portion of. Dad talks about work while mom pouts, and all I want to do is head up to my room, shower, and go to bed. I am so exhausted from today's workout that tweaking my documentary holds little interest. There's a first.

Probably because this one's personal. Ever since middle school I've focused on *them*. Whoever that happens to be. But this one's different. I know I need a piece like this if I truly want to go to film school—something brave, something self-revelatory. It serves two needs. I have to get to a healthy weight, and if I can succeed, then I'll have the kind of transformation people want to watch.

Instead of working I read a few articles, tweet my weight change, and log out. Then I go to Facebook.

I search for Alva. He comes up, but his page is locked down.

Makes sense; he's smart enough for security. I search for his partner in crime, Gilbey. His page is wide open.

I pore over his wall, searching for any mention of what happened yesterday. Nothing. He's just got links to stupid YouTube clips and one-line back and forth conversations with other guys from the team about girls at the school and lacrosse. Why would there be anything else? The bros are too solid of a unit to make mistakes like that. It seems like Callaghan's not at practice much, and I've yet to see Mallory. So the bros must police themselves, which means there will have to be more evidence.

I move today's workout to the folder and pull up the files I shot from the hall. I remember the douches chanting "Dun the Ton." But I don't remember the next.

It's my belly and by feet trudging down the hall. Shit, I must have forgotten to turn it off, and then it must have gotten wedged half in, half out of my pocket. Lockers slam and kids yell to one another. I'm wobbling along and the motion is making me nauseous. I stop at the water fountain and the phone dips lower, picks up sneakers and a conversation, audible just over my slurping. I crank the volume.

"Yeah, I think my rib's broken. At least cracked."

"Did you tell anyone?"

"Hell, no!"

"You know what will happen if we do."

"Yeah. I remember what he said, but still."

"Still, nothing! I only told you so you could watch my back. If you're gonna be a bitch about it. . . ."

"No. No. Sorry. I won't say shit."

"Come on, before Alva pops up. If he gives me a rib shot, I swear I'll fall apart."

The bell rings. I finish my drink, oblivious to the conversation that just occurred and a moment later the recording ends, but not before I catch where I was going. The computer lab. The end of the day. I was down in the freshman wing.

No one's face is visible, but their voices are clear. I could track them down.

What am I thinking? These kids, freshmen or not, they won't talk to me. Especially not about that. They're bros. Unless someone I know is willing to talk to them first. I file the clip under "Lax Bros" and try to still my mind so I can sleep.

CHAPTER 4

QUINN'S CAR SMELLS LIKE PERFUME. An overpowering aroma.

"I know, it reeks in here. This girl, Heather, she wears too much."

"You sure it's not you? Is there something you're not telling me?"

Quinn doesn't answer.

"Is Heather the same girl who texted you yesterday?"

Quinn drives. "Yeah, why?"

"Yesterday you said, 'It's just this girl. You don't know her.' So I figured it's the same one, because today you're using her name, and clearly *someone's* been in your car."

"We spent a long time in the car."

I look out the window, envisioning this. Sounds nice. "Was she trying to punish you or something? You choke her with your one-eyed monster?"

We stop at a sign. "It's not like that. Damn, Dun, you need a date."

"No shit I need a date. But don't change the subject. Who is this girl?"

Quinn opens his mouth, but I cut him off.

"And don't tell me that I don't know her."

Q purses his lips.

"What?"

"You told me not to tell you that you don't know her, so I'm not saying it."

"You are a serious pain in the ass. Does she go to our school? Is she older? Younger? Your cousin?"

"Let's see, yes, no, yes, no, no."

I retrace the questions I asked. "That's one too many."

"I agreed with the whole pain-in-the-ass comment."

We pull into the parking lot. "So that's all I get?"

"For now." Q shuts the car off.

I don't like it, but I realize when he intends to stay tight-lipped. "Hey, I got more footage."

"What do you mean? Nothing happened yesterday."

"I know. It was in the hall. Doing my thing." I don't tell him it was an accident.

Quinn scrunches his forehead. "Yeah, and that shit is going to get your ass kicked one of these days."

"Or make me famous."

"Doubtful."

"Anyway, I caught these two freshmen talking about Alva. One kid has a broken rib."

"What do you mean? Did you like interview them or something?"

I tell him about the recording and Quinn stares through the windshield. "If we figure out who they are, we could follow them, maybe see if this is really hazing. Let me see it."

"The video?"

"Yeah."

I open the Lax Bros folder and select the right one.

Before it plays Quinn points at the screen. "You've already got a folder for them?"

"Detective work."

The recording plays and Quinn asks, "Where was that?"

"Freshman wing."

"All right. I'll keep my eyes open."

I cannot ask for more, and I know he will find them.

* * *

I've never had recurring nightmares, which is kind of surprising considering the amount of shit I've taken. In sixth grade, after the cafeteria film incident, I lost what friends I still had, except Quinn. Everyone plugged their noses and said, "Phew, what is that stench?" every time I walked by. I began using deodorant, but it was too late. They saw my weakness and the jokes started flying.

In seventh grade, we had those flip-top desks and mine would somehow get filled with food so when I'd open it, shit just spilled everywhere. No one sat with me at lunch. Even Quinn. In eighth grade, I didn't get invited to any birthday parties and no one came to my graduation party. Quinn was on vacation. Throughout it all, the name calling ramped up and that's when I started filming them. No one ever gave a shit about what I showed them, but I kept recording anyway. And even if no one cared, *I* did. It helped me remember.

Like in freshman year when my locker was decorated with farm animals. I kept track of who was always around when the pigs changed to cows and then donkeys and so on. No surprise it was often the bros, but there were regulars who weren't on the team as well. And those same faces were around last year when Crisco and butter were duct-taped to my locker. Surprisingly, this year nothing's occurred, but everyone's off partying and hooking up, so maybe there's less time to think about messing with the fat kid.

In spite of all of this, there's been one constant that I cannot escape—the locker room. The smell alone is enough to make me break out in a sweat. I've tried everything from trips to the nurse's office to fake doctor excuses to get out of class, but it's never enough. I have to walk into that hell hole twice a week and stand in my corner and keep my eyes down while the jokes fly, laughs echo, and my body is on display.

Today is no different.

I move to the back, spin the dial, and take a deep breath. A kid nearby makes a fart sound with his mouth. Kids laugh. I take off my shirt. Someone says, "B cup. Maybe a C?" More laughter. I pull my T-shirt on and sit down. The bench groans and someone else says, "It's tapping out." More laughter. I face my locker, untie my shoes, and slide them off.

No one here is as big as me. Sure some of these kids are borderline, but most are max 150 pounds, with ropy muscles and flat stomachs. As much as I don't want them to look at me, it's difficult for me not to look at them, either. I'm envious of them, though, not repulsed.

I slide out of my jeans and have to stand in order to get my shorts on.

"His ass is eating his underwear. Dun, what part of you isn't hungry?"

I don't respond, I don't turn around. I give them zero satisfaction in knowing I'm hurt.

I wait for the room to clear out and I wipe my eyes on my shirt before I join the class.

We're playing floor hockey and it's about as much fun as getting kicked in the shin. I'm stuck playing goalie because of my size, but have the reflexes of someone hopped up on bath salts. Kids score left and right, and when that's not fun anymore they take moob shots or aim for my "gunt."

I go into a zone, just disconnect. But as much as I try to stay in this state, little douche Gilbey keeps coming into focus. He elbows one kid, trips another, and talks trash the entire time. He's not one of those followers who feels powerless without his leader. No, he assumes the role and is vicious. My PE teacher doesn't do shit. He coaches football, and Gilbey and Alva are superstars there as well.

Gilbey flies up and takes a shot that clips my leg and instantly feels like a charley horse. Someone grabs the ball and the game continues, but Gilbey lingers. "Thought all your working out would have helped by now."

I don't say anything, because the words, like me, are cornered.

"Keep it up, Dun. Just remember, we're watching your ass. Don't mess with us, because we'll fucking kill you. And everyone will think it was just an accident." He boxes my ear and trots off.

Fortunately, after class most kids are concerned with getting cleaned up and not smelling like ass for next period. No one showers. So it's fine that I saturate myself in Axe spray. Everyone else is. I still take my time, though, because milling around by the door before the bell rings just leaves me open for taunting. My corner clears out and I tie my shoes. The pressure from my stomach blows. I imagine it's what balancing on one of those big-ass exercise balls must feel like for regular-size people.

"Yeah, we take it easy every so often. Keeps them on their toes. Don't you remember JV?" Gilbey's a series of lockers over, but his voice carries over the wall of metal. All of me cringes.

"So are we fucking them up today?"

I don't recognize the voice.

"Not my call. You know?"

"Right. Alva."

"Yeah, but he gets his orders, too."

"What do you mean?"

I can hear Gilbey shuffling his feet. "Let's just say the word comes from a higher authority."

I stop breathing.

"What? You don't mean like God or some shit?"

"No, you asshole. Mr . . . oh fuck, never mind. Just follow me and Alva. Got it? If you're selected for next year, we'll tell you."

"Thanks, bro."

"All right."

The sound of them slapping hands echoes, followed by a muffled chest bump/back slap. The bell rings and they take off. I breathe. It doesn't a psychic to imagine that shit's about to hit the fan.

I get a text. Rice and sausage. Best bet for today.

I reply to Quinn, K. We have to talk later.

He doesn't reply and I head down to the cafeteria. I get the rice and sausage with a water, and make my way to my table. Oliver is already there.

"Hey, I hope you don't mind," he says.

I scowl but sit down.

"Seriously, Dun, if you want me to go, I will." He grips his tray.

As much as I know that's a good move, I don't want him to leave. I'm feeling screwed up from what just happened and would love to have someone to talk to and distract me.

"No, it's cool. Stay."

"You sure?"

"Absolutely."

Oliver looks relieved and examines my tray before diving into the mountain of his own. "You dieting?"

No other guys would have this conversation. Girls, sure. At least I think so. "Yeah." I don't really care to elaborate.

Oliver nods, his mouth full. He speaks around his food. "I tried that shit a dozen times. Woke up one night about a year ago literally eating my pillow. Haven't stopped eating real food since."

I've woken up with my hand in my mouth after dreaming about burgers. "Been there before." I scoop up the sausage and rice. It's not bad, but it's not pizza, either.

"So what's your goal? What you trying to get down to?"

Is he serious? We're not sitting together two minutes and

he's asking *that* question? I shake my head.

"Sorry, keeping it a secret?"

I'm not, no. I tweet about it, but I guess no actual person besides Quinn knows. "No, just nervous."

"What, of failing?"

Oliver's as straight shooting as they come. It's refreshing. "Yeah. Exactly."

He nods and eats more pizza. I return to my rice.

"The way I look at it, it makes sense to fear failing, but it's unavoidable, isn't it? Unless you're a cocky bastard." He laughs, but I hear pain.

"What's unavoidable? Failing or the fear?"

Oliver smiles. "Both, I guess. You ever really succeed at anything?"

I shake my head.

"Me neither." He drinks. "And you've already admitted to being scared, so there you have it."

I don't know if I agree with him, but he does have a certain logic.

"All right, I'll tell you my goal weight if you tell me why you're sitting here."

Oliver blinks, but continues watching me. He extends his hand. "Deal."

I shake it.

"I've got this grandfather," Ollie says, "he's a fattie, like us.

And he's sick. Diabetes and high blood pressure and all sorts of shit with his kidneys and whatnot. He's all about looking at his life and trying to find some meaning or something."

I cannot believe he's being this open, but I listen intently.

"Last weekend he asks me about school, the shit I put up with, the teasing and all, and then he asks about the lunchroom." Oliver laughs again, another sorrowful sound. "He says to me, 'Ollie, you can't eat alone. That's my problem. I got nobody, so I eat all the time. Food's my friend. Now it's killing me. I'm not telling you to quit eating. You gotta eat. But like drinking, just don't do it alone.'"

The cafeteria's loud as hell, but in spite of this, a certain calm washes over me. I know exactly what Oliver's grandfather means.

I look up and Oliver's waiting. I can tell he's ready to book it if he needs to, if I make fun of him like everyone else does. No way. Not after that.

"225. That's my goal."

Oliver smiles. "Balls."

"Exactly."

CHAPTER 5

BLINT'S BASICALLY GIVEN US THE CLASS to do whatever the hell we want, under the guise of working on our projects. We're all at our own computer stations doing bullshit. I pull up one of the blogs I like and catch up.

"Hey, Dun?"

I ignore the voice.

"Greg, hey?"

Same.

"Greg. I like that site, too."

Now I'm at attention. I turn, and behind me Ella's swiveled in her seat. "You read this one?"

"Yeah. That dude's great. He tears apart all the movies that are so *popular.*"

"I know, he's awesome."

Ella smiles and I realize what's happening, I'm talking to a girl. Shit, the sweat starts. She types an address on her computer. My next favorite blog pops onto the screen.

"His best was when he tore apart *Super 8*," I say.

Ella's jaw drops. She types another address.

"She's good, too, but gets a bit redundant."

"Totally. Huh? What about this one?"

I can already tell where she's headed so I finish the address.

Ella stops typing and turns fully around toward me. "Greg, how the hell do you know all this? I thought I was the only one."

"We might be the only two, then."

She laughs and I laugh and I am sweating worse than I did in PE.

"Are you on Twitter?"

I look over, check to see if anyone is listening to us. Blint's on his own computer, doing whatever. Everyone else is talking or checking Facebook.

"I am, but just to follow this stuff. No one here."

"Why would you follow anyone here?"

I wait for the joke but she's serious. "I don't know. People do, though."

"Who do you follow? Let me just look. What's your username?"

I hesitate. If she finds me, she can read my tweets. She'll see that I'm trying to lose weight. She could share that with the ass-holes at this school in a second.

"I'm Ellafaint," she says.

I laugh. It's a good username. She smiles and I feel in a way like I did with Oliver. There's something honest here. "Gregalicious."

Her mouth curls up and my heart slams even harder than before. I wait for the laughter, but she just nods, "You're rocking some confidence over there, Greg. Nice." She finds me on Twitter and begins perusing my "following" list. I breathe again.

"Seriously, we follow like all the same people. This is cool. You've got some here I've never heard of." She scans my tweets and I feel the blush rising. But she just reads and laughs over an article title I sent out, mumbling it, "'Why your films suck.'"

I do the same as Ella and check her lists. She wasn't lying, not a single person on here from school. I return to her profile and click FOLLOW. Then my heart seizes. What did I just do? I go to click UNFOLLOW as fast as my sweaty hands will allow.

"Hey, did you just follow me?"

"Uh, yeah." My voice sounds like I'm in sixth grade.

"Cool. I'm doing the same."

And just like that, we're connected.

*   *   *

Out in the hall, Ella takes off without a good-bye, but I don't blame her. Taleana and her crew are chatting away and Alva rolls up. I grab my phone and start recording while pretending to look at the outline for my portfolio.

Taleana and Alva nuzzle each other and smile and look like the happiest people in the world. Then Alva sees me.

"Dun the Ton, what's up, fucker? Your weight, I bet." I just give a little wave like he's so damn funny.

"You ever want to seriously drop that flab, let me know. Working out with Quinn is useless. But I'll burn it off you."

I have an image of him and the rest of his minions actually lighting me on fire. It's not that insane of an idea. "All right. Thanks." I pack up my shit and am about to take off when Taleana pipes up.

"Hold up. Hold the fuck up. Is Dun really working out?" She asks as if I'm not standing five feet away. "Please tell that stupid little Ella to record you for her project. Hilarious. Plus, you might pass out and fall on her. Probably kill her on impact. That would so make my day."

I try to stop myself, I really do, but the words are out before I can hit PAUSE. "If you want someone killed, I'm sure Alva will do it for you. That's pretty much all the bros are good for." Her face is flushing red, but that doesn't deter me. "Or just show up without makeup one day. We all remember how you really look under all that, but the shock of actually seeing it . . ."

The slap knocks the words out of my mouth and turns my head sideways. At least I don't drop my phone or stop recording.

"You say another word to me and I'll rip off your fat, fucking face. You hear me, Dun? You listening?"

The hall is quiet, everyone's watching, and I'm the entertainment. But I can keep my composure. For now. "Loud and clear," I say and move on.

*　＊　＊*

Since it's Friday I don't have to wait around in the computer lab. No, after getting smacked twice today, I get to head straight down to the weight room and get abused by Quinn. We really do have a screwed-up relationship.

The lax bros are already hooting and hollering when I arrive. Quinn's bent over, holding his stomach and staring at his log.

"You all right?" I ask.

"Yeah, of course. Just trashed my abs yesterday."

I wonder just what it would take to "trash" Quinn's abs. Mine, like two sit-ups. He's got the washboard look going on, so he must have done something insane. I start changing.

"You hear that shit?" Q asks. "Sounds like they're ramping up for something big."

"I heard Gilbey in PE today talking with one of the bros. Bet you're right."

"You find those freshmen? The ones from the hall."

Q shakes his head. "Hey, is there any way you could rig your phone so that we could, you know, film on the sly? That way we don't miss anything and I can still whoop your ass. Kind of protects us, too."

I think about it for a moment. "Yeah, we could. It'd be as tricky as hell to get the right angle, and it'd kill my battery, but I get your point."

Quinn looks at the gym door. "Yeah, muthafuckas!" blasts through.

"Shit, even if it's just audio, I think we'd be all right."

I grab my phone. "You tell me what we're doing and we'll sneak it in there."

Quinn smiles. "If I tell you, you might just go to Alva and beg to be tortured."

I open the door off the closet and we make our way beneath the bleachers. The bros are running laps, already sweating. Alva and Gilbey stand in the center as the team gallops past. I watch for a second, looking for the kid with the broken rib. All the young guys seem the same, though. The air is saturated with exertion and something else. It's not quite excitement but it's not downright fear. It's something in between.

I settle my phone in the foot well of the bleacher closest to me, angle it out, and turn it on. Here's hoping.

We return to the locker room and Quinn asks. "We good?"

"I hope so. There's good lighting."

"All right, let's get to it."

I put up a hand. "You're supposed to tell me first."

"Shit, right. Okay, but no freaking out on me now. Got it?"

I nod.

"All body-weight exercises, but for twenty minutes straight, no rest."

I swallow and remain stone-faced but can feel my heart already banging against my chest.

"It's a circuit, three stations, repeated as many times."

"What are they?" I manage to rasp.

"Five push-ups, ten bent-over rows, fifteen step-ups onto the plyo box."

He can't be serious. I can barely string together five push-ups as is. Same with rows. Step-ups make me feel like I'm about to fall off a wall. This blows.

"Don't worry," Q continues, "I've got a puke bucket." He, indeed, points to a construction bucket in the corner.

Who the hell knows where that came from, but at this point it's the least of my concerns. I look down and can't see my feet. I think of Oliver and how he's just given up. I refuse to walk that line anymore. "All right, let's go."

"Now we're talking," Quinn growls, and for the briefest moment I feel like one of the bros. That bucket may come in handy.

* * *

I'm lying on the floor in a pool of my own sweat. I can glide around on it. Which I am, as I try to catch my breath and will away the pain. I can't tell which part of me hurts more. By the end, the push-ups were singles from my knees, the rows, spotted by two benches, and the step-ups completed inside the squat rack for hand support. But I finished, with something like nine rounds.

"Damn that was good shit, Greg. Awesome work. You sure you don't need this?" He offers the bucket and I wave it away.

I roll over and sit up, squeezing my knees to my chest with my arms. But I can't hold that for long because I can barely breathe and my arms are noodles. "Where do you come up with this shit?"

"The workouts?"

"Yeah." I let go of one arm and now look like one of those Renaissance paintings with the fat ladies waiting to be fed.

"My dad. I just use his plans for one of his really overweight clients."

This comment negates the good feelings I had about myself. It's true, I feel really good about myself after these workouts, like I'm achieving. Then Q hits me with shit like that.

"That's right, it's time to play the pain game! Line up!"

Alva's voice comes through the doors. I don't know how he isn't hoarse all of the time.

Quinn offers a hand. "Come on."

I don't know how he gets me on my feet or how I manage to stay standing, but we make our way to the closet door and sneak in. The bros are all paired up. The younger kids stand with their hands behind them like they're handcuffed and the others wait with sticks loaded with balls.

I search for my phone, but I've dimmed the screen so much it blends in. I fumble around with my useless arms and make noise. All heads turn in our direction. Quinn grabs me and pulls me under the bleachers. We hold our breath as they all listen.

"Ha!" Alva laughs. "Even the rats are coming out to see if you're man enough to play for this team."

I wait for more, to see if he calls out to either of us, but he must be so confident because of the locked door.

"You will repeat our mantra while you and your partner play for points. Five for the chest, stomach, or legs. Ten for the nuts."

I find my phone and zoom in. Alva smiles like the Cheshire Cat and just as quickly the grin leaves his face.

"If you can keep speaking throughout the hits, you get the points. If not, they go to your partner. Gilbey and I will keep score. Losers get one last shot, close range."

Alva and Gilbey pick up whiteboards and markers and move to separate ends of the line. "Flanagan, you get double duty since what's-his-fuck isn't here. Hey, where is that bitch, Mayston?"

No one answers and I close a low battery warning. There's plenty left.

Alva paces the middle of the rows. "If no one tells me, this game is off, and the one we play will be far worse. Fuckwads," he says to the underclassmen, "you'll have no chance of winning."

"He's at the doctor's," a timid voice speaks up.

"Who said that?"

The upperclassman paired with the kid points at him. Alva moves.

"What do you mean he's at *the doctor's*? What for?"

The kid's voice is inaudible, but Alva repeats his answer. "A broken rib?"

Shit, that's the kid from the water fountain. I nudge Quinn.

Alva turns away and the kid he was speaking to looks relieved. "I'm only going to say this once. There is a difference between being *hurt* and being *injured*. If you are injured, you've broken or torn something. You need surgery. Everything else is just hurt! You play with pain! In fact, that is the entire point of this game. Balls up." Alva points at the upperclassman in front of the kid who spoke. His stick is held high. "Recite." Alva points to the kid, who stares for a second, but must see what I do, the vein growing across Alva's temple.

"Our allegiance is to the Warriors, our bodies are weapons, ready for sacrifice. We will . . ."

The ball flies and catches the kid in the stomach. He stops speaking and sucks air.

"Five points for Tim." Alva makes a mark on his whiteboard and the kid attempts to stand tall. The upperclassman retrieves his ball and the next pair gets ready.

I've been verbally tormented forever, but I've never experienced this. Quinn's torture doesn't count, because it's good for me. This, this is just bullshit. Pain for the sake of pain. Maybe I don't know because I never played sports, but I understand right from wrong and exactly on which side this lies.

The game continues with only one underclassman able to continue speaking. The pairs repeat two more times with kids taking shots to the nuts and crumpling to the ground, Alva and Gilbey laughing and high-fiving the upperclassmen. But still, this one underclassman, in spite of a nut shot, keeps going. He wins and Alva decides to leave his winning shot for last. The upperclassman just laughs it off and the rest take their swings into the already messed-up underclassmen.

The room is silent except for the moaning and coughing of the underclassmen still trying to recover. And soon even that ends, I think because these kids want to see one of their own exact revenge.

The kid, Kyle, gets his stick while his partner is relieved of his. Gilbey takes it and his smile is disturbing, like he's about to watch porn.

"Got to hand it to you, Kyle," Alva says. "You seem to be one tough motherfucker."

There's hatred in Kyle's eyes but a smile on his lips. I don't understand the contradiction.

"Patrick here is one of our stars," Alva continues and the team stares at the upperclassman. "Well, used to be, at least." Patrick's face darkens but Alva ignores him. "However, I need to check something first." In a flash, Alva's fist rockets into Kyle's crotch. Kyle doesn't flinch, but Alva comes away shaking his hand.

"That's what I thought! That's what I fucking thought, you little piece of shit freshman. Even though I said no cups, you kept yours on. You little douche. You thought you could get away with this shit. Fuck you! That's not how this game is played. Take it off."

Kyle's eyes are enormous and I feel an overwhelming urge to go save him. Out of the corner of my eye I see Quinn as twitchy as some kid tweaking. I grab his arm and he pulls away. He can't mess with this shit. Not yet. I need just a little more, just enough on film. The low battery warning pops up again. *Get on with it, Alva.*

Shit, that's an awful thought.

Kyle stands still, breathes deep, and doesn't touch his waistband or in any way make a move to remove his cup. Alva nods to Gilbey, who moves behind Kyle. "I'm going to count to three and then we're taking it off, whether you like it or not."

As the countdown begins, Kyle tightens his jaw and he shakes his head. The underclassmen are all standing now, bodies taut, thoroughly afraid. The upperclassmen are tense, a few pace. Some murmur to Kyle, "Just take it off," but the kid just stands there, either stupid or brave.

"Three." And like that Gilbey has Kyle in a full nelson. Kyle resists but it's useless. Gilbey's arms look like the harness on a roller coaster around Kyle's shoulders. Alva snaps his fingers and two upperclassmen move to Kyle's side. They grab his shorts and pull down, his white jock and cup now on full display. Q growls.

"Now be a good boy and don't kick or this will just get worse."

The two upperclassmen grab the waistband of Kyle's jock and begin to pull. Kyle hunches down and bucks against Gilbey, striking out wildly with his feet. He catches one of the goons in the face.

"Fuck, my eye." The kid grabs his face and moves away.

Alva watches him and then his back flares. He charges and the punch is fast and blood sprays. Kyle screams and Alva steps away. "Why didn't you listen to me? I don't fucking make idle threats. I told you this would get worse and now you've got a busted nose."

Kyle gasps for breath against Gilbey, whose face is now spattered in blood.

"Make another move—kick, headbutt, anything—and you won't be able to walk out of here. Understand?"

Kyle just keeps gasping.

"Understand?"

The slightest nod. Gilbey looks up and it's like seeing a demon. I watch through the safety of the lens and feel my legs go soft.

Alva points to another upperclassman, who steps in to help finish the job. They tear off Kyle's jock and leave him exposed in his compression shorts.

Alva steps to Kyle and cups one hand under the kid's junk. The battery warning flashes again. I can't have much time left. *Come on.* Shit, I'm sorry, Kyle.

"This is for not listening." Alva cocks back his arm. Gilbey smiles. The bros all stand silent. Q bites his hand, and I hold down a scream.

"Alva, what's going on here?" Callaghan walks in.

My phone dies.

"Mr. Callaghan?" Alva puts his arm down, but Gilbey keeps Kyle locked up. "We were just finishing up." Alva sounds like he's a parent talking to a child, trying to stay calm and not lose his shit in front of everyone.

Callaghan steps in front of Kyle and looks at Gilbey. He waves his hand and Gilbey releases Kyle. Kyle staggers forward, his nose still dripping.

"What happened?" Callaghan asks, but it's impossible to tell who he's speaking to.

Alva answers. "Kyle, here, fell on his face during a drill. Seems like he broke his nose. Gilbey was trying to keep him upright."

Callaghan looks down at Kyle's feet.

"Why are his shorts around his ankles? Pull those up, son," he says to Kyle, who obliges.

"We were, uh, going to use them to stop the bleeding. You know, as a rag. He'd already bled on them, so . . ." Alva doesn't finish. The younger bros now move back and forth, shifting weight from foot to foot. The upperclassmen stay still.

Callaghan surveys the room, and when his eyes sweep past us, Quinn and I drop back into the shadows. Q notices the phone pointing at the floor.

"What's up?"

"Battery."

Q looks like he'd like to punch me in the face.

"Alva, please make sure this boy gets that stopped before he leaves. And find him some clean clothes. Now, a word."

The pair moves out of earshot, but even in the dim light it's clear that Callaghan is not pleased. Alva nods sharply at our principal's words. Meanwhile, someone has gotten towels and Kyle is getting cleaned up.

A door creaks open, and just as soon as he arrived, Callaghan's gone. Alva walks back to the cluster of bros. "Practice is over. Ice that shit, Kyle." He walks away and soon the bros start to follow, including Kyle.

CHAPTER 6

"THAT WAS BEYOND CRAZY. It was bad enough with what Alva was doing, but then Callaghan showing up? What the hell?" Quinn sits on my bed and looks as dazed now, an hour later, as he did when we bolted so we could get out before any of the bros saw Q's car in the parking lot.

"We can go to the cops," I say. "I'm sure that they'll help out. We've got two pieces now. I wish I'd gotten Callaghan, though. Damn battery."

"But the cops, though. Shit, that's scary."

"I know, but who else are we going to go to? Callaghan didn't seem the least bit fazed by what he saw. I doubt going to the assistant principals will help. They'd just go to him. So who else?"

Quinn squints. "The superintendent?"

I know that's the chain of command. Plus the school board. It's a possibility, but it seems like too much with too little. I need to go slow, or risk fucking it all up. "Yeah, let me think about it. Maybe if we get one more."

Q sits up. "You're just going to keep saying that and you know it. At some point *we* have to do something. The longer we wait . . ."

"Yeah, the worse it will become." Story of my life. I waited until I was already crying in the bathroom before I said anything to my parents about the bullying. By then the teacher had pegged me as overly sensitive and I had started seeing the school's therapist. Who cries in sixth grade? Which was exactly the point I tried to make. There must be a reason. Not one anyone wanted to hear, though.

But as much as I hate to think it, part of me wonders: *Why do we have to do anything?* Or, better, why *should* we? We don't know everything that goes down with the lax bros. Maybe this is just how they roll.

"All right, think it over. If you don't want to go to the cops, which I agree might not be the best move, we can't do anything until Monday anyway?" Quinn stands.

I nod. "Where you off to?"

"Date."

"Really? With Heather, the girl who I don't know, but you know, who may or may not be your cousin?"

Quinn laughs. "I told you she wasn't."

"Do I get to meet her?"

"If the timing's right." He reaches out and I reluctantly slap his hand. "Good work again today. Stay clean with that diet this weekend. Take a walk or some shit; you'll be less sore on Monday."

"Gotcha. Thanks."

A minute later Mom appears. "Why'd Quinn leave? I thought he was having dinner with us?"

I am sure I just ruined her evening by not being good enough friends with him. "Date."

"Oh." She pauses a beat. "Who's the lucky girl?"

I do not look at her because I know where she's going to take this. "Haven't met her yet."

"Huh? Well, you'll have to see if Quinn can set you up with one of her friends. Maybe she's got someone like you in her life, just like Quinn does."

"I highly doubt some girl who's dating Quinn has some fat chick she hangs with." I look up now. She's horrified. "Just saying."

"Gregory Francis, that is no way to think of yourself. You're a beautiful boy and any girl would be happy to have you as a boyfriend."

I've heard this spiel a thousand times. She's a thousand times wrong. I know she blows up the ego of all her precious little runny-nosed four-year-olds, but I'm a bit older, in the world of reality, where not everyone is your friend, and girls call you "heinous" and "disgusting," and threaten to rip off your "fat, fucking face." Yeah, Quinn and I are in two completely separate dimensions.

"Someday, Mom. But that day has not yet arrived."

"Maybe you need a little more time out there rather than in front of that screen."

I reach up and slam my door in her face. I regret it as soon as it closes. "I'll be down in five minutes," I say.

She makes exasperated sounds on the other side of the door but ultimately marches away. My eyes sting like they did back in sixth grade, and like then, I have no one to turn to.

* * *

It seems like the entire world is out doing something: movies, parties, shows. At least that's what I see online. Not me. I'm here. So I check Twitter.

I scroll through the feed, searching for those I like best, read a few articles and take mental notes of movies I should see and ways I should edit. Then I notice something at the top of the screen, under the envelope tab. I click it. I have a direct message. There's a first. Probably spam.

I click. **Hey, Greg, it's me Ella. If you're not busy I could use some help editing my trailer :)**

I read, and reread. Is she for real? I guarantee she could edit her video blindfolded or with just her toes. But what if? Shit, why not?

I reply, Sure. Let me know when and where. I'll be glad to help.

I click SEND and again read and reread. Do I sound pathetic? Needy? Too willing? Aren't you supposed to play girls?

I log out of Twitter because I don't think I can handle it if Ella gets right back to me, but Facebook is still open.

In spite of the fact that I'm an overweight piece of shit, I have a lot of Facebook friends. I friend as many people as I can because we all know it's just a way to flaunt your shit or eavesdrop. Since I have nothing to flaunt and eavesdropping and filming go hand-in-hand, it makes sense. What amazes me, though, is how many people are willing to friend me. I do get taunted here, too, so that could be part of it. But it's so easy to just delete.

So I head to Gilbey's page. Alva won't friend me. He may be just as smart as he is evil.

Gilbey, however, is a blabbermouth. It's no surprise that I find a message to the bros. Good practice. Hope Kyle's doing all right and that Mayston comes back. We need a solid JV for the next years. Stay strong and keep it under the bucket yo.

I read the stupid-ass replies about devotion to the team. Bullshit. I search for Stephen Mayston, find him in a second, and send the request. He's a freshman, so there's a good chance he's on. Sure enough, he accepts. My avatar isn't of me, it's a plate of nachos. I need to change that. Or maybe not.

I head to his wall, scroll though for a moment, and find what I'm looking for.

Kyle: hope ur ok, man. practice was f'd today. we should talk.

Stephen: i heard. you going to dr?

Kyle: no. maybe. idk.

Stephen: i hear you. broken rib. doc wanted to know how. not sure if he believed me.

Kyle: shit.

Stephen: xactly. got 2 b crful. Lax is dangerous.

Kyle: yeah. that's only half of it.

Damn, I like this Kyle kid. Smart and looking out for his friend. I could use this. I take the screenshot, add it to my collection of "evidence" and resist the urge to find the superintendent's email. In time. Everything in time.

CHAPTER 7

MY MOTHER IS SLAMMING AROUND in the kitchen, making pan-cakes and bacon. I grab a banana and a glass of milk. She watches me out of the corner of her eye. I force myself to sit at the table and peel the banana. The bacon is practically giving me a hard-on.

"Is that what you're going to eat? I'm making breakfast." She points as if somehow I could have missed the scene on the stove.

"I see that. I'm good with this."

She huffs and slams something against the backsplash. "I just don't understand, Greg. I mean, I do, but you're a growing boy. . . ."

"Yeah, but I'm growing the wrong way." I cut her off and feel bad, but she needed it. She would have gone on and on about how I *need to eat*.

"You're fine, Greg, but if this is what you're choosing, then I'm going to have to ask you to pitch in here. Make your own meals. Because I'm not a short-order cook." Her voice is rising and Dad comes in with a mug of coffee and the newspaper.

"Hey," he says. "What's going on?"

I stand. "I was just helping Mom with breakfast." I toss the peel into the garbage, down my milk, and place the glass in the dishwasher. "All done." I walk away before either says anything to me.

Back in my room, I swallow my fear and check Twitter.

> **@Gregalicious** Come over around noon. I'm at 15 Stony Brook.

I know exactly where she lives. I reply: **@ellafaint** Noon it is. See you then.

Shit, what am I going to do for the next three hours besides deep breathing to calm my nerves? I tweet my updates to #weightloss and play around online, mostly checking out Ella's followers. I don't have many of those, just a handful who I think automatically follow back. But she's got history with some of these people. They've tweeted back and forth. Unreal. Why the hell does this girl want to spend a moment with me? This "date" is starting to feel more and more like a trap.

* * *

I arrive at Ella's at exactly noon covered in sweat. Fortunately, I have an extra T-shirt in my bag.

Ella answers the door and is adorable as ever in this black tutu with crazy mismatched knee socks, a bright purple shirt, and cat-eye glasses.

"You wear glasses?" I say and want to punch myself in the dick.

She laughs, though. "Yeah, but I never wear them to school. Come on in."

Her house is pure funk. None of the furniture matches. There's no TV anywhere that I can see. There's some reggae music playing and the smell of cookies. Her dad's on the couch clicking away at his laptop.

"Dad, this is Greg."

He gets up and shakes my hand. "Nice to meet you. Working on the film project, yeah?"

Usually when I meet adults they say something like, "You're a big boy, huh, Greg?" As if I've never seen myself. They typically ask what sports I play and size me up. Then they look all let down when they realize I'm not athletic, just fat. Ella's dad does none of this. He just looks into my eyes with that same piercing interest his daughter possesses and politely waits for my response.

"Yup. I guess Ella wants help, but I really think she's going to teach me something." I laugh and he frowns. Shit, that sounded awful. "I mean, I'm good with editing and she knows a ton about film, so we should be good together." His frown deepens. "I'm going to stop talking now."

Ella laughs and smacks her forehead. It's such a kid move but it's perfect. "Jesus, Dun. I hope you edit better than you string together sentences."

Her dad looks between us and I expect him to tell her she's an idiot for having me over, but he says, "Just let me know if I can help. All right?" He smiles again and heads back to his laptop.

I'm saturated now. "Where's the bathroom?"

Ella directs me, and behind the closed door I bite my fist and let out a small scream.

I change my shirt, stuff it into my bag, and compose myself.

Back in the hall, Ella leads me to her room, which is a disaster. Clothes are everywhere, along with empty water bottles and a few two-liter bottles of soda. No dishes or empty boxes of food, however. Which, of course, I look for because, well, red flags. Ella doesn't seem to give a shit. She just kicks crap out of her way and carries on. "The problem's pretty simple. I have all of this footage, but I have no idea how to tell the story without giving too much away."

I focus on her words, on the task at hand, because if I think about the fact that I'm in a girl's room, I may have a full meltdown. "All right, what's your film about?" Ella gives me that soul-searching look and I sit in the chair near the desk after removing two sweaters from it.

"Promise you won't laugh."

"Sure."

"No, say it." She snaps her mouth at the end.

"I promise not to laugh."

"All right," she says to herself and takes a deep breath. "I'm filming about the different cliques at school."

I don't understand what there is to laugh about. But because she's obviously distressed about this, I stay quiet. I'm good at that.

"It's so cliché, I know." She raises her hands over her head. "But I want to show how if you changed the clothes or the music or the body styles, it's all basically the same. We all do stupid stuff because that's what our group does, and no one's innocent of that."

I think for a moment before I answer. "First, it doesn't sound like a cliché to me. It's pretty insightful, really. Second, speaking of cliques, you should be careful around Taleana and her crew. She has some lethal ideas for you."

"What?"

I tell her about getting slapped in the hall.

Ella rolls her eyes. "This is exactly why I want to do this film."

"So she can try to kill you?"

She laughs and I cheer on the inside. "No, because she thinks she's the biggest badass. There are other girls like her, running their own cliques. She's not unique. Hopefully, people will see my work and understand that."

She might be right. A lot of people have been ruthless to me over the years, from all walks of life. But the bros and Taleana, they stick out in my mind as the worst. Possibly because they're the most wicked, or possibly because I just need to believe that. Shit, Ella's work has me thinking and I haven't even seen any footage.

"So, what clique am I in?"

"Um, well, Dun, in case you missed the memo, you're kind of in the fat boy club."

I know I shouldn't, but I laugh. I laugh and it feels like snot's going to shoot out my nose.

"And since you're with me, you're kind of a film geek, too."

Now I just nod. "Yeah, I guess that's true. So shit, what am I guilty of?"

She sits back in her chair. "The first is kind of obvious. But I guess you're working on that?"

"Huh?"

"Your tweets. You working with someone to lose weight?"

The hell with it. It's not like this is some kind of budding romance or a setup—at least I hope not. "Yeah. My friend Quinn's training me. So far, so good."

"That's awesome, Greg. Really."

It's awkward hearing this from Ella, but cool at the same time. "Yeah, so since I'm a film geek, too, how about I check out your goods?"

Ella tilts her head. "Yeah, we gotta work on that. My *goods*? Really?"

I'm blushing from head to toe. "Sorry."

"Just playing. Come on, slide that chair over and let me show you what I've got." She tosses me a quick grin, and I feel a thousand times better than I have in years.

. . .

"The way I see it, you need to sell this as an exposé." I glance at the screen, where I've just watched a few dozen clips of interviews and candid shots and narrated pieces about the various cliques at our school. It's good material, but it doesn't sizzle. It's way too intelligent.

"But it's not." Ella frowns.

"*I* know it's not, but that's not the point. The idea is to hook the audience, make them want more. And most people want the gossip, the sleaze, you know?"

Ella bites her nail. "Yeah, because people are stupid."

She said it, not me, and I'm glad. "Right. And because of that, trailers fulfill a certain expectation that fits with that level of intelligence."

"Is that a quote from somewhere?"

I think of the recent blogs I've read. "Might be."

"So I should lie?"

"Just a white lie. Something that people will maybe not

realize until the end and hopefully forgive you for."

"Like what Michael Moore does?"

It's tough to admit, but I say it. "Yes. And me, too, I guess."

"What do you mean?"

I stare at the screen because it's easier not to look her in the face while I talk. "You took Film Concepts One and Two, right?"

"Yeah, they're prereqs for Mechanics."

"Right, so you've seen these."

I log onto my YouTube account and pull up one of the two projects that got me suspended. I glance at Ella. Her face hasn't changed, but her body is screaming. She may know where this is headed, but there's only one way to find out.

I thought a film about a no-grades policy would be interesting, until it wasn't. All the teachers I interviewed really didn't want to talk, and those who did said grades were necessary. So I did what I know how to do. I went into stealth mode, recording conversations when teachers didn't realize, and all their talk about how much grading papers and labs and quizzes suck made its way into my video. I used their still images and posed the question: *Is this really what we want?* Then I provided all sorts of stats on schools with a no-grading policy, the morale, the success, etc. But no one saw that because Blint bugged and shut it off. Callaghan saw, though, and I got suspended. Ella has now watched as much as everyone else, so I hit PAUSE.

"So, yeah, that's as far as that got."

Ella shakes her head. "Greg, Blint shows this as a warning for what *not* to do."

"I've heard." I look at the floor, because this is more embarrassing than I expected.

"The second one?"

I look up.

"You interviewed the school board?" Ella's staring ahead, but I bet she's seeing my other video in her mind.

"Here." I move back to the computer and pull it up. "Watch."

This one landed me in some serious shit because I lied about what people said during the school board election, which apparently, is way important. How was I to know that my mash-up of quotes of who said what would get viewed so many times and cause so many people not to vote because they didn't feel they could trust anyone? The candidates all said the same things, so I just used a typing audio background, scrolled in their quotes and turned it into a "matching" game. Of course the "answers" at the end were incorrect. That was the point, and I found it funny.

Callaghan didn't. Neither did the board president. Nor the cops.

The video ends and Ella asks, "Why?"

"Why the election?"

"No. Why lie like this? They aren't exactly *white* lies, are they?"

"It's more interesting than the truth," I say, because it's the safest answer I can offer.

Ella looks away, out her window.

"*I'm* not going to lie, Greg. I'm not going to be that kind of person."

"You mean like me?"

Her face goes dark. "That's not fair. Don't put words in my mouth."

"I'm not. It's just logically the most sensible conclusion."

Ella bites her nail. "Are you a liar, Greg, like in real life?"

I like how she posed that question. She gets the difference between film creator and the everyday. "I try not to be."

She leans back in her chair. "That's probably the most honest answer anyone can give." Ella points at the computer. "How are those still around? Didn't you have to delete them?"

"I did, but then changed the titles and put them back up. How did you know I'd have to delete them?"

"Dad works for an investigation firm. All retired cops. He's tech support, and this happens all the time. So don't be surprised if he goes searching for you online, now that you've met."

"Balls."

Ella laughs and I like the fact that I made a girl laugh, not *at* me but *with* me.

"I don't know if I should be taking your advice then, Dun. Sorry."

"All I'm saying, speaking strictly as a film geek, is that if you want your film to pop, promise them they're going to see something they've never seen before. You're not really lying. Most of the kids in our class probably have never seen the nerd herd's lair in the computer lab. You've got awesome stuff here. Just splice it with quick cuts of everyone doing or saying ridiculous shit. Like the cheerleader asking about how to use a tampon. Then do voice-over narration, leading everyone down the path."

"Okay, but then when they watch the film . . ."

"That's not the point. Not now. Like I said, now you hook 'em." I'm sitting on the edge of my seat feeling pumped. I literally have never had this detailed of a conversation about film. I have in my head, asking questions of articles and blogs, agreeing and disagreeing with the commentary, but that's not the same, because I'm here with Ella and she's actually listening.

"But don't you think it's kind of messed up being so deceitful?"

"No, you don't get it! That's not the point!"

"Greg, why are you yelling?" Ella's voice is so small it makes me feel even more enormous.

"I'm sorry." I hate where my voice just went.

There's a knock at the door followed by Ella's dad. "Every-thing all right?"

"Yeah, dad. Had the volume too loud. Sorry."

"No problem."

I stare at the floor and wish there were enough clothes on it so that I could disappear.

"Greg? What just happened there?"

The tingling behind my eyes is overwhelming, as is the tension across my face. I'm about to lose it. But I can't. That would be the end of whatever this is. So I laugh it off, which is a hell of a lot less obvious than lying, but it's the same thing.

"Just got a little carried away. Sorry." I hold up my hands. "I have way too many thoughts about all this than the average person."

Ella smiles, but I can tell she's playing along. "That's why I wanted your help. So, no worries. For the sake of creative differences, let's agree to disagree. All right?"

"I can do that."

I wish I had Ella around to talk me off the ledge all the time.

•　•　•

Instead of heading straight home, I take a longer route, walking a good three miles more than I need to. With every step I try to pound down the memories that surface. The times that I behaved just as I did with Ella. On the playground. In class. After school. At parties. It's not just being fat that has left me so alone. It's me. All of me.

I walk in, covered in sweat, no less angry.

"You all right, Greg? Sit down." Dad grabs my coat and slides out a kitchen chair. I sit. "You're dripping. What happened?"

"I just felt like getting in a little extra exercise. That's all."

Dad frowns. "You sure? Because you seem inside your head."

"I am. Just thinking about my own project now that I helped Ella."

"All right. I understand." He hangs up my coat and gets me a glass of water. "So how did it go? You help her?" There's an attaboy laugh tinging his words and it's so contradictory to what really went down that it's perfect.

"Sure did. Hopefully she'll need some more."

"There we go. That's the spirit." He claps my shoulder and I try to ignore how he has to wipe his hand on his pants.

"Yeah, we'll see." I push away from the table. "I'm going to shower."

"Good job, Greg."

I don't look at him because I don't think I can stand to see the smile that's across his face. Here he is thinking I may have stepped into a bit of "normal" territory. Here I am happy that Ella is so forgiving. Maybe we're both idiots. Or at least me.

I strip off my clothes and keep my head down so I don't see my reflection. I crank the water as hot as possible and step in and force myself not to wince. I deserve this. I lather and am disgusted by the stretch marks and moobs and folds and red splotches and the overall sausage-like appearance of my body. "You are disgusting," I say and want to rip the shower head off the wall.

I dry and change and lie on my bed. It's Saturday afternoon. I have no plans. Never do. I'm going to sit in front of my computer and vicariously watch the world go by.

I hop on YouTube and scroll through my videos. I've gotten a fair amount of hits, especially for the two that got me suspended. White lies.

On Twitter, there's no light indicating a message from Ella. No reason there should be. I read my newsfeed, check some fan pages, but then start thinking about the lax bros.

Am I going to lie again? Am I really even going to do something with any of the film? I don't know, but I have this nagging feeling that I need to get to the bottom of this, to find out if what I'm seeing is really the truth. And not something I edit to represent what I think that is.

CHAPTER 8

ELLA'S AT HER DESK IN BLINT'S CLASS and our eyes meet. She doesn't look away. I do. Shit, I have to figure out how not to be so awkward around her.

The bell rings and Blint comes into the room. "Trailers are due next week and today I'm conferencing with you on your projects."

The class groans.

"The dates are all in your packets, so this shouldn't come as a surprise." Blint places his hands on his hips and looks even more birdlike than usual. "Head over to the lab. I'll be around momentarily."

Kids get up, moving like zombies into the next room. I sit and wait and watch Ella. I always go last because by that time kids are already into logging on and I can move as undetected as possible.

Ella stands. "Come on, Greg."

I struggle out of my desk. "Are you ready to blow Blint's mind?"

Ella smirks. "I don't think there's much up there to begin with. Should be easy. What about you? You going to be okay talking to him?"

"No, no, I am not."

Ella squeezes my arm. "Just remember that you're the expert on this subject, not him."

Ten minutes later, Blint approaches with a clipboard, a checklist, and his pinched face.

"Mr. Dunsmore, how is your trailer coming along?"

"Fine. I'm done, really, just need to tweak."

"Excellent." He checks off a box.

"Now, about the project overall, what are you doing again? Remind me."

I doubt he's forgotten. He's probably just hoping that I've changed my mind. When we initially conferenced I told him it was going to be a personal documentary. He shifted about and adjusted his tie and told me I should think "big," "beyond just myself." And, as always, to be careful. The irony.

"I'm doing a personal documentary, like I said before."

"Right, right. On what, now?"

I can't be sure the kids in here are paying any attention to this conversation, but it's possible, and that is enough to make me feel like crawling out of my skin.

"On my weight loss," I mumble behind a cupped hand.

"What now?" Blint bends down.

"My weight loss," I say a little slower and a bit louder. A couple of heads turn.

"Oh, your weight loss. How nice." Blint scribbles a note and looks me over. I would bet my laptop that he thinks I'm lying to him. I don't really blame him, but can't he feel the sincerity? A few chuckles pop around us and a bead of sweat runs down my back. Blint moves on, and I avert my eyes from anyone who might be looking. Guess I'll have to prove myself.

Twenty minutes later Blint stands in the front of the room. "Your attention, please."

We give it, but I stare at Ella and wonder how she pitched to Blint. Did she use my advice or keep true to herself?

"As if the grade on your project isn't enough motivation, this year we are creating a contest." Blint pauses, seems to wait for a reaction, gets none, sighs, and carries on. "First place receives five hundred dollars, second, two fifty, and third, one hundred."

Now the room sits up.

"You mean I could like win cash for just doing this project?"

"Yes, Tom, that's *exactly* what I mean."

"Sweet!"

Ella raises her hand. "Why?"

"Why what, Miss Jenner?" The beginnings of Blint's smile fades.

"Why are you doing this, running some contest for something we should want to do well on anyway?"

Kids shoot her looks but she just stares at Blint.

"I agree with your point, but artists deserve credit for their work, so why not use a grant that we received to do just that?"

I expect her to let it go, because that is a reasonable answer, but Ella's anything but the expected.

"That just devalues the entire product. You're turning it into something else, a game."

Blint stares at her and I can't tell if it's hatred or empathy.

"Yo, if Ella wins, I'll take her money. For real," Tom says.

The class laughs, and Ella stares at her desk.

"Yes, well, I doubt you'd be the first on her list for charitable donations." Blint looks us over. "Anyway, the deadline is the same for the contest as it is for the project. You simply need to let me know if you want your work considered. This is completely *voluntary*." Blint says that last part real slow, but Ella doesn't give him any indication that she's heard, or that she gives a shit. I silently cheer for her.

Then Blint adds. "I have also been in conversation with the film schools nearby. This winner will have his or her work reviewed by their departments."

If I were as brave as Ella, I'd raise my hand and ask what that implies. Does that raise the chances of getting into the school? Could there be a scholarship? Because if there is . . . My heart's racing. The moment passes with the ring of the bell.

We spill out of class and I want to wait and check on Ella, but I see Quinn. It's weird because I never see him once we're in school, but here he is, down in the communications wing, where he has no classes. Then I see who he's with and it makes sense.

Stephen and Kyle stand against their lockers, Quinn with his back to me, guarding them. Stephen is stooped and talking close to Q's ear. Kyle's wearing a splint on his nose and the bruises that spill from beneath it are deep blue and purple.

I feel like I shouldn't approach, like this is some kind of moment between the three that I shouldn't intrude on, but Stephen sees me and nudges Kyle, and then Quinn waves me over.

"What's up, Q?"

"I know you wanted to talk to these guys, so I figured I'd get to them first, because you aren't the smoothest. You know?"

I nod because it's tough to hear, but my track record *does* suck.

"I'll bring you up to speed later," Quinn says to me, then turns back to Stephen. "So you were saying?"

"Yeah, right. Well, I get your point about the cops and all that. I do. I'm just scared. If we do this, what's going to happen to our reputations?"

"That's really the last thing you need to worry about. These assholes will be gone next year. This is your chance to make them pay instead of letting them earn some scholarship or shit. Right, Dun?"

I'm startled by the question. "Yeah, I guess. But it's not as if there won't be shit to deal with. This is larger than just the bros."

Quinn looks at me like he wants to kick my ass. I understand. I've tipped my hand a bit, which is not like me. Maybe it's all this talk about having to lie versus wanting to tell the truth. Or maybe I just needed to say it out loud to see if I believed it.

"That's my point." Kyle bounces on his feet. "Let's just have them get in trouble with the school. If somebody wants to do more with it, that's their decision. No cops."

"I agree. But why don't you just quit? Walk away from all this shit?"

"Do you have any clue what lacrosse means to my dad?" He turns to Stephen. "Our dads." Stephen nods. "They grew up here, played for Callaghan, lost their shit when Mallory's son died. They literally have tattoos of our mascot. Their entire team got them. We've got no choice."

I remember Kyle from practice, defiantly wearing a cup and not backing down. "Seems like you're thinking about making one, though."

"Yeah, guess we are. It just ain't right. I like the game. Love the attention. You know, the perks. Maybe a scholarship and all that. I just don't want the rest."

Quinn shakes his head. "I don't agree. We all know Callaghan won't do shit. But it's your life. Talk to G."

Kyle narrows his eyes. "What do you have? He keeps hinting that you got dirt."

Now I look at Q liked I'd like to kick *his* ass. But I understand these two need proof we're not fucking with them. I doubt they trust much. "Some of the hazing. During practice."

"And you're just sitting on it?"

I shrug, but it's a ploy. I didn't want to do *this*. I wanted the whole story before we got here.

"That's kind of fucked up, yo." Kyle gives me a hard look, and combined with the splint and bruising, he looks like a badass. But to hell with that.

"This is your first piece of the bullshit around here. Not mine. You let me do what I do and this will work out. All right?"

All three look at me differently, like I'm not the stupid blob they believe me to be.

"Maybe. But *we're* the ones dealing with this and it's just . . ." Kyle fades.

"It's just out of control," Stephen says, his voice a piercing whisper. "Callaghan doesn't even seem to care."

"Which is why Dun wants as much evidence as he can get and why we're going over Callaghan's head. Don't worry, we'll take care of it. We may just need you to speak about it. Cool?" Quinn puts out his hand and the guys pound it.

"For now," Kyle says and we part. I feel a mix of anger and pride. I turn to Quinn.

"Thanks for finding them. I didn't realize you cared so much."

Quinn sets his jaw and speaks out of gritted teeth. "We all have our thing, right? This is mine."

"The bros?"

"No. The weak. You said this shit was bigger than just the bros. Why's that?"

"Just putting the pieces together, that's all. Think about it. Alva's evil and so is Gilbey, but Callaghan didn't seem shocked at what he saw the other day when they were beating Kyle."

"True. But your point?"

"I don't know yet. If they talk, maybe it will make sense. Until then . . ."

"Until then, we keep our eyes open. And that includes on you as well. No way I'm letting you slide because of the fucking bros." He storms off and I'm left feeling thankful for just how right he is.

CHAPTER 9

I EAT THE POTATOES AND WISH they had more butter, same with the beans. The roast beef is cold and tasteless without the gravy, but compared to the sacrifices of others, I have nothing to complain about.

Ollie appears, tray in hand. "Hey, Greg. Is it cool if I join you?"

"Absolutely." After what he's told me, there's no way I'm letting him renege on his promise to his grandfather.

Oliver chews his lunch slowly and steadily. Between bites he cracks me up with fat kid jokes and stories about his home life.

As I watch him, I can't help but feel like I owe him something. Maybe it's my guilt for potentially using Kyle and Stephen, but regardless of the reason, I blurt out, "Hey, you want to train with me?"

Ollie sets down his fork. "Did I miss something?" He looks skeptically at me. "I'm not interested in losing this man-bulk here. It's taken me sixteen years to get this." He pats his belly. I guarantee he's pushing 365.

"Maybe not, but I'd like the company." I want to say something about how his grandfather would want this, but that might be going too far.

Ollie looks at his plate. "Let me think about it, all right?"

"Sure. We'll be in the weight room after the late buses."

Oliver nods and I wonder if he'll show. Shit, I wonder what I'll do if he does. We'd have to let him in on what we're filming. It's not like he's just going to sit there while we run off to film the screams going on within the practice gym. Shit, I didn't think this through.

Ollie burps. "Awesome. More room."

. . .

I hope I've achieved my goal weight, but I hope just as much that Ollie will show. In spite of what it may mean to have him here.

Q is ready, reading over his workout notes, sweat drenched. "What do you think?" he asks.

"About what? How awful you smell?"

He frowns. "Really? I'm sure you realize what a cesspool you make of yourself. This," he pops his shirt, "smells like a man."

I laugh and parrot "like a man" until I feel light-headed and have to sit. Q frowns and waits. "I'm sorry. That was just funny shit. You work out already or something?" I ask.

Quinn's eyes are furtive for a moment. "I missed my morning run, so I hit a little something, here."

I know Quinn goes from here to his dad's, so that means one thing. "You work out twice a day?"

"Yeah. Why?"

"Uh, well, you're not fat."

Q tosses his book down. "It's not only about losing weight. Strength and staying fit are equally important."

He sounds like he's getting ready to teach a spin class or some shit. "Are you telling me I have to keep this up forever?"

"Yes." Quinn claps once. "All right, your weight, that's why we're here. What's it gonna be?"

It takes me a moment to come out of my fear of the future, but I hedge a guess. "329."

"So you're feeling confident? Good. Let's get you up on that scale."

I strip to my underwear and T-shirt and give Q the phone. I stop, though, because it's so quiet. In spite of the soundproofing for the gym, it's always obvious the bros are practicing. Their voices are everywhere. Not today. "The bros?"

"Scrimmage," Q says.

Quinn starts recording, does his intro like I do with the journals and then I take a deep breath and get on the scale. 324.

"Hell, yeah!" I scream and high-five Q, and as I do the locker room door opens. I suddenly feel like I'm naked. I hop off and cross my arms over my moobs. Q stays cool and steadies the phone at whoever's walking in. He's learning.

"I heard screaming, so I had to come." Ollie's all smiles. "What's all this yelling about?"

I uncross my arms. "324. That's what."

"No shit? That *is* awesome." He pounds fists with me and then puts his out for Q, who looks at me.

"Did I miss something?"

Ollie lets his arm drop, and his face follows suit.

"Yeah, I was about to tell you. I invited Ollie to be my training partner. Figured he'd be good to have on board."

"Having him *on board* means a lot of things, G."

"*I* know that, but I think it's worth it."

Ollie puts up his hands. "Hey, if this isn't going to work, no worries. I thought maybe Greg had talked to you first."

Quinn shakes his head and aims the phone at Ollie, but not before looking at me and mouthing, *Shit.* He hits record and speaks to Ollie. "So you wanna train?"

"I guess. I mean, we'll see."

"No. Give me a real answer. Commit or don't." Quinn sounds just like his dad, and he'd kick my ass on the spot if I said so.

"Look at Dun, there. Almost thirty pounds in less than a month. You want that?"

It's such an unfair question, and on film, nonetheless. But as much as I want Q to put the phone down and give Oliver some space, I want Ollie to answer. I want him to say yes.

Ollie looks at me and I nod. He nods back. "Hell yeah, I do."

Quinn pounds fists. "Welcome aboard."

"So what's first? We running?"

Quinn shakes his head. "Let's see where we stand. Get on that scale."

Oliver looks at it and sighs. "I hate those things, but okay."

He strips down and seems less embarrassed than I do. In fact, he seems to look better as well. He's more "husky" than fat. He's probably athletic and about to whoop my ass. Great.

He steps on and the digits pop: 372.

"Quinn, you've got your work cut out for you," Oliver says and steps down.

Quinn smiles. "Not me. The two of you."

And like that, Ollie and me are a team, and unlike the shit-sticks that make up the bros, I think we're good. At least we're not under the thumb of some deranged ass and his henchmen. Which I guess we'll talk to Oliver about next time. Because there will be a next time. I can tell.

•   •   •

I go through the motions of dinner with my parents, offering brief answers to their questions and asking none of my own. The chicken is bland and the vegetables are just thawed out from a bag. I realize Mom's trying and I appreciate that. But still, the cafeteria food tastes better than this. I might need to buy her a cookbook.

I head back to my room and settle in front of my computer, feeling like a cat must when they find that perfect perch. Ollie worked hard and we had a good time. Quinn seemed pleased, too. Asking Ollie to come on board was a good call.

And my mind's more clear on what I need to do with the lax bros piece. I want it to be good to go if Kyle and Stephen decide to talk. Yeah, I'm moving in the right directions.

I pull up the lax bros and watch the hazing all over again. I make sure to amplify the whacks of the sticks cracking across the kids' backs. I have a tight shot of blood trickling down one kid's side. I throw in slow-motion footage of the "pain game" and kids crumbling to the ground. Then I speed it up with what they did to Kyle and, of course, the punch. I score it, too, with their stupid chant. It builds like a crescendo in the background until it's the only sound. It ends with a still shot of Alva's face, contorted and crazy.

I sit back and stare at the screen. It lacks something, a finality. Possibly that's Kyle and Stephen. Possibly it's something else. Maybe I'll see if Ella has footage of Alva. Would he open up to her?

My mind puts it all together, but I know the difference between fantasy and reality, so I turn my attention to my trailer.

It's the shit. Yeah, I'm biased, but whatever, it's true. I've got this awesome mash-up of these scenes I've pulled from YouTube and elsewhere. It's a mix of beautiful images and ugly ones. Like bodybuilders and supermodels followed by flabby shits like me and the homeless. I keep the theme going with scenes from tropical beaches and star-filled nights, then split to animals dying in a drought and scenes of war and dead bodies. I finish with images of our school, those I've captured on my phone, of the hot girls, the studs, the goths, the wallflowers, the jocks, the nerds, the metrosexuals, the homosexuals, the poor, the rich, the obese. All of it is scored with "Immigrant Song," but not the Zeppelin version, the one Trent Reznor did for the movie about the girl and the tattoo.

I finish with a brief interview of me stating that "I know where I belong, but I'm trying for something new," and slide in snippets of my workouts with Quinn and digits from the scale. It's ballsy. And it scares me as much as it excites me. Someone's going to say, "Oh my God, you really do weigh like a ton." Someone like Taleana. But to hell with her. I want to make this statement. And if this gets me into film school, what an awesome statement that will be.

On Twitter, there's a stream of conversations under #thebestdirector comparing David Lynch to the Coen brothers. That's like comparing *Monty Python and the Holy Grail* to *The Exorcist*. All right, that's a bit of a stretch, and probably why I shouldn't chime in on the subject. However, I have a message.

It's from Ella. Greg, can we get together? Just wanted to review my trailer with you. I can bring my laptop to school. Let me know. K?

Ella's a saint for being willing to chat with me about her work after how awkward I was last time. I'll be better. I'll control myself. I reply, Of course we can! Tomorrow, after school?

I send the message and shower, and when I return she's replied: Perfect.

CHAPTER 10

I GIVE ELLA A WAVE when I walk into Blint's. She waves back and my stomach knots, but in a good way. Blint actually walks us through an interesting presentation on how documentaries often "construct a reality." His main point is that documentaries are still just stories and that we are choosing what pieces to show, what perspectives to present, because we can't include it all.

The bell rings and we head out and Ella waits for me at the door.

"You still available this afternoon?"

"Of course."

She smiles and I feel hot. "Can we meet after the late buses?"

"Uh, uh . . . well, that's, uh the time when, well, you know, Quinn and I . . . we . . ."

"Shit, you're working out. How did I forget? After?"

I'm a jumbled mess, but manage to say, "Yeah, that's fine. I'll be swamp of sweat, though."

"No worries. See you then." She takes off and I make a mental note to check that I have enough Axe. I'm so lost in my thoughts I almost miss the commotion across the hall.

"I'm not sure what you expect. You missed the scrimmage." Alva's voice sounds a lot like Callaghan's.

"But my nose is broken. You broke it."

I get my phone in position and hit RECORD. Alva and Gilbey have Kyle and Stephen pressed against their lockers. If I could I would, but I can't help them in any other way.

"Shut your fucking mouth unless you want something worse. Remember what I said about you not being able to walk? That wasn't a fucking joke." Alva presses into Kyle.

Taleana stands at Alva's side and smiles her glamour-girl grin and I make sure I aim the phone in her direction.

"What do you want?" Stephen asks.

"Really? Are you like retarded?" Gilbey says and smacks Stephen upside his head. Kids in the hall look, but keep on walking. "You come back to practice. You're part of the team. That's all there is to it."

"What if we don't want to?" Kyle's voice is low and controlled.

Alva laughs. "That's not a choice you get to make." He puts his knuckles into Kyle's chest. "Understand?"

Kyle grimaces and nods. Taleana's face seems to flutter with enjoyment.

"Good. That's the end of this conversation. Period." Alva straightens himself and looks around the hallway. He sees me.

"Have you been recording us, Tubs?"

My heart stops. My legs cramp and a wheeze escapes my lungs.

"Hey, Dun, the fuck you doing with that phone? Better be prepared to eat it." Alva's moving across the hall.

"No, I was just texting, that's all."

"Who the fuck would text you?" Alva reaches out. "Let me see."

I turn away. There's no way in hell I'm letting this monster touch my phone.

"The fuck you doing?" Gilbey's in my face now, pawing at the phone. Fortunately, I'm big enough to tuck it under my armpit and away from either of them. But they keep reaching and barking shit like, "Hand it over, Dun." "Give me the phone before I fucking break you." No one's stopping to help and it's only a matter of seconds before they destroy the one thing in my life I need besides food.

And so I do what I have to in order to survive. I reach behind me and wedge my phone in between my ass cheeks. And then I clamp down. Hard. It seems as if all the squats have paid off, because it doesn't slide at all.

I lift my arms and Alva and Gilbey look at me like I'm a magician.

"Where'd it go?" Gilbey asks.

Alva pins me to the lockers and pats me down. He even lifts my belly to check the fold. Embarrassing, but thorough. He stops at my crotch and looks up. "Tell me you didn't put it in there."

Gilbey follows his lead. "That's fucking sick."

Alva doesn't take his eyes off me, and I feel like I'm looking at a younger version of Callaghan. "Pull it out, Dun."

I press my ass against the wall. There's enough padding. "No."

Alva tilts his head. "Did you really just say no?"

I don't know why I feel empowered in this moment, but I do. Possibly because this is the one time I have something that they want, and it feels good to withhold. Or quite possibly it's because I finally get the chance to say no and have it matter.

Alva stands, and I can now see the rest of the hall. There's a decent crowd. A bunch of bros, Taleana and her bitches, and a handful of randoms. No one dares move.

"That's not how this works, Dun. Hand it over now."

"And you know that will never fucking happen." I look him straight in the eye, just in case it drives home the point of *never.*

My balls shatter beneath his fist. I fall to the floor, but have the presence of mind to keep my back to the wall, my phone safe. Kids linger and then go at the bell. Alva and Gilbey talk shit when they go past, but I hear none of it. I sit in a crumpled heap and I see myself, not in the here and now, but in the future, after I have won. After I have beaten these assholes.

This will all be worth it. No lies, because I don't need them. No deceit, because it's not necessary to convince anyone. Just honesty. I reach back and grab my phone. Unscathed. Fuck the bros. I'm just getting started.

* * *

My balls still hurt. I just want to see Ella and go home and edit what I captured on film. But Ollie's pumped, and it's not as if I don't need this. "Come on, Ollie, let's go lift something."

"Deadlifts today, boys," Quinn says.

I feel like something dead. Perfect.

When we finish with Quinn, I'm drenched, but towel off and shake the can of Axe. Plenty. I douse myself, and Q and Ollie cough.

"You angry?" Q asks.

"Huh?" I wave the mist around.

"You trying to kill us with all that?"

"Uh, no, I just have a meeting?"

Quinn asks, "Yeah, with who?" he sounds genuinely interested and for a moment, I feel awesome. That is ended by a loud scream, followed by a thud.

"No! I'm not eating it!"

"What the fuck is that?" Oliver asks.

Quinn and I share a glance, and I say, "Don't make a noise, and don't do jack shit. Got it?"

Ollie's confused. "Okay?"

"Come on." Quinn nods and I get out my phone.

Ollie doesn't say a word as we pick our way through the janitor's closet and behind the bleachers.

Inside the gym, Kyle and Stephen are lying facedown on the ground. An upperclassman sits on top of each one. Gilbey stands before them holding a bag with a spoon. Alva has his arms crossed and is shaking his head.

I zoom in on their faces and then the bag. There's something brown inside.

"Yes, you will fucking eat this." Alva squats down and pats Kyle's cheek. "Sometimes you gotta eat a little shit to prove that you're part of the team. You *are* part of this team, right?"

Neither answers. Alva stands. "They are a part of this team, right?" He addresses the rest of the team.

"Right!" they answer in unison.

I pan to them and their faces are a mix of emotions: fear, apathy, disgust, excitement. It's awful.

"The hell is going on?" Ollie whispers.

Q and I both raise fingers to our lips, but then I whisper, "You think this is on purpose? Some setup to catch me because of today?"

"You give them way too much credit. They don't think you're capable of taking them down."

I think about the hall and how *never* felt in my mouth. Q's right.

"Of course you are a part of this team, because we won't ever let you go," Alva says. "Gilbey? The spoon?" Gilbey hands it over, and on my screen I can see the shit, moist and rounded, like pudding. But not pudding.

Alva pushes it toward Kyle. He shakes his head and screams, "Fuck you!" Alva snaps his fingers and another upperclassman appears.

"Squeeze his mouth open."

The kid pries at Kyle's face and opens his lips. Kyle strains, but this boy is big and seems like he's done this before.

"Enjoy," Alva says and pushes the spoon in.

The big kid forces Kyle's mouth shut and Kyle twitches like a fish out of water. I have to look away. Vomit rises in my throat and I swallow it, but I will myself to hold it together.

"Next," Alva says, as calmly as someone at a doctor's office. The process repeats and the only difference is that Stephen is crying before they punch in the spoon.

We all turn away as soon as it's over because Quinn's about to explode and Oliver looks like he might pass out.

Back in the locker room my ears ring, and I go to the water fountain and wash out my mouth as if *I've* just eaten shit.

"Holy fuck. Holy fuck," Ollie says over and over. "What was that?"

CHAPTER 11

WE HIGHTAIL IT TO QUINN'S CAR. But this time, Ollie sits in the back, looking so lost, it's like we picked up a hitchhiker.

"Could one of you please tell me what the fuck is going on? I'm totally freaked out right now."

"Take a deep breath, G. We gotta tell him."

I listen to Quinn and do just that. "Ready," I say, and we begin.

It takes a few minutes, and hearing it out loud, each of the events strung together, with the hint of Callaghan knowing, sounds insane.

"But why haven't you guys done anything?" Ollie asks.

Q eyes me, his eyes smoldering with anger.

"That's my fault. I held Q back because I wanted to get as

much evidence as I could." I pause, because I know what I'm about to say is going to sound horrible. "I was also afraid to stick my neck out for them. They *chose* this. No one made them. So if I was going to do anything, it had to be because things were really fucked up."

"Is this fucked up enough for you?" Ollie points toward the gym and holds his head. "Shit, the *whole thing* is just insane. I just, I don't . . ."

"It is enough. But even before this, hearing Kyle and Stephen talking about how their dads *need* them to be a part of this team . . . they probably went through this, too." I look up. "This entire town sickens me. Which is why I can't wait to get out. Everyone lets shit slide because of the money they bring in."

"You're right, Greg. The town does suck. Because of the money and because of the tradition and because of the devotion to Mallory's hero son, Max," Quinn says. "But I don't think they do this, what we saw today, all the time. Kyle's and Stephen's dads didn't go through *this*. Not this far, Greg. That was some special kind of awful in there." Q's eyes tell me he knows what he's talking about, and I have every reason to agree.

"You're right. And if I'm being honest, besides doing the right thing by them, I still didn't know what was in it for me."

"So what's it going to take, G? Or am I going to have to do this myself?" Quinn asks.

"I have to win."

Q tilts his head.

"For me, videos, making film, next to food, it's all I have. If I mess this up, get shot down because of whatever connection Callaghan has to all this, I'm done. There's no more for me. The old *three strikes, you're out*, I'm way the fuck past that. If what I have on the bros doesn't bring their whole damn *business* down, it won't be worth it. They'll clean up this mess and then turn my life into hell. I need to destroy these assholes in spite of their past five years of winning States and their ability to bring in so much fucking money that they built the tech wing."

My words drift through the sweat-drenched fog inside the car, and I wait for what will come back at me.

"You go this far, you kill the tech, which fucks you, but you also piss on Max Mallory's memory, which kills the team, and this town," Quinn says.

"Well, if we are built on such a rotten foundation, then I say cave it in."

Quinn stares at me and I can't tell what he sees, but he nods slowly after a moment. "Something's changed in you, G. I don't know if I agree with you, but you sure did grow a set or something—maybe a new pair. I don't know if this is another one of your suicide missions, but I like your conviction."

In spite of all of it, I grin big, because he's right, in so many ways.

Ollie shakes his head. "I don't know half of what the hell you are both talking about. I'm still trying to recover from what I saw. But you're going to make good on this, right, Greg?"

"I promise, Ollie."

"Good." He wipes his face. "I'm not sure what I would have done if you had said no."

"You think going to the super will cut it?" Quinn asks. "Will he be enough for your plan?"

"I don't know. Cops, lawyers, somebody like that is probably better."

"What's the but, G?"

I sigh. "I don't want to screw over anyone who's not at fault, you know? If I succeed, a lot of people get hurt."

"True, but it's dangerous to second-guess if you truly believe."

"Just thinking it through. And please, tell me one thing about all of this that isn't dangerous."

Quinn laughs. He starts to speak but laughs harder. "I got nothing."

I laugh with him.

"What's wrong with you two? You're all happy about this little plan of yours, but you didn't even think about kicking some ass in there?" Ollie rocks the car back and forth, he's so agitated.

"I feel you, but you don't get it." Quinn's tone is cool. "Those kids would have put you in the hospital. I know you saw what they just did. Seriously, you want to fight with *that*?"

Ollie shakes his head. "Still feels like we pussied out, and I mean *we*. I'm not throwing you under the bus alone. I just can't understand. . . ."

Quinn clasps his shoulder. "Trust me, I'm with you, but leave it to G, here. Once it's all pulled together, his video will do more damage than any punches we could have thrown."

Ollie and Quinn are wearing the same deviant expression. "It would've felt real nice, though," Ollie says.

"Damn straight," Quinn replies.

*   *   *

As soon as I get home I tweet, **@ellafaint** Sooo sorry. Something came up and I got stuck. If you let me, I'll explain. I have no idea how she'll respond, if at all. But I hope I get the chance to make up for this. All of it.

My door opens. No knock. Mom pops in, looks around. "You feeling all right? You seemed upset when you came in."

"Fine. Just needed to check on something."

She frowns. "Everything all right?"

I so want to tell her. I just want to get rid of this burden, because in spite of all I just said to Quinn, I'm terrified. Why did I ever think I could pull this off? I should have figured out who to tell after that first incident.

"Yeah, just school."

"Junior year is like that, sweetheart." She squeezes my shoulders, and my sore muscles sing at her touch.

"Yeah." It's all I can manage.

"How about I make you a little something for dessert? That should help."

"Chocolate." I say the word, automatically, no thought, but it's immediately followed by a jolt of concern. It's subdued by her hands rubbing my back, taking care of me.

She pats me and says, "Done," and I feel weird, like some part of me just lost a battle. She leaves and I decide to shower. Maybe that will get my head straight.

At the table, I dive in, eating barbecue ribs and mashed potatoes covered in butter. I squeeze the tiniest bit of salad onto my plate but just shove it down for looks. I have seconds and Dad says, "You're really packing it away, huh?"

I can't judge his tone because I'm so focused on how good this food tastes and how happy I am to have that full sensation back. It's like a friend I haven't seen in a while, and I love her. So I say, "Yeah, Q suggested I eat a big meal. We deadlifted today. Lot of energy needed to rebuild."

"Okay." He definitely wants to say more, but my parents have reached a point where they shut up and just let things slide. At least in front of me.

"Save room for dessert. I made brownies." Mom squeals a little and Dad shakes his head.

Drool spills at the corner of my mouth.

Mom clears the plates and brings out the brownies. She serves me first, and the brownie she gives me is the size of a slice of cake. She sprays whipped cream on top and says, "Enjoy."

I bite into a forkful and the brownie's warm and the Cool Whip cold, and I close my eyes it's so damn good. I understand the meaning of *savor*. I eat another bite and another, and in no time, it's gone. I sit back, full to busting, so satisfied I could die and Mom says, "Another?"

Dad coughs. "Don't you think that's enough?"

"But he said he needed energy. All that lifting."

"I think he's covered it."

I feel sick. Because of the lie? Because of the food? Because of their exchange? Because of the brown smear on my mother's lip that reminds me of this afternoon? I push away from the table. "I'm good. Can I be excused?"

Mom says, "Sure," and Dad, "Please," and I know they're going to have a talk. Meaning Dad will lecture Mom. Wonderful.

I put my dinnerware in the dishwasher and feel miserable. And then I hear them.

"Seriously, what the *hell* was that? Do you even *see* how good he's doing?"

"Don't talk to me like I'm a child. Yes, I see, but excuse me for showing him some love."

"What's that supposed to mean?"

"Nothing."

"No, really. Explain. Do I have to make my overweight son

brownies just so he knows I care? Huh? Is that your logic?"

Fuck my life.

I head upstairs and the light is shining, a message. **@Gregali-cious:** I'm all ears.

I stare at my keyboard and listen to the argument downstairs and feel the swell of my belly. I can't think of a response. I slide to my bed and lie down. I rub my swollen stomach and think about puking or telling Q he needs to whoop my ass tomorrow. Then I realize just going to school may make both occur. I should just stay home sick. No, then my mother would be all over me, making soup and Jell-O and all sorts of bullshit I don't need. The murmurs turn sharp and I reach for my phone, because it chimed with a text, but it's just past my grasp. I rock toward my nightstand and still can't reach. I rock some more and stop. I can see myself, this fat shit too big to sit up, wobbling like a turtle on its shell. *I did this.*

Dad yells, "You should know better!"

He might as well be talking to me. Because I do, so why do I mess it up?

I force myself up and grab the damn phone. It's from Q. Don't know if you can read his wall, but if so, check out Gilbey's. I head to Facebook.

Gilbey's written, Bros, good work today, specially Kyle and Stephen. Really stepped it up and bcame part of the team. Diffrence btween men and boys is what we're willing to suffer.

I slam my phone down and open my cloud and find today's footage, a thumbnail of unspeakable behavior.

Downstairs Mom is now crying and Dad apologizing. I just ruined all of today's good with one meal, dissed the only girl who's ever wanted to talk to me, and now have to piece together something that will undo a team of maniacs.

I've suffered enough by Gilbey's stupid standard. Through their logic, I'm a man a hundred times over. Time to prove it.

CHAPTER 12

THE SUPERINTENDENT'S SECRETARY is on the phone, but she eyes us and gestures to the seats against the wall. Q and I sit and look around. It's so businesslike and sterile that it doesn't even seem connected to the school. Except for the enormous lax bro team pictures turned posters, and the accompanying logo: IS THE WARRIOR SPIRIT IN YOU?

I sure as hell hope not.

"Can I help you?" the secretary asks, setting down the phone and writing a message, not looking up.

Quinn nudges me. "We would like to see Dr. Philmore," I say.

"Do you have an appointment?"

My face burns. "Well, uh, no, but it's important and just came up, so, no."

The secretary sets down her pen. She has the severe lips of someone who does not enjoy people. "I'm sorry, Dr. Philmore is in a meeting. May I take a message?"

She's not the slightest bit sorry, and there's no way we can leave a message. This was a complete waste of time. I stand and a second later, so does Q. "That's all right. Is there a better time for us to come back? Possibly schedule an appointment?"

The secretary stares at us. "No. He's a very busy man. Issues at each school are first dealt with by the principal. Do you see any other students here?" She grabs her pen again. "Names?"

"I, we, don't have a message. We'll do what you said, talk to Mr. Callaghan. Thanks," I say.

"Names," she says as if I haven't spoken.

"Like I was saying—"

"You are here during school hours," she cuts me off, "so you'd better give me your names so I can contact Mr. Callaghan and let him know who you are and that you are here. He will decide if there will be any punishment for truancy."

"Shit," Quinn whispers and the secretary snaps her head in his direction.

"Excuse me?"

Quinn doesn't look at her. He coughs. "I'm sorry, I'm Andrew

Alva and this is Dennis Gilbey."

I feel light-headed. What is he doing?

"Mmm," is all the secretary says as she writes down our "names." When she finishes she says, "You may go now."

We climb back into Quinn's car. "So, *Alva*, what the hell was that about?"

Quinn backs out. "There's no way I was giving her our names. Sure, if she calls Callaghan he'll know it wasn't his evil sons, but he'll have to guess who we really were."

"Yeah, it'll take him forever to figure that out once his secretary says, 'This really pasty but jacked kid, and his ogre friend.'"

Quinn doesn't respond. I sit in the silence as he drives and can't fathom how bad this is going to get.

"You really think I look jacked?" he says as he parks.

"Yeah. You don't?"

Quinn shrugs.

"There's no hope." I open my door. "I *do* look like an ogre, and we're going to get killed because of what your *jacked* ass just did."

Quinn climbs out and stares at me across the roof. "I'm sorry," he says, but walks away like usual, leaving me to huff my way into school, late, without an excuse. Although, I do huff a little less.

After I get my pass, I take my time. I have no interest in history, but what am I going to do, cut after being late? Up ahead, the chronically tardy slackers shut lockers or slide toward class, sipping coffee. Taleana is one of them. I pass and she tsks.

"I'll get the Shop-Vac and needle. You won't even need to pay me. That lipo will so be worth it." She cracks up and so do the rest of the kids with her. I wish I got that comment on film.

I round the corner and my classroom sits just up ahead. I picture me entering and having to stand in front of the room to give the pass to Mrs. Olmstead. In my mind, she has to cut her lecture and deal with me, which will piss her off, and as much as the class will be half-alive, someone'll make a crack, and then she'll get more pissed and assign extra work, and somehow it will all be my fault for being fat, for being late, for just being me.

I head into the bathroom and sit in the handicapped stall. It's the only one I ever use. I just need to get my head straight.

I pass the hour scrolling through Twitter, not even really reading anything, just distracting myself. I should have responded to Ella, but I can't now.

The bell rings and I swallow and feel enormously full.

*　　*　　*

PE is the same shit, different day. Except Gilbey watches my every move while we play this stupid-ass game called "hockey tag." Since I can't stickhandle the puck, I'm "It" immediately and am stuck bumping into kids for the rest of class and never once stealing their pucks. Gilbey purposely weaves toward me and puts his puck within reach. It's an obvious challenge, but I don't take it. He laughs and moves on only to pop up again and again.

In the locker room, I wait out the class but Gilbey sticks around and follows me into the hall at the bell. He doesn't say a word, just laughs that twisted sound of his. I'm sweating so bad I get goose bumps. Or maybe those are just from fear?

Text from Quinn: G, turkey sandwich w/mustard not mayo. Apple or banana.

I get my food and Ollie appears and chuckles. "Man, stress makes me eat more. Not you?"

"I had a date with a brownie last night, if you know what I mean?"

Oliver chews his sandwich, dripping with mayo. "One of the best girls I've ever dated. She only agreed to get with me, though, after I'd already stuffed my face." He grins a knowing look that makes my loathing feel like a side dish.

"She's filthy that way, but if that's the price you have to pay to get her, well, it's worth it."

Ollie laughs and smacks the table. "I like you, Greg. You get this shit." Then he opens his mouth but immediately shuts it. His eyes go wide and he tries to motion with his hand, but it just flops back to the table.

"What is it?"

"Me, you little fuck." Alva slides into the seat at my side.

My mouth goes dry. "What's up?"

"I know that you, your inflatable raft here, and that douche

Quinn have been working out. What I want to know is, where's the change? You're still disgusting."

I don't speak but do feel my lunch coming back up.

"That's fine, don't talk. I'll just fill in the blanks for you." Alva clears his throat. "I also know that you and Quinn stopped in to see Philmore this morning."

My heart seizes and I look over Alva's shoulder at the defibrillator.

"Surprised? Don't be. There isn't a fucking thing that goes on at this school that we don't know about. Shit, in the entire town." He leans closer. "I also know because of how close that shithole of a gym where you work out is to us, that you probably have questions about what we do. Let's hope for your sake that for once, you keep your fat, fucking nose where it belongs: out of other people's business."

My mind goes in too many directions for any clear thought, but I manage to say, "And if I don't?"

Alva draws even closer, as if he's a snake trying to wrap around my body. "You know what I'm going to say, so do I really have to say it?"

"Yeah, you do," Ollie pipes up.

Ollie's staring at Alva as hard as he can. But Alva just laughs.

"Fine. I'll make your life so miserable you'll want to kill yourself. Unless you already feel that way. Then maybe we'll just push you to do it." He claps my back hard enough that I feel the welt rising as he walks away.

"You okay, Greg?" Ollie's voice sounds as scared as mine.

"No. You?"

"Greg?" Ella's voice. She's between our table and the entrance to the cafeteria. I start to smile at her but freeze. Just beyond her is Callaghan.

Ollie speaks out the side of his mouth. "Go. See her. I'll distract him."

"'K."

Ella shrugs but I just keep moving forward with Ollie at my side.

"Mr. Callaghan?" Oliver says, and Callaghan takes his eyes off me for a moment, long enough for me to slip to Ella.

"So?" she says.

It takes a moment to get my brain to transition to her, but I manage. "So, yeah. Yesterday. I got caught up with Quinn and Oliver." I point toward Ollie, who sounds like he's talking a mile a minute about some new school club.

"You said that."

"I did? Shit, sorry."

She shifts her weight. "I just assumed it was with them. Sorry, I'm not trying to be a bitch, it's just, what the hell, Greg? Blowing people off is rude. You could have texted."

"Right, right, but I don't have your number." I laugh like it's hilarious, but Ella just stares at me.

"So put me in your contacts."

I fumble with my phone.

Ella gives me her number, and then asks, "So what were you doing? Still working out?"

Oliver is no longer speaking. I hear him coughing but do not turn around. I know Callaghan is there, listening. If I were smaller, Ella might see him, but I'm so wide he's eclipsed. "Working out, like you thought, but Quinn got sick and we had to get him home."

"Really? Is he all right?"

I can feel Callaghan on my back. Shit, maybe this is amusing for him, listening to me trying to talk to a girl.

"Yeah, stomach bug or something. He thinks it might be something he ate."

Callaghan cracks a step to my side. Ella jumps and I feel like I might piss myself. "Miss Jenner, if you don't mind, I need Mr. Dunsmore for a moment."

Ella says, "Sure," but since he wasn't really asking, it's not necessary. I see Ollie move to her. I hope he doesn't say too much.

Callaghan angles me toward the wall and looks straight into my eyes. His are gray and open so little it's as if he's just woken up. "Why did you and Mr. Casey go to Dr. Philmore's office this morning?"

"I, uh, wanted to."

Callaghan waits and leans in, just like Alva. "I could suspend you for what you did, using someone else's name like that. There are security cameras there, Greg. I figured someone with your *interests* would have figured that out."

Shit, he's right. "I'm sorry. That won't happen again."

"Oh, I know that. Because if you have anything you need to talk about, you come to me. And if you don't, I'll know anyway. Think about that." Then he turns on his heel and is gone.

Ella and Ollie come to me. "Greg, what was that all about?" Ella asks.

I look quickly at Ollie. He seems to understand what I'm looking for from him. "My project. Apparently Blint's been talking to him. He was just wishing me good luck."

Ella looks shocked. "Wow, that's so not like that creep, but good for you." I brace for a fat joke. None comes.

A pit opens up inside, deeper than the one I try to stuff with food. This is all too much at once. I'm not good at holding things together. At some point, either I will break something, or I will just break.

And then they will have won.

•   •   •

We're presenting our trailers in Blint's class, which I totally forgot, but it's probably good because I'm scared shitless of the reaction. We've already watched half from the class, and they've either been terrible or halfway decent. The good topics have ranged from small businesses in the area getting started, an inside look at the police force, and an account of one kid's grandfather's tours in Vietnam. The shitty ones were about some handbag company, the cheerleading squad (Taleana's), and that stupid show on the Jersey Shore.

Blint gave us all these rubrics to complete for each one, I think in an effort to keep us awake. There's no way in hell he's actually going to use these for grades. Then again, he's barely awake, stuffed up on his stool, appearing to take notes. He could just be doodling.

"Ella?" Blint says, and Ella rises. I'd like to whisper "good luck," but I'm not sure how she'd react.

She loads her trailer and the opening image is frozen on the projection screen. A collage of students, but with dividing lines that look like concrete and barbed wire, a concentration camp. I don't know how she did that, but I need to know. Someone near me says, "So fucking creepy," and I'd like to strangle her, but Ella begins.

"My documentary is about the cliques here at school. I'm interviewing as many as will let me, and filming them when they hang out and come into contact with other cliques, especially ones that don't get along. My aim is to see whether we're all really that different, or truly more the same than we realize."

That right there is the kind of eloquence I'm going to need with Callaghan. I'm taking notes.

The initial image rumbles like an earthquake has hit and then a piece of the collage pops forward and takes over the screen. It's of the chic girls, the rich and beautiful. The clip plays. Lots of laughter and perfect teeth. *"It's not our fault that our parents have a lot of money, so I'm not going to walk around being all ashamed of who I am. Why should I? Would you ask some hot girl to not be happy about her boobs?"* The girl laughs and looks like a model. *"Oh, wait, that's us, too."*

The scene slides back into the puzzle and another pops up: the goths. *"Yeah, we don't fit in. That's the whole point. We dress this way to make a statement about not being a part of anything."* Ella asks a question off camera that is inaudible. I make a note to tell her to type the questions for subtitles. *"I guess. Sure, we're a part of us, but that doesn't mean we're accepted."* The girl sneers and her face slides back behind her barrier. This is the most intriguing piece so far, even better than mine.

Another brick, the bros, Alva as spokesperson. He smiles at the camera but does not blink, just stares, and it's unnerving. *"Yeah, of course we're the best here. We've won State the past five years in a row and have been in the top five for the past fifteen years."* He pops his collar. *"And beyond the field, we're everything. Coach Mallory's donated more to this school than anyone else, all because we have the most successful tournament in the state, and because he's the embodiment of what it means to be a Warrior. Name one business that doesn't have our roster and schedule in its window. You can't."* Again, another question from

Ella. Alva's smile falls a fraction. *"Sure, people don't like us, but that's just jealousy. I'd be jealous of me if I was someone else."*

Ella's trailer finishes with scenes from the nerds, the jocks, the gays, pretty much every group we have, except for the film geeks—because I think that's just the two of us. I score her rubric and clap. Only a handful of other students joins me. I look around the room and all the slackers and stoners shoot her dirty looks. Same with the party kids, the snobs. I guess they didn't like the reflection in the mirror.

Ella steps away from Blint's podium and Taleana says, "Fucking slut!"

"Excuse me?" Ella stops next to her desk. I can't believe how controlled her voice is.

"You heard me." Taleana whips her head as she speaks. "I see what you're doing and it's bullshit. Rolling up on our boys. Trying to make us look bad. You don't knock my girls. No one does."

Blint moves slowly, as if he just wants this to resolve itself.

Ella smiles. And it looks genuine. "One, your *boys* disgust me; they're all yours. Two, *you* don't get to tell me what to record. If you don't like what you saw, change." She half turns to Blint, who's now standing and squeezing his temples. Ella has to say, "Right, Mr. Blint?" to get his attention.

"Yes. Yes. Taleana, I'm sorry that you didn't like this piece, this exposé . . ."

I almost laugh at his use of the word. I was right. Right?

". . . but you were all given freedom to choose your topics. I see nothing wrong with Ella's work."

Taleana looks at our teacher and then at Ella. She wads up the rubric and throws it in Ella's face. "Well, fuck that!" Taleana stomps out of the room without turning when Blint squeaks her name.

Ella takes a deep breath and moves down the row to her seat. I smile at her when she's close, but she doesn't see me. She's inside her head, looking at that scene, playing back the details. I wonder what she sees, because I'm thinking courageous, but she looks more vulnerable.

"All right then. Next?" Blint says. He resumes his perch and some kid gets up and delivers his lackluster presentation on growing hydroponic plants. I have a suspicion that he works better with another variety of herbs, but at least he was smart enough not to film them.

And now it's my turn.

I take a deep breath and drown out all sound. If I don't, all I'll hear are the whispers and jokes. No point in that. I'm about to show them how they should be prepared for a change. A new me.

Blint tells me to begin, and I steel myself and proceed. I'm not nearly as smooth as Ella, but I manage to deliver the details. I'm fat, we all know it, and it's about time I did something. Here it is.

I play my trailer and when the last beat drops there's an image of me on the floor covered in sweat, writhing from the pain. Badass if you ask me.

The laughter begins as a few pops, and the kernels burst at a rapid speed, and soon the entire room is losing their shit. All except for Ella. Blint halfheartedly tries to stop them.

All that's left for me to do is return to my seat. I sit and stare at my desk and ignore the "Greg?" I hear from Ella every few seconds. If my goals are laughable, pathetic, what does that say about me? If the idea of changing isn't going to affect how I'm viewed around here, why bother? I'll just stay Dun the Ton and to hell with all the rest. I'll eat and make films, or just eat and then maybe someone will make a film about me getting buried in a piano box after having to cut down the wall just to get my corpse out of the house.

The bell rings and I'm out in the hall and there's pressure on my arm. "Greg, are you okay?" Ella's voice is soft against the noise.

I nod. I thought my piece would be awesome. I thought it might change some perceptions. How could I have been so wrong? Fuck me.

"There she is." Taleana's voice cuts through everything and she's by Ella's side. "So are you planning to enter that piece of shit film into the contest? You wanna have everyone at school all over your ass. Is that what you want, you little bitch?"

I am amazed by two things. One, how strong Ella seems. She's listening to Taleana with her eyes straight ahead. Two, that Taleana paid enough attention in class to realize that the school will be watching and voting on these films. Maybe she isn't a complete flake?

"Are you finished?" Ella asks, and it sounds like she's talking to a telemarketer on the phone.

Taleana opens her mouth, says, "As if."

Ella sighs. "Yes, I am entering my film into the contest. Is that a problem for you? Are you going to *do something*?" Ella shakes her hands at her sides in mock terror.

Taleana laughs. "Don't you realize who I am? The fucking cheer captain at this school." She bends down to get level with Ella. "And do you realize how much of a hard-on our principal, this school, this town has for sports?"

Ella doesn't answer.

"Didn't think so. Because if you did, you'd know to keep to yourself, mind your own fucking business, and stay the hell outta my way."

I'm surprised Ella doesn't ask Taleana if she's finished again. She so looks like she wants to. A small crowd has gathered and I'm sweating over this conversation. This is the exact wrong place for me to be at this moment, but it would take a Mack truck to move me from here.

"And apparently you can't tell that I. Do. Not. Give. A. Fuck." Ella steps closer to Taleana.

Taleana's face turns so red I'm afraid she might literally explode.

"What the fuck is going on?" Alva's voice surrounds us, and

then he slides in, poised and confident, even while pissed off. Asshole. Sick, psychopathic asshole.

"Your girlfriend has a problem with my film project," Ella says and sounds more annoyed than angry.

Alva scoops up Taleana, who goes from angry to being caressed in a second. It looks so much like bad acting on a soap opera it's disgusting. Alva sees me, and smiles.

"Wouldn't it figure that *you* have something to do with this, fat fuck?"

"This has nothing to do with Greg. This is my project."

Alva looks at Ella. "Right. We all know Dun the Ton walks around with a phone in his hand because he can't find his dick. Don't protect him."

"I'm not. You're wrong, that's all."

Again, Ella's voice is harsh, defensive. Still, I don't like how quickly she jumped away from my defense.

"Am I?" Alva has shifted Taleana and is leaning toward Ella.

"What the hell is wrong with the two of you? Are you really this stupid?" Ella says. "Listen. Your girlfriend is pissed because I'm showing people who she really is and who you and your douche team really are. If she doesn't like it, then she should work on that. This is *my* film, not Greg's. If you can't wrap your brain around that concept, it's not my problem. Do you follow?"

There's a gasp in the crowd behind Alva and Taleana. It punctuates exactly how I feel. *What the fuck is she doing?*

"Yeah. I follow. But you need to remember one thing, you little twat. This is *our school*. It seems that *you've* forgotten. Just ask Dun, he'll help you remember."

Alva and Taleana strut away, and Taleana says, "Warned you. I'll check your ass later."

I'm sweating so bad I should go and change my shirt. Ella spins toward me. "What, Greg? What did he mean?"

I look away and the scene from yesterday flashes before me. Across the hall, the lockers that should have Kyle and Stephen at them, grabbing books or watching us, are closed. They're not here today. Alva's right. This is his school. Quinn's right, too. It's the team's town. "You know what he meant. Just that we shouldn't mess with him. He thinks we're working together or some shit."

Ella purses her lips. "No, that's bullshit. You know something."

I stay silent. But down the hall, where Alva and Taleana have paused, there's a squeal.

"Of course! That's it. That little slut is fucking Moby! No wonder she's protecting him."

The laughter echoes up and down the hall, followed by the whispers that will keep the rumor alive.

Ella's eyes are brimming with tears. I don't know what to do. If I reach out to her, it will only reinforce what will soon be the school's "truth." If I don't, and I let her suffer, what does that say about me?

"Ella, I'm sorry." I reach for her.

She pushes my arm away. "Fuck you, Greg! I don't need *that*! I need you to be honest with me. Of all the kids in this school, I never expected *you* to lie to me." She clenches her jaw against the tears. "So tell me the goddamn truth."

I swallow and nod. Shit, I wish it didn't have to come out this way. I wish I could have kept her in the dark. But why? To protect her? She doesn't seem like she'd want it. Or need it. But now, with what Taleana just said, maybe we both do.

"All right, Ella. But not right now. It's not safe out in the open like this."

"'Not safe.' Greg, what the hell?" She wipes tears from her face.

The words lodge in my throat. "Something I recorded."

Her eyes grow large. "What? *Tell* me."

I rub my face with my hand. The bell's going to ring any second. Now is not the time to have this conversation. "Later."

"What, after school, so you can blow me off again? Not now, because you don't want anyone to see us together?"

"No. It's not like that."

"What then? You want me to come see you while you're working out?"

It's absurd, but Q and Ollie know what's up, and if I'm going to bring her into this weird fold, why not have us all on the same page? We're there already, us outcasts, including Ella. Because if she wasn't before, she certainly is now. Shit. "Yeah. Trust me, it's the only way."

"Trust you? That's asking a lot, Greg. So give me a hint. What did you record?" Her words are hushed.

I know there is no other option. I need her help, and she needs to know. "Would it surprise you that the bros are hazing one another?"

Ella stares down the hallway. Back to where Alva and Taleana were. To the spot where the first ugly rumor about her took shape. I have no clue what she's thinking, what's going on inside her, but now I want to know more than ever.

"Greg, there's not a whole hell of a lot that surprises me. I've seen more than you understand."

Her words reach into me and hold fast. I've seen it all. Haven't I? "I don't understand."

She turns to me and smiles. "You give me your story, and I'll let you know mine."

There is nothing more in this moment that I would love to hear, or that I am afraid of.

CHAPTER 13

OLLIE AND I ARE CLINGING TO EACH OTHER for dear life, just trying to keep the other one standing.

"One more set, boys. One more. Thirty seconds," Q barks and we separate, then move to our respective medicine balls. Quinn's had us throw them overhead, against the wall, like a thousand times, and right after, swing a kettlebell for another insane amount of reps, and then do some disgusting number of sit-ups. We've already done this four times, and each time, Ollie and I have had to peel each other off the floor. If Quinn didn't make this up as some sort of punishment for bringing in Ella, then he's just a sick asshole and I want to crush him with all my blubber.

Because it was my call to make. He didn't see what I did. She's in this as much as we are. So I laid out all the details, and once we're done working out, we're all going to figure this shit out. Whether he likes it or not.

"Go!"

And we do, and it burns, and we grunt and sweat flies all over the place and I'm sure if Ella closed her eyes this would sound like some real nasty sex scene. But she's stuck around and Ollie and I have no choice but to sound like we're banging or dying.

We lie on the floor and Q chucks us our towels. "Good work, guys. Really nice job."

Right now the lax bros could kill me and I'd be fine with it. But I help Ollie up and we both collapse onto benches. Q hands us water bottles and we down them.

Ella clears her throat. "Guys, seriously, that was some badass shit. I may need to add you to my documentary as a separate clique—"

"So what are you thinking?" Q sits with us and glares at Ella.

"What, you trust me now?"

"You know everything, so either I have to trust you or watch out for what you'll do." Quinn smiles, but it's not warm.

"That's some quality insight, Quinn." Ella smiles right back, but hers is genuine. "But before we go there, let me ask Dun something."

"What is it?" I say.

"Earlier. Taleana. That go anywhere?"

We all shift, uncomfortably. I'm not surprised they've heard it, too. "Yeah, but don't worry. No one in this room believes her."

Q and Ollie nod at this. Ella points at them. "Doesn't really matter what they think, though."

She's right and there's nothing else for me to do but agree.

"Shit," she says, but no more.

We've got some enormous shit we're dealing with and now this development with her. What do we handle first?

Fortunately, Ella finds her way through. "Forget about that bitch for now. I have a question about the bros and you." She waits until we're all looking at her. "Why?"

"Why, what?" I ask.

"Why do any of this? Expose them? What they're doing is fucked up, but you're risking a lot. So why?"

"It's not just exposing them, it's doing the right thing, for everyone."

Ella takes it in. "I like that, and that you don't want to burn this whole place to the ground in the process, but picking and choosing might be real tough."

"That's what I said." Quinn points at his chest.

"Great minds, Quinn, you and me," Ella says.

I check on Ollie because he's been so quiet. "You all right with all this?"

"Maybe?"

Ella stretches. "I'm just saying that once you have what you think is enough, you'd better consider what you want do with it. Clearly the super isn't your outlet." She frowns. "But don't think for one second I'm trying to protect them. I hate them, now even more than before, but I won't let that affect what I see."

"What do you see?" I feel like I've cut her off, but I had to ask.

"I see you, Greg. Not Dun the Ton. You. You might be in your own way, trying to pick and choose the story, when, really, you just need to let it unfold."

We sit in silence for a moment, and if Q and Ollie are thinking the same as me, their heads must hurt. "I create in my own way, and sometimes shit goes sideways. But if I get the message out there, who cares?"

Ella nods. "That's exactly my point. You can't do the same as you have. *This time*, there can be no question whether you're telling the truth. If you're going to see this through, you have to get comfortable with that."

"Why? Why does it have to be like that?" I'm a little pissed, but mostly uneasy.

"I don't make the rules. If I did . . ." Ella trails off but then picks it back up. "You have control issues, Greg. No worries, we all do. You *can* control film. You *can't* control how people react."

"But isn't that the opposite of what you just said?" I look to Ollie and Q, but they seem as confused as me.

"Yes and no. At some point, you'll get that the story is already telling itself. And the craziness is that those are the best stories."

"Shit, this is just . . . wow! I went from just being a fat shit hating life, to working out with you two, to getting caught up in a hazing scandal, all within a week. What do you have planned for the rest of the year?" Ollie says.

We all laugh, but I feel a little nagging sensation. He's right, this shit is snowballing. But what gets me is the part he implied, the *us*. That's not real. Q barely hangs with me. I barely know Ella or Oliver. Has something changed or am I, again, just wanting to believe that it has?

The worst part is, even though I've manipulated things, I'm used to throwing everything away. But if I do that this time, it's not just about me. Everyone will feel the fallout.

Someone coughs, and I look up.

"Greg, are you all right?" Ella asks. They're all looking at me.

"Sorry, I was just thinking." They wait for more. "What, is this the point where we're all supposed to pile hands and yell something inspirational?"

Ella laughs. "I'm totally researching that. How many times does that happen in movies?"

"Too many," I say.

"Damn, I was pumped for that scene." Ollie chuckles. "My grandfather likes this saying. *The best thing about the future is that it comes one day at a time*." Ollie stares ahead. "I think, like with losing weight, or building a film, or exposing psychos, we do our work one day at a time. Whatever the hell that is."

I pull into myself at this, his openness. It's painful.

The gym is quiet, no yelling lacrosse bros, no kids getting tortured. And I let myself believe in Ollie's words, and quite possibly, Ella's. Tomorrow will be completely different, and I'll take it as it comes. And that's as tragic as it is inspiring.

· · ·

Home, after dinner, in front of my computer, I finally have a moment to think. The bros could have been waiting for us instead of practicing outside in the melting snow. Q could have flipped seeing Ella. Ollie could have just bailed because this shit is crazy. Ella could have gone into hiding because of Taleana. None of that happened. I am one lucky son of a bitch.

There's a rare thought.

I scroll through Kyle's and Stephen's Facebook walls. Not much happening but typical bullshit back and forth. Neither has posted any status updates, but that doesn't mean shit. Time to follow up. I send them both the same message: Guys, we need to talk. Wherever and whenever you want. Let me know.

I tweet my results to #weightloss. I read other people's success and want to reach out and retweet or give them props, but I'm not there yet. I check some of my favorite film sources and read some posts and am about to actually do some homework when I get a text from Ella: Hope all is cool after today. Thanks for hearing me out. And for not asking too many questions. I never did swap stories with you.

Don't worry, it's fine. Thanks for helping us figure
this out. And I'll help you with the other thing,
if you want. If I can.

I don't know if you can, or if you should. You've
got enough right now. But we'll talk. Promise.

I blush. Weird. She's nowhere near me. Whatever works for you.
Thanks.

I wait for her to reply but she doesn't and that's fine. I look
back at my screen and Kyle's messaged me: I'll talk, but not Steve.

Shit, I wonder what that's about. K. When?

Now. the park near your house.

All right. Give me 10.

I don't know what I'll say to my parents, but screw it, this
game is on.

I head downstairs and they're watching TV. "Hey, Quinn
thinks a short walk before bed is a good idea. You know, rev up
the metabolism and all that. All right?"

They both nod and Dad says, "Enjoy."

I head out the door and am at the playground within five minutes. I check my phone, no texts, so I sit at the picnic table and wait.

Footsteps crack behind me. "Kyle?" I call out.

"Yeah," Alva says, stepping out of the shadows. Gilbey smiles at his side.

My stomach plunges to my knees and I'm frozen. Not that it matters. I can't run away, even if I tried.

"Stand up, fat ass." Alva looms over me, cracking his knuckles. Gilbey watches.

Shit. My legs are numb when I stand and my ears are ringing. But I'm ready. Being fat has, ironically, prepared me to be less than everyone else.

The punch comes quick and into my ribs. It stings and I double over, but I do not fall.

"Now, you'll tell me the truth or I'll keep punching. Got me, Dun?"

I slide my hands to my knees and push myself to standing.

"God, you're pathetic," Alva says.

"Yeah, maybe, but look who's talking."

"What's that supposed to mean?"

"You said you wanted the truth. I'm just being honest."

"Fuck you!" Alva steps closer. "What did you want to talk to Kyle about? Like I said, there isn't shit I don't know."

"Did you force him to text you if I reached out, is that it? Or do you have his password?"

The second punch takes the wind out of me and I wheeze to get it back. Alva laughs.

"You're not the one asking questions. I am. You ready to answer?"

I nod and stand, as much as it hurts.

"So answer."

"What he ate for his snack yesterday." I know it's a huge risk, but it's one I had to gamble. I've been trying to control, trying to be safe. Time to let it rip.

Alva's nostrils flare, and I'm positive I'm looking at the face of insanity.

"Figures you'd want to talk about food." Alva pulls me by the front of my sweatshirt. "You will never have that conversation. Understand? So don't even try."

I swallow. "And if I do?"

"You like that Ella slut. It'd be a shame if something were to happen to her."

I think I say, "Fuck you," but I could be wrong. The fist slamming into me takes away everything.

The ground is cold and wet, but I don't immediately try and get up once I regain consciousness. My head is swirling too much. I look around just in case they're still here. But I'm alone, lying on my face, because Alva punching me in the back of the head was the answer. The question now is whether I accept it.

CHAPTER 14

AFTER A VERY BORING FILM CLASS, Ella and I walk out together, and Kyle and Stephen are at their lockers. But Gilbey, Alva, and Taleana are clustered around them, a barrier.

"He's gonna flatten you like a pancake and then eat your ass," Taleana says. A volley of laughter follows.

Ella ignores her and keeps walking. I do, too, but catch Kyle's eye and he doesn't turn away. After I got home last night, created an excuse for my parents—black ice—and showered, I lay in bed thinking about Kyle and Stephen. I bet they saw the message. They knew but understood there was nothing they could do.

"Dun the Ton, how's the dome?" Gilbey laughs and rubs the back of his own head. "How long you think you were out?"

I keep walking but he stays at my side.

"Huh, how long? A minute, two? More?"

I ignore him but cannot ignore how Ella is looking at me.

"Lot can happen in a minute, fat fuck. Know that you're not the only one with a phone."

I understand what he's hinting at, but the implications are vast.

"Yeah? Well, let's see it." Ella practically climbs up my arm to get in Gilbey's face.

"Wouldn't you love to." He smiles and grabs his junk.

The crowd moves closer. "Come on, Ella, let's go," I say. She keeps her eyes on Gilbey.

"Huh, no balls, all talk. Figures." Ella flips her hair. We move away, but in a flash Gilbey is in front of us, holding out his phone, the screen showing some image that's too dark for me to discern, but Ella's eyes pop.

"No balls, my ass, you bitch."

"Gilbey, no! Put that fucking thing away!" Alva's voice booms from behind and Gilbey slides his phone into his pocket. He looks like a little kid who's just been scolded.

I pick up the pace, and Ella stays at my side.

"You need to explain that," she says.

"I will. It was a sucker punch."

"With his balls?"

"What did you just say?"

"The picture he showed us. Didn't you see it?"

"No. The angle."

Ella scowls. "It was you on the ground, being tea bagged."

My skin crawls and I bolt. The bathroom's down the hall and I crash into people as I go. Fuck them and whatever they're saying to me. I pull up to the sink and start scrubbing. I lather and rinse and repeat. I lose count of how many times. I showered last night, but still. Why couldn't I have just stayed some fat shit? None of this would ever have happened. Not to me at least. Shit, Kyle and Stephen had worse, and if I weren't around no one outside the bros would know. Or at least no one would have evidence.

I've got enough. I've had enough.

* * *

Hard shell tacos, not soft. Only vegetable toppings.

I get my two tacos and sit. Oliver has two hard and two soft. "I can't just eat two puny tacos. Not yet."

"You're on the plan, too?" I pat my phone.

"Yeah, I figure why not go all in?" Ollie takes a bite, and half the taco disappears.

"I'm thinking we need to move ahead," I say.

"Why? What happened?"

I shake my head but hear, "I'd like to know that, too." Ella sits next to us with her salad and water. I bury my face in my hands.

"Whenever you're ready, Greg. Oliver and I will wait."

They chat and their food crunches and my stomach growls. I peel my hands away but don't look at them. Instead, I devour my tacos in four bites and wipe my face. They're both staring.

"Had to get that out of the way. Sorry."

Ollie laughs. "I figured you could put it away, just haven't seen it. You and me should hit up the buffet restaurant. We'd destroy shit."

"No, you shouldn't." Ella nibbles her salad and looks so small and sounds so pious next to us I feel like telling her to stick it.

"All right." I sigh. "So last night . . ." I tell them the story and try not to embellish my bravery.

"You all right, Greg?" Ella asks when I'm done.

"No."

"I don't give a shit, I'll kick either of their asses right now. Gilbey or Alva by himself doesn't scare me." Ollie puffs up, but it's all for show.

"You know it would never be just one of them. It'll never be a fair fight; that's why we need to move ahead now."

"Look at you. Ready to throw it in just because you got played." Ella's voice is deadly calm.

"What?" I sit up and can hear the tinge of anger in my question.

Ella leans across the table. "Greg, stick with our plan. Work with us to get the entire story. Don't do what you've always done, walking away from shit because you're afraid of the rest."

I don't even know what to say to her. I don't know if I'm angry or shocked or hurt. Maybe *betrayed* fits best?

"Listen, Greg," Ella continues, "I'm not trying to be harsh—"

"But you are," Ollie cuts her off. "Go easy, huh?"

I'm relieved, sort of.

"Noted," she says. "Okay, so I'm sorry if that was blunt, but here it is: you run now, you'll never get them. You don't even know *who* to run to. Now, I'm sorry that you got punched and tea bagged. I really am. But you can't tell me that's the worst thing that's ever been done to you."

"What? What the hell happened to you, Greg?" Ollie asks.

I close my eyes. "Last night. It was a setup, and I got knocked out. Gilbey tea bagged me."

Ollie's fist booms off the table. "No! No, Greg! They can't get away with this shit."

I know he doesn't mean just what's happened to me. But we can't discuss that because there's laughter in the distance, and someone saying, "Me mad. Me want more tacos." Another, "That would be the worst threesome ever. Terrible way to die."

Ella hears it. Ollie hears it. We all go silent.

A minute passes and Ella says, "Like that." She points toward the assholes and their comments. "We're all in it. So you can't make the kind of move you want until we know it will work."

"But what if I can't wait? What then?"

"Come on, Greg," Ella says. "You're stronger than this. I think your problem is that you've looked at yourself in the mirror through your own lens for too long." She stills. "It's time to harden the fuck up."

"What do you think I'm doing with Q and Ollie, prancing through a field? 'Harden the fuck up'? Who are *you* to tell me what to do?" I'm hovering over my seat, leaning over the table toward Ella. Ollie's eyes are big, watching me. I sit. "Fuck, I'm sorry."

Ella's frown deepens. "Damn, you've got issues. And I don't like *that* one. Getting yelled at is not my thing. Remember that. All right?"

I nod, thoroughly ashamed of myself.

"But you can use that energy for what I mean. Deal with that shit, on the inside, or you'll always be the fat kid."

I clench my jaw and resist the urge to unleash on her again. One, because she's right, and two, because no one has ever spoken to me like this. Not my parents. Not the doctors. No one. "How the hell would you know? Did you already get your degree in psychiatry?" I try to ask calmly, but my voice is still simmering.

Ella does not blink. She pulls something laminated from her bag and flips it onto the table. It's a picture. Of Ella, but not Ella.

"Go ahead. Look."

I pick it up and Ollie looks on with me. It's a printout of a picture that's been Photoshopped. In it, Ella is covered in words like "slut" and "whore" and "cunt." She's been made to appear naked and is surrounded by a group of guys, also naked. Even though I know it's Photoshopped, there's a moment where I question what's real and what isn't.

"That was on Facebook at the start of eighth grade. Worst year of my life. Mom had left us, and I was so out of it that I didn't really connect with friends over the summer. And when school started, I had lost them, and I'd become something else."

"A slut?" Ollie says and blushes. "I mean, that's what they were saying about you?"

"Exactly." Ella looks down. "I thought about killing myself every goddamn day. Fucking Bethany and Misty and Chandra. Those bitches made my life miserable. We used to be tight, and then . . ." She trails off. "I have no clue what changed. Still don't."

"So what happened?" I can't help but ask. The story is playing out in my mind and I need to know.

"I tried. Dad found me with the note and bottle of sleeping pills. Those medics were at the house before he hung up the phone, he says. Pumped my stomach, kept me in the hospital, ended up at an in-house psych ward."

"Did that help?" Ollie asks.

"No. I learned how to cope, but I was still a hot mess. Every day I wondered if there was something about me, something I'd done to make people think I was a slut. I hadn't even had a boyfriend. It was just so out of the blue."

I'm on the edge of my seat, breathing heavy. I so understand how the tide just turns. "So, what happened?"

"Dad dug around while I was in treatment. Looked at everything online, found out what was going on, had some conversations with people, teachers, cops, doctors, got an idea of what to expect." Ella pauses and looks around. "He'd already moved when I was released. I went psycho. I had prepared myself to confront them. It was all I thought about. So it took me a month to even speak to my father, two more to listen to him explain. I still don't know if I've ever really accepted it, even though it was for my own good. I doubt I would have changed anything. Just me."

"But I remember you in eighth grade. You were quiet but normal," I say.

"Looks can be deceiving."

"Fuck, I never would have known. Never thought that." Ollie rubs his face.

"And that's my point. Don't go feeling sorry for me. I don't need that. But I do need the both of you to man up and roll with whatever comes at us. That's what I'm doing now. You heard Taleana. Those pricks just now. The rumor mill's at it again. Like me, you owe it to yourselves to fight this."

"About that. This *getting tougher* shit, why do you get to suggest that? It doesn't seem like you ever did? Your dad moved you away from the problem," I say.

"Exactly. But it's not as if I had a choice, so here's my chance to make up for it. Do you think I like girls like Taleana calling me a whore and aiming to kick my ass? No. I want to expose them, and the guys that do the same. I owe it to *myself*. Got it?"

I do, and just when I thought I had a way to edit the story, Ella pulls me right back in, demanding more.

*   *   *

I work on my project in the computer lab, piecing together weigh-ins and workouts. I'm going to have to do another round of trans-formation shots.

The shadow appears before the clacking shoes and I don't look up, just minimize the screen.

"Mr. Dunsmore?" Callaghan is behind me.

"Working on my project. That's all."

"I didn't ask, but thank you for offering. Let me see." He motions toward the mouse.

I realize how I just sounded. And it's because of Alva. Is he really that connected? Because if so, the man responsible for those connections is standing next to me. I hesitate to play the video, but it's school property. He has the right. It's raw and choppy and I look like a mess on screen. There's no way he can be enjoying what he sees.

Callaghan nods. There's a knock at the door. We both turn and see Coach Mallory. I've rarely seen him in person, but have at enough events to know that he has a perma-scowl. But right now he looks downright pissed, as if maybe Callaghan forgot to meet with him or something. The principal stands and mutters, "Keep it up, Greg," and moves to the ex-marine. They exchange a few words and move down the hall.

I stare at the screen. I know it's a work in progress, and I know I intend to add more, but still, something's missing. I need to make it work. Period. All of this. I pack up my shit and head to the gym.

I change while Quinn scribbles into his workout log. He's sweaty again.

"You miss your run this morning?" I ask.

"No, never. Why?"

I stop tying my shoe. "Didn't you work out here because you missed your run? That's what you told me last time."

I can see Quinn's eyes behind the corner of his notebook. He's shifting, trying to remember. Did he lie to me?

"Oh, yeah, I may not make it to Dad's gym, so I figured I'd take care of things here."

Total bullshit. Quinn spends more time at his dad's gym than at home. I'd ask what the fuck is going on if I had the energy to think about one more issue.

Ollie and I weigh in and Q does his intro for me. I'm 320. Ollie is 368. We warm up, and it still baffles me how no one else is ever down here. Yeah, the equipment is old and kind of shitty, but still. Although, Quinn has told me how many guys from school are members at his dad's gym.

"Just squeeze your belly like you're about to get punched and keep that ass tight, no knee bend."

We use Quinn's cues and finish the sets, move on to more pressing with the dumbbells "for volume," as Quinn says. Like we need more of that? We finish with bent-over rows and my shoulders burn as if I've been out in the sun.

"Nice job, guys." Q leans on a bench. "And I'm glad you're on board with the diet, Ollie. Big changes are coming. As my dad always says, 'You can't out-train a shitty diet.'"

Ollie and I look at each other and laugh.

"So glad you two find this amusing. How about—"

"That was the shittiest performance I have ever seen! Yesterday you made us look like a joke! Today, you pay!" Alva's voice cuts through our conversation. We all turn toward the noise.

"Shit, G, hold up. They kicked your ass because they know you know what's going down."

"Your point?"

Alva yells again, and someone falls to the floor.

"You could be getting played again. There's no guarantee that if you walk through that door it'll be some hazing. It could be them *waiting* for you to come in, phone in hand."

"Then they've got you, Greg. Quinn's got a good point. You can't record people the way you do," Ollie says.

I look at my phone and listen at the door. Damn soundproofing. "I don't know what to do."

"I got this, G. Hold up."

"What are you . . ."

But Q goes to the regular door, the one that's always locked, and is through it before I can finish asking.

Ollie's eyes bug. "Get ready to call 911."

We hold our breath and we wait, but hear nothing.

A moment later the door opens and Quinn returns. "Just dropping their equipment and making them put it all back on. Like a race or something."

"They see you?"

"Oh yeah. But I kicked my sneaker off when I got in, pretended I was looking for it, then held it up and said, 'Assholes around here looting my locker.'" Quinn looks at me. "They were waiting, G. Alva and Gilbey, standing across from the door with *their* phones."

"Greg, what Ella said at lunch, listen to her. Don't trust anyone else," Ollie says.

I nod and wonder if I should even trust myself.

CHAPTER 15

ALL EVENING I'VE BEEN OBSESSING over how to get to Kyle and Stephen. It's better than obsessing over food, but I'm getting nervous, because I have no answer. They might be willing to talk, to give me some way of cracking things open. They might not. But I'll never know unless I can reach out to at least one of them. And I don't think showing up on their doorsteps is a good idea. Not considering how this town talks and how connected their dads are to the bros' legacy.

Fuck it. Even though Alva's probably monitoring their accounts, I send them another message. No point in trying to hide when they already know.

Kyle and Stephen, Hey I know you aren't allowed to talk to

me, but if you need to for any reason, I'm here. Hope to
hear from you.

I stare at what I've written, and it drives home how truly
messed up today has been. Ella's story, now ongoing. Q saving my
ass. My life feels tipped at some weird angle.

My phone chimes with a text. Ollie. You all right?

Hanging in there.

It's weird how much he cares. Or maybe it's completely normal
and I've just never experienced it?

Well, make sure your feet are on the
ground o_O

I laugh, even though that's some twisted-ass shit to say.

I text Ella. Thanks for what you said today. About yourself and
about me.

Really? Ur welcome, I guess. But it wasn't
too creepy that I still have that picture?

Totally creepy, but I wear my reminder
of things, so no judging here.

> You'll succeed, and then you'll have your film :)

Someday. Thanks. I caught her up on what happened today as soon as I got home. She wasn't surprised. Even though they are so totally different, there's something so similar about her and Quinn.

There's a knock at my door and it opens. Dad sees me latched onto my phone. "Bad time?"

It may be. I have no idea what he wants. "No, what's up?"

He sits on the edge of my bed. "You feeling okay?"

"Yeah, why?"

"You didn't go out for a walk tonight. You barely ate. Just checking."

I should have just said I wanted some fresh air and not attached my going out to Quinn's advice. "You're right. I should have. Just busy with schoolwork, and I really wasn't that hungry. I'm good."

He looks relieved. "All right. If you say so. But you let me know if something's up. We're here for you, your mother, and *me*. That may sound weird after I was such an ass the other day, but it's true."

"Sure," I say. "I know." But inside, what he said before, it's sticking around. I don't blame him for being disappointed with my screw-ups, but it doesn't mean I like hearing how much it bothers him.

He looks around and stands. "Don't stay up too late."

I nod and wait for him to close my door, but he says, "Do you mind me asking, how much weight have you lost?"

It's funny how he didn't give me a chance to answer the first part of the question before asking the second. Regardless, I'm proud enough to be honest. "Thirty-two."

His eyes widen. "Really? That Quinn, wow. He's something else."

"That's an understatement," I say.

"Yeah, you're right." He chuckles. "Well, keep it up."

I check for messages from Kyle, Stephen, or Quinn, just in case. Nothing. No surprise. It's not always easy reaching out, asking for help or being honest. I have yet to succeed at any of those.

● ● ●

Quinn is quiet the whole ride in this morning. Doesn't say a word about yesterday, which I appreciate. What he's doing for me, and now Ollie, is pretty awesome. We just have such a weird relationship. But I know there's something under the surface that *he* needs to get off his chest. In time, I guess.

Then it is weird in the halls, too. Nothing worth recording. Everyone's quiet. Which makes me nervous. A quiet school is dangerous. We're all like animals here. We can sense danger even if we have no idea what it is or where it's coming from. But unlike the animals, we've got nowhere to hide.

I head into the PE locker room and no longer feel like I've lost more than thirty pounds. I feel as if I ate someone else. Kids eye me as I head to my locker, whisper, laugh, say shit. And I stuff it all down.

"Yeah, so I told the kid he'd better not mess with me or I'd break his fucking face." Gilbey's voice pours over the lockers and I tense. Normally, I'd think he was just talking shit, but after what I've seen, who knows?

"What'd he do?" some kid asks Gilbey.

"He didn't fucking listen. Got in my face and asked what I was gonna do. I had my mini stick in the car, so I grabbed it and the dick just laughed. Guess he thought it was a toy or something."

"Yeah?"

The entire locker room is listening now. Most have stopped changing. Even me.

"As soon as I cracked him across the face he knew what was up. Caught him right in the jaw. Couple of his teeth were sticking through his cheek."

"Did he run?"

"Tried to." Gilbey laughs and it's ugly. "I caught him in a knee and he went down. And let's just say, he won't be walking right for quite some time. If ever."

"Holy fuck."

Holy fuck is right.

Kids lace shoes and file out. I change as quickly as I can, but I'm still last. Which means laps. Eh, I could use the extra work.

I turn the corner, and Gilbey is waiting. "What took you so long, Dun? Have trouble tying your own shoes?" He laughs and I step around him. Or try to. There really isn't enough space in the narrow hall leading to the gym.

He grabs me, spins me around. "Hey, fuck face. I need to ask you a question."

"What?" I stop because it's just easier to get it over with.

He sneers. "Did you not understand the message we sent?"

I play dumb. "What?"

"Your meeting with *Kyle*? Did you not understand or do you just like the taste of my balls?"

More than being angry, I wish I had my phone. Since I don't, there's no point in engaging this asshole. "Got it," I say and turn away. He grabs me again.

"I don't think you do, cuz if you did you wouldn't have messaged Kyle and Stephen last night." Gilbey gets closer and under the fluorescent lights somehow looks smaller. "What, you think we aren't watching that shit?"

Of course I knew it was a long shot. But I still wonder if Kyle or Stephen saw it. I still wonder if there's a chance.

"Are you fucking listening to me, you fat fuck? You remember what we said about your sweet little bitch. The things we could do to her. Damn!" Gilbey clips me off the back of my head. Just an open-handed slap, but it does the trick. It drives home just what he means.

These assholes are capable of anything. They will do whatever they feel like in order to preserve their cult and their standing. I don't give a shit how much they hurt me. I started this. But everyone has a fucking line, and mine seems to be Ella. Not just because she's a girl, but because there's some shit you just don't do. And what Gilbey just said, combined with what I know they're capable of. No. No goddamn way I'm ever going to let that happen. He'll have to kill me first.

And in this moment I see just how little space he has behind his head and the brick wall, and just how big I am, and how strong I need to be. I charge.

We hit the wall, and his head bounces as I thought it would. "I'm listening, you psycho. But don't think I don't know what's going on, or that I won't do anything about it, just because you and Alva don't want me to."

Gilbey squirms like a bug, but can't reach me with his hands. He's fuming. "You're in for it now, Jabba."

I revel in having him pinned like this. "Yeah, just what are you—"

Gilbey lands a knee so perfectly in my junk that I fall like a tree. I squirm, try to catch my breath, and don't hear what he says. I can guess though. But I'm not afraid. I know the truth, and regardless of whatever he or Alva does, I'll make damn sure I'm not the only one.

I manage to get to one knee and stand after a few minutes.

Class is already in progress. I can hear Coach's whistle and don't even see the point in going. But if I cut, that means I'll have to answer to Callaghan. No, thanks. I massage my bruised balls and limp into class.

Coach sees me and blows his whistle. "Dunsmore. So glad you decided to join us. Ten laps."

I nod and start trudging. Every step is painful. My nuts feel like they're up in my belly. I keep my head down, but feel eyes on me for the first few laps. Hear the laughter. Then it's just me and my sweat and Gilbey, who is looking every time I peer around. He's found his target, and I have a sense of what those newbie lax bros must feel. Yet, unlike them, I'm going to build a way out.

CHAPTER 16

QUINN TEXTS WHAT TO EAT and Ollie and I sit with the same lunch. Ella shows up and notices me wincing. I tell them both about PE and Gilbey. None of us has any answers. We all know that we're in over our heads. But the only thing to do is move ahead.

I spend the rest of the day dreading after school. I don't think Alva or Gilbey will have a problem roping us into practice and using our bodies as goals.

Quinn's with Oliver when I arrive in the locker room. They both look at me as if someone in my family just died.

"I take it Ollie told you," I say.

"Yeah. I'm not surprised. Alva's controlled, Gilbey's not. And it's obvious they're egging you on. Don't take the bait."

I set my bag down. "I don't plan on it."

"Good. I'm just going to eavesdrop, in case. Squats today, if your nuts can handle it." He walks into the weight room.

"Jesus, Greg, you've had a rough day. Maybe you should sit this one out?" Ollie shrugs. "And what is it with the bros and balls?"

"No idea about *why* the balls, but mine are fine." I pass my phone to Ollie. "Guess we'll record our own weight today."

Ollie records while I step on. The digits pop: 315. Holy shit. A couple of weeks and I might be sub-300. Ollie and I high-five and then he weighs himself: 365.

"Shit, Greg, we're kicking ass and taking names."

We head into the weight room. Quinn's at the regular door, has it opened a crack, and I almost ask what he's doing, but I hear the voice speaking and turn my phone back on.

"The pain game? I don't think you boys have been doing it right. Not based on what I've seen on the field." The voice. It's not Alva and it's not Gilbey.

Quinn turns, sees the phone, and locks eyes with me. "You want me to go?"

I could say yes, let him take the heat, but that's not right. I need to face this. "No. Together."

We move into the practice gym through the other door, and in the middle of the floor, with his tie tucked into his shirt, stands

Callaghan, lacrosse stick in hand. I freeze, but fortunately Ollie nudges me in the side. "Greg?"

I get our principal square in the center of the screen and focus. The upperclassmen stand across from the underclassmen, as before. The first kid starts with the chant: *Our allegiance is to the Warriors, our bodies are weapons . . .*

"Watch and learn, boys," Callaghan says, and fires the first ball into a lax bro.

The kid falls to the ground. There's a stunned silence, but Callaghan takes no notice. He moves onto the next and when the kid doesn't say anything, he just whips the ball at his head. He, too, goes down.

"The words. Let me *hear* them! Your tournament is right around the corner. Without discipline, you will disappoint. If you disappoint, this will only get worse." Callaghan grabs the next stick in line and the JV player starts reciting. Our principal leans against the stick and listens, his eyes closed. The kid continues, is close to the end. ". . . dominate at whatever cost to our opponent or to . . ." Callaghan pounces, and flicks his wrist so fast that the kid is either caught off guard and stops, or the ball to the stomach ends his words.

"We have the best lacrosse program in the state. This is not opinion, but fact. If you rise to the challenges we set, all of you have a high probability of playing in college, receiving a scholarship. But you have to *earn* it, here!"

Callaghan continues through the rest of the line, and when it's all over he hands the stick back to an upperclassman and pulls his tie from his shirt. "Boys," he says. "If you cannot bring that kind of intensity to practice, you will never have it during the game. And this game can save you. If you let it. Put away your fear of being hurt and replace it with your desire to inflict pain. Then, and only then, will you ever succeed." He looks at Alva, nods sharply. "We all have eyes on us, gentlemen. Not just on the field. At all times. Best to always bring one hundred percent."

What the fuck does he mean? Is he . . . are they? There's no time to tease it through, though, because Callaghan walks away, and is headed toward the weight room.

I set my phone on the bleachers and then nod toward our door. Ollie and Q both look at my phone, but I wave them on and we are back inside the weight room.

"Quick. We have to look like we've been working out," I say.

They don't hesitate, but run to the squat stand. Ollie puts a bar on his back, and Q starts critiquing his form. "Butt back first." The door opens and the shoes come toward us.

Ollie racks and I get into position.

"Boys." Callaghan's voice is an invitation for us to stop and give him our attention. We oblige. "Greg, where is your phone?"

My insides churn. "I, uh, I left it home." The words feel stale coming out of my mouth.

Callaghan steps closer. "I saw you with it today."

I know better than to say I ran home after school. If he saw me with it, he might know I just had it in the computer lab. But I have to stand my ground. He has the power to fuck this all up.

"Feel free to check my bag, all our bags. It's not here. You may have thought you saw me with it, but you didn't."

Callaghan scowls. "Are *you* calling *me* a liar?"

"No. I think you are just so used to seeing me with it, you thought you saw something you didn't."

Ollie hops in. "What do you need his phone for?"

Callaghan stares at Ollie. "Greg *is* making excellent progress, and I want to see the evidence." My head is scrambling to make sense of this. Is he onto me? But then he finishes his statement and I understand. "*All* of it."

Callaghan walks out.

We all take a breath, and I sit down on the bench. "Shit, that was close."

"Your phone, G. You better get it."

"I'll wait until they're done. It's not worth the risk."

Ollie gets in my face. "Are you out of your mind? Don't you realize what you have?"

I nod, still amazed at what's on there.

"What? G, that was Callaghan, whipping kids in the head with a lacrosse ball. *That's* all the evidence you'll ever need. Combine that with the bros, and it looks like he's in on all of it."

"Here's hoping. I'll be right back."

As quietly as I can, I slip into the gym. The pain game appears to be over. Kids are lying on the ground, holding themselves in various places, much like I did earlier today. I wonder how any parent could not see what's going on. In the same moment, though, I feel my weight and know how much my parents must have turned a blind eye.

"Dun the Ton?" Alva's voice booms behind me.

My knees buckle. I've been spotted. My phone's in my hands. Callaghan's probably nearby. Gilbey will probably go get him in a flash and that will be it. But not if we can get away.

I slam through the regular doors. "Q, get your keys! They're coming!"

And I'm off and into the hall. Quinn and Ollie spill behind me and Q takes the lead. Ollie's on my heels huffing like an asthmatic but not stopping. I'm running on pure adrenaline as well. No way in hell I could ever have moved this fast before. I don't even bother to see who's watching or if Callaghan's around or if Alva or Gilbey are giving chase. I just follow Q out the door into the parking lot. He starts sprinting and unlocks the car with his remote. He pops the back door, and gets behind the wheel. The car starts just as Alva and Gilbey appear on the far end of the lot. My legs buckle again, but Ollie yells, "Don't stop, Greg!"

He passes me and I find a burst of speed. The bros see us and then Quinn's car, and sprint. It's down to a footrace and there's no way we can win. But Q backs up and slams on the brakes. "Get in!"

Ollie and I reach the car and pull our fat asses into the back, barely getting the door closed as the bros descend. Alva punches the window, and Gilbey tries the back door. Locked. Quinn screams, "Fuck you!" and floors it, leaving a cloud of burnt rubber and the bros behind us.

It's not until we're out on the main road that anyone speaks. Quinn looks at me in the rearview. "You got your phone, right?"

I hold it up so he can see.

"We're going to pay for this, I just know it, but let's go see your skills at work. Time to edit before it's too late."

* * *

Dad doesn't even knock, just pops his head in. "Greg, there's a girl here. Ella?" He can't hide his grin. Quinn, Ollie, and I all respond at the same time, "Send her up." Dad shakes his head, and in a moment Ella's walking into my room. I don't think I ever thought I'd see this. Her face slides into business mode, and she pulls up next to the computer.

We grabbed chairs from the kitchen table after I explained to my parents that we had a project due immediately. I grabbed one for Ella, too, because I knew she'd be here. Mom's only question was what class were we all in. I answered, "Blint's," and that seemed to suffice. She eyed Ollie like she does me, as if she's amazed a boy could be so large. She told Quinn it was good to see him again. I have no idea what she said to my father.

I play the video for Ella, and she bites her nails. "Holy shit."

"Exactly," I say. "So with this last piece, along with the rest, what do you think?"

Ella takes a moment to think and I'm glad. Quinn and Ollie were practically begging me to send it once I pulled all of the pieces together, but they don't know shit about film and how it's analyzed. However, everyone here knows my reputation with it. And we can't ignore that. Period.

"I don't want to be a bitch, but, Greg, is it enough?" She looks at me as if we're the only ones in the room.

"What do you mean?" I ask, even though I see it as she does, from the outside-in.

"Think about it. What do you really have?"

"Uh, I don't know, kids getting beat and force-fed shit for starters. Then our principal trying to kill someone." Quinn tilts back in his chair. "Least that's what I see." His voice is so condescending I'd like to smack him.

"Sure, because that's what you want to see." Ella doesn't seem offended. Amazingly. "Objectively, you've got some kids completing drills that are no worse than what other sports do. 'Bull in the ring' for football, 'Knucklehead' in soccer, 'Face slam' in volleyball. I've got video of all of these and interviews with the kids after. They don't seem to care."

"But the shit eating?" Ollie asks.

"Could be pudding."

Ollie and Q grumble at that, but she's got a point. "It's true. If no one on that team will say it's shit, then it could be anything. They are all under Alva's thumb."

Ollie and Quinn nod. Then Q says, "True, and it's not as if they'll even *let* Kyle or Stephen leave. It's like a cult."

Ella throws up her hands. "And that's all the more reason you shouldn't send this shit! This is exactly what I was saying at lunch."

Ollie shifts forward. "So what are you going to do, Greg? You know we can't get any more evidence. There's no way Callaghan's letting us anywhere near the gym now."

I look at Ollie and am frightened by the implication. Not only are we cut off from recording, we're cut off from working out.

"Like Ella said, this has to work or I'm done. There's no time left."

Ella sighs. "That's not the only thing I said, but you're right, you have only this card to play."

This is my call. *I* have to decide. This is when I make a move that shows all I felt today with Gilbey, with Callaghan. I refuse to be afraid of them. And I won't prove that by playing it safe.

I pull up the school's website and copy Dr. Philmore's address. I paste it into my email and write, Urgent! Hazing video attached, for the subject.

Quinn and Ollie help me word the email. Ella stays silent. I attach the video.

In all my years of facing the administration at school for the films I've made, I have never been this scared for one that seems so cut and dry, so honest. Yet, at the same time, one that I know could be easily distorted.

I take a deep breath and click SEND.

CHAPTER 17

I'M SWEATING AND MY MOUTH'S DRY as sand when I walk through the school doors. It's been like this for a week. Nothing from Philmore.

I wait a second, as if Callaghan is going to pounce on me as soon as I'm here. Nothing happens, except kids running into my back.

"Move it, fat ass."

"Dun the Ton, what the fuck are you doing?"

I need to move, if only to minimize the attention I'm drawing. I step to the side, tease the lens out of my pocket, and hit RECORD. When it's like this, faces are usually cut off. But there's something about it that works. Trying to figure out who's talking shit to who.

I walk on and it's a typical day.

"Yeah, so I told that bitch to step off. I don't know who she thinks she is. I'll steal her man and anyone else's. I'm looking out for me. Sorry if you can't handle that."

"Yeah, she's totally into fat guys. Who knows why. But if she'll plow Moby, ain't no way she'll say no to me."

"Bobby? Give me your homework. Bobby, I know you can hear me. Bobby, homework. You know I didn't do it and you always have the answers. Bobby? We're boys, right? Come on. Bobby, don't make me."

I slide into Blint's class and am relieved to see Ella already there. "Hey."

She's staring at her phone. "Hey, Greg." She snaps her head toward me. "Did you hear anything?"

"No. Still nothing."

"Don't worry. Something like that might take more than a minute. Just watch, you'll be in the office before the day is over."

"Is that supposed to make me feel better?"

"No, maybe help you get prepared? You recognize this number?" She holds up her phone and the text. **Gonna stick my foot up your ass and kick you back into place.**

"Shit, that's rough. But I'm sure we can both guess who it's from."

Taleana and her crew make their racket as they enter and I try to ignore them, but it's nearly impossible. Taleana's got on a knee-high pair of boots. "Ready to kick some shit," she says, and looks right at Ella.

"I thought you were going to . . . hold on." Ella looks back at the text. "Kick me back into place."

Taleana moves closer. "The fuck you just say? You accusing me of something?"

Ella doesn't answer. She folds her hands and watches Taleana.

"Bitch, I asked you a question."

"I'm sorry, I don't speak your language. What was that?"

Taleana wrinkles her forehead. "You're speaking English right now."

"Not that." Ella, still sweet. "I meant *ghetto bitch*. Which I only partially understand. You're not from the ghetto."

Taleana moves down the aisle. Kids move their legs out of the way so as not to get trampled.

"Who the fuck do you think you're talking to?" Taleana's face is red, her arm cocked at her side.

"Your name is, uh, Taleana, right?"

Taleana's face twitches. "That's right, bitch."

"Well, then I'm talking to you, Taleana. I'm Ella. So nice to meet you."

A few kids risk a laugh and I would, too, if I weren't so close. Ella is not giving Taleana any way in. Most girls are petrified and start kissing her ass on sight. Just like with Alva. Taleana hears the laughter and turns. She glares at the room and Blint walks in.

He whistles and heads behind his desk, oblivious.

Taleana leans close to Ella. "This ain't over."

"Really? Because it seems like it is. There's not much more for you to say, especially because your vocabulary's so limited. But thanks. It was a nice chat." Ella finishes with a little wave.

Taleana burns a deeper red but walks away.

"Careful, Ella," I say.

"Isn't that the pot calling the kettle?"

"Yeah, it is. But who's the pot and who's the kettle?"

The bell rings and Taleana's friends try to console her, but she just shakes them off like they're flies and locks her jaw in place.

"So, as of today, your projects are due in five weeks. Which means you don't have much time to finish gathering material because we're going to spend a lot of time editing. You have to bring your work here, even if you're editing at home. I need to see what you have and give you the points you deserve. All right?"

No one answers. But I think about what Blint just said. Everything has to be here, on the school's server, essentially their property. And they can view it at any time. He's never made that demand before. Is it his rule, or someone else's?

"Okay then, let's move on to best practices when interviewing."

I would rather get kneed in the nuts again by Gilbey than listen to this shit. My phone vibrates with a text. It's from Ollie. **Just saw Dr. Philmore. He went into Callaghan's office.**

My entire body clenches and Ella looks over at me. I put up a hand as if to say I'm fine. Blint says, "Remember, the most important part of interviewing is leaving room for your interviewee to speak. Open-ended questions are good, but make them about your topic. Let us hear what this person has to say. Remember, if they ramble, that's what editing is for."

·　·　·

I'm in study hall when the phone rings. Everything slows. I watch the teacher grab the phone, listen, speak, and turn. Her eyes sweep the room and fall on me. She nods twice and I see her mouth say, "Yes." My heart seizes and I wonder if passing out would work in my benefit.

"Mr. Dunsmore?"

I look up.

"Mr. Callaghan would like to see you."

Kids murmur, but not like when it's for someone who always gets in trouble, say Danny Martone. Then it's fun because the class places bets on what he did and how long he'll be gone. Sometimes Danny even gets in on the action. With me, they just laugh. Because I'm a joke. A big, fat, fucking joke.

I gather my shit and walk toward Callaghan's office. My head's spinning and my stomach's churning and everything's sweating. The hit catches me completely unawares, and I bounce into the wall, dazed.

"Ha, ha, fat boy. Good luck!" Gilbey spits his words and

moves down the hall as if we've just pounded fists. He knows where I'm headed. And if he knows, and isn't afraid . . . I breathe. It's all I can do.

I walk into Callaghan's office and his secretary is decked out in our school colors. She's holding a pen that's shaped like a lacrosse stick. How the hell did I forget that today is the bros' first home game? Callaghan's going to gut me and use my intestines to string a new head on his STX. The secretary presses a button on her phone. "Greg Dunsmore is here, sir."

"Send him in."

She waves toward the door and I catch her earrings: lacrosse balls. I turn the handle and shit myself. Not literally, but pretty damn close to it. Standing at Callaghan's desk is Superintendent Philmore. Both men look at me, but Philmore's eyes are as kind as Callaghan's are vicious.

"Greg, have you met Dr. Philmore?" Callaghan's all business, there's even a trace of pleasantry in his voice.

"Uh, no, I haven't." I stretch out my hand, which is dripping in sweat.

Dr. Philmore takes it and winces the slightest bit as he shakes. "Nice to meet you, Greg. I can only imagine you're here for praise from Mr. Callaghan?" He discreetly wipes his hand on his suit coat and turns to my principal.

"Yes. Greg here is one of our budding film students."

My stomach drops into my nuts.

Dr. Philmore smiles and nods at me.

"In fact, that's why I called him down, to talk about his latest project."

Philmore says, "That's great." Holy balls, I'm screwed.

"Well, Jeremiah, Always a pleasure." Philmore shakes Callaghan's hand, nods again at me, and walks out of the office.

I'm so confused, so scared, so undone that I say, "Huh?" when Callaghan tells me to sit.

"Sit," he says again. Not a question.

I fill one of the chairs before his desk and could punch myself. I had Philmore in front of me, and I didn't say a word about the email. I could have just asked if he'd had a chance to look at it. Because maybe he hasn't? And asking would have made it stick out. But I didn't because I thought he knew. What's wrong with me? Callaghan may be evil, but he's smart, and he's onto me.

Callaghan looks out his window over the playing fields. "Would you care to explain yourself?"

A wide open question, so open-ended I could ramble for hours. Great if the person wants to talk. I shake my head.

"What's that?" Callaghan turns to me.

I shake again.

"This will go much better for you if you speak. Am I clear?"

I doubt that, but I say, "Yes."

"Good. Let's try this again. Please explain yourself. Why are you here?"

I want to say because my mom and dad banged and nine months later, holy shit there I was. "I don't know."

"You don't know?" Callaghan sounds like he just ate something rotten. "I find it impossible to believe that you don't know that you sent an inflammatory video that you labeled *hazing*." Callaghan searches my face and I look away.

How? How did he see it and not Philmore? Did I paste the wrong address?

"Does that ring any bells, Greg? Do you have an idea, now, why you are here?"

I've got two options: tell the truth or lie. I know what's right, but I also know Callaghan isn't. "No, I don't. Could you explain?"

Callaghan bends at the waist and places his hands on his desk, like an animal gearing up to pounce. I swear he sniffs the air. "Are you honestly going to sit there and tell me you didn't send the video?"

Yes, I am. "Uh, I don't even know what *video* you're talking about, so yeah. I haven't sent you anything." There, I technically haven't lied.

Callaghan stays in his crouched position for another moment. "Then we have a problem, because last night I received an email that originated from your address." He holds up a hand. "I already had it traced to your IP."

I'm sweating but hold on for dear life. Some part of me knows that he wasn't supposed to receive that email, that I didn't make a mistake, and that he shouldn't be talking to me about it. "That doesn't necessarily prove I sent it."

"GDuns@gmail isn't your address?"

"It is, but you do know that people can hack into accounts?"

"Do you really expect me to buy that?"

I swallow and collect my words, because this next piece has to work. "Feel free to investigate. I didn't send *you* anything. Why would I?"

Callaghan's jaw stiffens and his eyes narrow. Damn, maybe I should play poker? I'm good at bluffing.

"All right, I'll do just that." He smiles and I know my bluff was for shit. "In the meantime, in order to keep my athletes safe, you and your friends are no longer allowed in the weight room after school. Alva told me everything."

"What? You can't do that! None of us has done anything!" I have to pretend that I haven't thought of this already. Let him think I'm stupid.

Callaghan stares me down. "Then if you're innocent, you won't mind allowing me time to investigate and to clear your name? In the meantime, in order to protect your academic standing and to ensure the athletic climate for our lacrosse players, I have every right to make sure you don't go anywhere near them." I force myself to keep looking at Callaghan. "Do you understand me, Greg?"

I do, but don't give him the respect of answering. I stand and walk out.

CHAPTER 18

"NO, HE DIDN'T?" Ella's mouth hangs open.

"He did. For real." I poke at my lunch, tuna casserole. It was the healthiest option according to Q, who I still need to tell what went down. Too much to text.

"We knew it might happen, but where are we going to work out?" Ollie pokes at his lunch as well.

"I don't know, but it's not my top concern. Callaghan somehow intercepted that email, I know it. And if he did that, then what the hell is going on?"

I'm not feeling pumped, not energized like I'm some underdog. I am an underdog, but this isn't a movie. Callaghan just shut my ass down. I have no superpowers to reclaim my position.

Ella speaks around the apple she's chewing. "All right, so now you know that avenue of emailing the super is closed. You're going to have to go to him directly, or skip him altogether and go to the cops."

I want to pick her brain about this, but Alva and Taleana are heading our way.

"Aww, look at that, little fattie has a friend." Taleana hovers. "Maybe he'll crush you with his flab, slut."

Ella just raises her middle finger.

Taleana laughs a forced, mean-girl, horse sound. "Good. I'll break that one first."

Alva stares at me. "Nice work, Dun. Somehow you manage to fuck everything up, don't you?" Now he laughs and they move past and I feel like I've been kicked repeatedly.

"I'm gonna mess that girl up," Ella says into her sandwich.

"You can't be serious. You versus Taleana? That girl's hard-core. She's with Alva, so she might as well worship Satan."

Ella sits up straight. "Remember, Greg, I spent close to a year calculating ways to get back at the bitches who fucked me over. And I never got the chance to do a single thing. I'm more than prepared."

I hope she's right, on all fronts, because I thought I was good to go, until I wasn't.

• • •

I wouldn't even be here if Quinn would just return my text. I gave him the lowdown: We can't use the weight room. I'll explain. What now? Apparently he's too busy to respond.

I half ass my way through my homework in the lab, because for the first time in forever, I have no interest in looking at anything film related. I hope this is just a phase, because I can't lose my ticket out.

The bell rings for the late buses, and I head down to the locker room, hoping I'll catch Q. Ollie agreed to come down as well. We won't go in, but at least we have each other's backs in case we get jumped. The bros have a game. They may also want a sacrifice.

Ollie comes around the corner. "Hey, you heard from him?"

"No. Hopefully he'll show."

"I still can't believe what happened, Greg. I'm sorry."

How is he so nice? I seriously need to meet his parents. "It's all right. It'll work out. Right?"

"Always does. At least that's what they say." He laughs.

"Who is 'they' anyway?"

"No clue."

The locker room door opens and I cringe, but it's Q, with our bags. "Figured you guys would want these."

I forgot all about them in the melee of yesterday. I take my bag and say, "Thanks."

"No problem, G. Here you go, Ollie." He hands his over. "So, what happened?"

"Long story. But Callaghan's mixed in. Not good."

Q frowns. "So what now? Any ideas?"

"Maybe, but let's go outside. It's crawling with bros around here."

They're filing down the hall with their sticks and grins. It's impossible to understand how they can look past all the shit they've seen, just for some stupid sport with a stick and a ball. Then again, for the upperclassmen, this is probably ordinary, which sends a chill along my neck.

We exit the school and walk to Quinn's car. I think I'll go home and nap. Or eat a carton of ice cream.

"So here's what I'm thinking," I say. Q leans against his car and I tell him what went down.

"Shit, you really think Callaghan funneled the email?"

"It's the only way what went down makes sense. He didn't seem nervous. He wanted me to crack."

"I'm glad you didn't, G. Maybe this training is toughening you up." He smiles and it's hard not to join him. "I don't know what to make of the Callaghan situation, but I *can* help with keeping you active. I guarantee you're about to spiral out, and losing the gym is the worst thing for you."

Shit, no ice cream, I guess.

Q looks at both Ollie and me. "You can do a lot of cardio and bodyweight stuff, but that gives us problems. One, we'd have to find a good place to do that, and there isn't another track in town, or stadium steps or really any good hills to challenge you."

"I'm fine with flat terrain," I say.

Quinn shakes his head. "Not if you're going to succeed. Just running isn't going to do it. So if we're going to do pull-ups and push-ups and jumping and climbing exercises, we're going to have to do it here."

We all look toward the track, where adjacent to it, the opposing lacrosse team is warming up.

"That ain't happening," Ollie says.

"No shit," I say.

"Yeah, kind of what I thought. And seriously, you guys need weights. You're big and flabby and weak, just a terrible combination."

That stings.

"So what do we do?" Ollie asks, seemingly not nearly as offended as me.

Q sighs and sinks down on his car. "My dad's gym."

"What about it?" I ask, knowing full well that this is some big shit. Because as little as I know about Quinn, even though we've been "friends" for so long, I know even less about the family business.

Q looks into the distance. "He'll let us work out there."

"You've talked to him?" I ask.

Quinn nods. "Yeah, I did. We saw this coming, so I played the odds and brought it up. He hasn't said yes yet, but he will." His voice is strained.

"But, Q, you don't want to bring us there. We're not like the rest. We'll just get memberships somewhere else."

"And once word got back to my dad that I'm training two guys somewhere else, how do you think that would go over?"

"Still, you don't have to."

Quinn stands up. "I know. But I want to. He doesn't exactly believe in me, so . . ."

Quinn's obviously putting his neck out for us. Or is he just trying to prove something to his dad?

"Quinn, man, that's awesome," Ollie says.

"Truth," I agree.

Q smiles, but then his face clouds. "Is that Ella?"

We turn, and sure enough, Ella's wobbling toward us. Her hair's askew as are her clothes. She laughs and yells, "Hey guys!"

We wave, but each of us tenses. She pulls up to us.

"So, she kept her word," Ella says, and she sounds like she's downed four or five Monsters.

We all shrug.

"Taleana. Look." Ella holds up her hand and the middle finger she used to flip off Alva's girlfriend is bent to the side, overlapping her index finger. "I would say *that* is definitely broken."

I look past Ella, at the swirl of bros and their families arriving. They're greeted by Callaghan, and then move along to the booster tent, filled with shirts, bumper stickers, water bottles, and more paraphernalia than any other sport here. Inside is

Mallory with his reluctant smile and cash register.

Three cop cars roll up, and the police jump out. They band together around Callaghan, and then Mallory, who comes out of the booth to shake their hands. There's a lot of back slapping and laughing.

Shit is majorly broken around here.

CHAPTER 19

IF THE LENGTH OF A DAY had a weight to it, I'm sure it would be over 300 pounds. Because I can feel it pressing on me, and it's almost enough to keep me rooted in place. Almost.

My parents are up, watching the news, still drinking coffee. "Saturday workout?" Dad asks.

"Uh huh." It's difficult to hold a conversation while eating a banana. And kind of embarrassing.

"Really, the school's open for that?"

"No, we're going to Quinn's dad's place."

Mom sets down her coffee. "You mean Peak Fitness?"

"Yup." I look out the window, hoping Q will be early. I slept like shit last night, kept having dreams about people breaking my limbs. Which were undoubtedly brought on by Ella's incident and our trip with her to the hospital. I'm going to pass out later, but now I want out of here.

"What's that cost, Greg? A membership? Because I'm not sure we have the extra cash. That place is expensive."

We didn't talk about money, but I have the sense that it's not an issue. "Dad, he's the owner's son, training the two of us. It's like good publicity. You know?"

He looks at Mom, who raises her eyebrows. "Well, all right. Have fun."

"Yeah. Fun." I throw away the peel, and Quinn's horn sounds from outside. "See you later."

"Good luck," Mom calls at my back.

Ollie's in the backseat, so I climb in shotgun. "Morning." I turn back to Oliver. "You could have ridden up here."

He shrugs. "That's your seat, not mine."

Quinn pulls away. At the first light, he finally speaks. "All right, so just stay with me, and we'll see how this goes. Dad's not fully on board with what we're doing."

"What do you mean?" I ask.

"He doesn't understand why we have to train here and not at school."

"What did you tell him?" Ollie asks.

"Renovation. He told me that was bullshit. That schools only renovate in the summer."

"He's right." I shift and my shorts feel loose around the waist. There's a first.

"I know. That's why I want you to just stick with me, do what I say. We need to look like we have our shit together."

Peak Fitness is big and beautiful. There are two levels, one with machines and free weights and studios for cardio kickboxing and Zumba and whatever else hot chicks in tight pants do. I've seen the commercials. Then there's an entire cardio deck on the second floor. Treadmills, ellipticals, StairMasters, and mountain climbers. There's another separate area in the back completely devoted to spinning. Watching the people up there, pounding and gliding, makes me feel as if they're powering the place with the exertion. And Q's dad is just the kind of guy who would harness that free energy.

He looks us over from behind the front counter, biceps encased in his ultratight polo shirt, not a detectable speck of flab on him. His chiseled cheeks underscore his penetrating eyes, and I have to look away. It's as if he can see beneath my clothes, can calculate the amount of fat I have and just how unacceptable it is.

But he puts out his hand. "Boys, welcome." Ollie and I shake and he says to Quinn, "You've got your work cut out for you, eh?"

Q fidgets, won't look at his father, so I speak. "I've already lost forty-two pounds."

"Yeah, fifteen for me," Ollie says.

Quinn's dad looks at us again. "Phew, it's worse than I thought."

Sweat breaks out across my back, and I see Q's cheeks flush. This feels like an enormous mistake.

We leave Quinn's dad and all his handsomeness and head over to a squat rack. There are a handful of guys pumping iron on another. They're older, like fifties, and ridiculously strong. This may be even worse than I imagined.

"All right, since we never did get to squat the other day, let's do so today and then get a quick burner on the cardio deck."

I look at the squat rack and then at the women above me, like sweaty angels, and I say to Ollie, "You go first."

Even though he doesn't have to, Quinn walks us through the squat setup from the ground up, all over again. "Feet, just outside hips, weight in the heels. Send your butt back first and keep your chest up. Belly tight and elbows pinned to your sides. Look at the wall in front of you, not the floor."

The men tossing around weight nod knowingly, and I catch Q's dad watching. So far so good.

Ollie does a warm-up set and Q tweaks, but it's pretty good. I get under the bar and am suddenly nervous. I forget half the cues, end up on my toes staring at the floor.

Quinn has me rack the bar and puts a hand on my shoulder. "Relax. Watch Ollie again."

My heart's already hammering, and I ignore the chuckles I hear around me.

Ollie does another set, and I try to pick up the subtle nuances. Then it's my turn.

"All right, G, all I want you to do is pretend like you're sitting down to take a shit, while watching TV at the same time."

The guys nearby laugh now, not even trying to hide it.

"What?" My voice has that nervous quaver to it.

"Forget the guys who are *experts* and who forgot what it's like to learn." Quinn speaks over his shoulder, "All right, G, all you."

I get under the bar and step back two steps, tighten my belly, pin my elbows, and hear Quinn say, "Shit and watch TV." I send my butt back, as if I'm reaching for the toilet and I pretend the wall is a flat screen and beautiful girls are rubbing oil on one another. A moment later I can feel my belly settling inside my thighs. My chest is still up and I can feel my weight in my heels. Shit, I've gotten to the bottom. Quinn says, "Stand!" I do and repeat the process another nine times and rack the bar.

"Nice, Greg." Ollie slaps my back. The old guys grumble and resume their sets.

Q grins wide. "All right, boys, let's add some weight."

We finish our five sets of five and my legs are trashed. The old guys have moved on from squats to deadlifts off some box. I don't ask Quinn what they're doing because I never want to do that. But I do see his dad still watching.

"Awesome work. Nothing like the squat to work the entire body. So now that burner." Quinn waves us over to the stairs. Ollie shakes his head and we separate, each taking a railing and pulling ourselves up behind Quinn. "In here."

We follow Quinn into one of the studios and he grabs a stopwatch. "This one is simple. One exercise, for ten minutes."

"No problem, Quinn, we got this." Ollie seems way too excited, but when I look outside the studio, Quinn's dad is leaning against the railing. Fuck.

"Burpees," he says and demonstrates.

It's a squat thrust with a push-up and a jump. *Not bad*, I think. And then I do one. Going down is easy. It's getting up, fighting gravity, that's a bitch. Ten minutes of this and I'll be dead.

Quinn flips a switch and music starts pounding. It's up-tempo, hip-hop shit and Quinn immediately switches to something heavier. "Ten minutes, guys. Make me proud."

Ollie and I share a look and Quinn screams, "Go!" and we're after it.

Two minutes in and everything burns: my legs, my arms, my chest.

Five minutes in and I can no longer feel the pain in my muscles because my lungs are on fire.

Seven minutes in and I think my banana's coming back up.

Quinn's cheering us on and I'm trying to match Ollie for reps, but I've lost count at eight minutes. Can I push for another two?

"Time!" Quinn yells and kills the music.

I roll on my back and feel worse, so I roll over into the fetal position. Better, but it still feels as if my brains are trying to escape through my ear. Quinn pats my side. "Awesome, G, just awesome." I raise a thumb. I hope that was good enough for his dad. Then again, if it wasn't, maybe that's not so bad. I've never felt this torn up in my life. I don't know that I need this again.

Ollie and Quinn peel me off the floor, and Q starts mopping up my sweat. I sway but don't fall and notice the gorgeous woman talking to Q.

"Thanks, Quinn. That's a big puddle." She points at the ground and looks at us, as if we're strays in a pound. "Damn, looks like you almost killed them." She sets down her bag and water bottle.

"That's the point, right?" He leans toward her and she does the same and there's a spark there. Even in my addled state I can sense it. Go, Q.

"Guys, this is Heather, one of the trainers here." Quinn extends his arms as if he's showing us the best part of the gym and gives me an extra wide grin.

Ollie and I wave, too gross to touch this vixen. But she's real. *This* is Heather.

"You two seem like you did an awesome job. I hope we get to see more of you." She smiles and she's model quality beautiful.

I try to stutter an answer but a line of middle-aged women

starts shuffling in, each with a yoga mat and water bottle. Quinn nods toward the door and we follow. Outside I manage to speak. "So, Heather?"

Quinn can't keep the smile off his face. "Yeah. Yoga instructor."

"Burpees, huh? After squats?" Q's dad emerges, much like Callaghan does. Q doesn't look back, or answer. "Not exactly how I would have done it, but you are working on rapid weight loss."

Still, Q stays motionless.

"All right, but let's keep it to off-peak hours."

"Right, wouldn't want to get in the meatheads' way," Quinn says.

"Let's not go there, Quinlan." He looks at us. "Boys, good work. I'll see you next week." With that he bounds down the stairs and heads for the counter where clients are looking to get protein shakes.

Quinn closes his eyes and takes a few deep breaths.

"You okay?" I ask.

He thinks for a second, looks in the studio at Heather. "Maybe."

*　　*　　*

It's awesome to work out somewhere I can shower immediately afterward. The stalls are all private. The water is scalding. I think I'm falling in love with Peak Fitness.

I dress and head out to the front counter. Quinn and Ollie are already there. No sign of Q's dad. We walk out and I feel so much better than when I came in.

"Am I still dropping you off at Ella's?" Q asks as he gets behind the wheel.

"Yeah, if that's cool." I try to sound aloof, but if he's decided not to bring me, I may just torture him by wrapping my sweaty underwear around his face.

"Fine with me. She should be checked on after what happened."

Ella and I had a brief text exchange last night. She couldn't type much because of her hand, but she wanted me to drop by today. We never did get to talk about her plan. I think I can handle it now.

We drive and Ollie and I both thank Q for what he's doing and ask questions about Heather. He dismisses our thanks and says nothing about Heather. I get the message. "So what about those meatheads? They a pain in the ass or something?"

Q's entire face shifts and he swallows hard. I've never seen this. "Yes," he says.

"Something happen?"

Quinn looks down the street. "Aren't we near Ella's?"

"Another mile or so."

"Right, right."

I don't say another word until he's dropping me off at her door. "Thanks, for the ride and for today."

"You're doing the work."

"Greg, you doing anything later?" Ollie calls from the backseat.

"Probably not. You?"

"Nothing. Text me."

Neither of us says anything to Q about getting together. They drive off and I turn to Ella's house.

"Stay cool. Stay cool," I say to myself. Sweat's already spreading across my back.

Ella answers the door, her hand in a splint and bandage. "Hey, how was your workout?"

"Terrible, but, you know, in the good way."

She laughs. "Whatever you say. Come on in."

I follow her up to her room and navigate through the clothes all over the floor.

Ella sits on her bed, and I take the chair at her desk. "How's your hand? What did your dad say?"

"Not bad," Ella looks at the splint as if it belongs to someone else. "I told him I got it sandwiched by a bathroom stall door."

"So how did it really happen?"

"Taleana sandwiched it with a bathroom door."

"Holy shit." She says it so deadpan, I'm not sure what surprises me more.

"Yeah, she's as crazy as they are, possibly more so. It's probably for the best that you got booted from the weight room."

I think of Peak Fitness and hope she's right. "So what do we do now?"

"You mean about the two of us, the whole hazing shit, or our projects? Pick."

I didn't know there were so many options. "Let's start at the beginning."

Ella smiles. "I figured you would."

I'm sweating through my shirt already.

I think Ella senses my discomfort because she asks, "Seriously, Greg, are you all right?"

I'm not. At all. Fuck it. I wipe my hands on my jeans. "Here it is. You make me nervous. I'm this fat kid, always have been. But it's not as if I don't feel the same things other people do. I guess I just don't know how to act when emotions bubble up, because I've never had a chance. And then I end up doing or saying something stupid." I look at Ella and she's looking at the floor. "Shit, am I making any sense?"

She nods but doesn't speak.

"You're adorable and I'm a slob, but I'm trying to show people I can change. I can take care of myself better. I'm not just this enormous pile of meat."

Neither of us speaks for a moment, but Ella sits up and looks at me, her eyes unwavering. "Greg, thanks for being so honest. I understand. So let me give you my advice. I'm not saying you shouldn't lose the weight, because you should. It's good for your health. But don't do it because you're trying to prove anything to anyone. Don't do it just because you're making a stupid film for Blint's class. Do it because it's your choice. For *you*." She keeps looking at me. "I've had a lot of time and therapy to think about this shit, so trust me when I say you'll figure out how to deal with your emotions like everyone else. We're all fat kids or skinny kids or loser kids or poor kids or kids from broken homes. You know? That never changes."

Her words are more true and powerful than any I've said to myself. "Thanks," I say. "Now is this where I swoop in and kiss you?"

"No, this is when I show you what I've learned. Get on my computer. Typing with this hand is horrible."

I'm relieved. If she had said yes, I don't know what I would have done. I have zero experience. I've never been to any bases. Shit, I've never stepped foot in the batter's box. Computers, though, I've scored grand slams with. Shit, that's awkward.

Ella directs me to a file on her computer: "Lax Bros."

"I have the same one on mine," I say. But when I open it, I quickly realize she hasn't filled hers with stupid videos of the assholes, but articles and links and pdfs. This is like a research paper on steroids.

"Open the folder and go to the subfolder, 'Mallory, Max.'"

The folder is a time line of our town hero's academic, athletic, and military history. I know most of this, but Ella directs which file to open and I read. I start with the videos and watch all his interviews. He's smooth, poised, and doesn't seem like the current lax bro model. Then I read the articles about him. Most of what is here is new to me. I whistle at a line I read.

"What is it?" Ella asks.

"So Max was good at lacrosse, like really good. All-state by sophomore year. And then he found his niche in technology. He built his own computers and edited people's film projects for them. Like, way the hell before Movie Maker. He attributes his skills to the, hold on," I skim the newspaper article and find the line. "'The unique discipline of the sport. The lineage of lacrosse and what it brings out of the individual.' Callaghan must have loved him."

"You think?" Ella says. "Which is why, when you look into the other folders, you'll see that Mallory started the booster club during Max's sophomore year. The next year was the first of the 'Fucking tournament, brah.'"

I laugh at her bro speak and wish I had a collar to pop. "So what's this all about? Why are you digging around in it?"

Ella shifts on the bed. "You know how it is, you go searching and then find a thousand different avenues to pursue. When I started reading all this, things started to crystallize. Like *why* Mallory is so eager to give money to the school, specifically the tech program. He could just save it all for the bros."

It makes perfect sense, and I guess I've never really cared why he's done it. If there's anything good that comes from the bros, I'm all in. We certainly pay for it. "You think there's anything deeper?"

"How so?" Ella squints.

"I don't know. I saw Mallory and Callaghan together the other day, and Mallory seemed wicked pissed. And the more I think about it, you never see them together. You would think with the team as tight as it is, that'd be the case."

"Good point. I'll see if there's anything more with Mallory or tech or whatever, but first, go check out what I do have on the top minions."

I find folders for both Andrew Alva and Dennis Gilbey. I don't know how, but Ella managed to hack into their school records, including disciplinary and medical. And it is exactly what I expected: fighting, bullying, cheating. None of it, however, past middle school. That's because Callaghan never punishes them.

But then I open Alva's medical file. Broken arms and fingers, lacerations needing stitches, tons of bruises, a cracked eye socket, multiple broken ribs, and a couple concussions. I realize I'm holding my hand to my mouth when I read, "Injuries are reported to stem from lacrosse training or games, but many have occurred in the off-season. Principal Callaghan, however, has spoken with the parents and there is no cause for concern. Andrew may just be injury-prone."

"I know, Greg. It makes it hard to hate when you see that."

"Those were all from when he was an underclassman. He hasn't had an injury in two years," I say.

"Same for Gilbey, but he hasn't had as many as Alva, overall."

"Guess that's what it takes to be a captain."

"You have no idea how accurate that is."

I look at Ella, and she's not smiling; it's saddened her. "You don't mean Max?"

"I do. The one and only."

"But how, Ella? How did you get all this, and if what you're saying is true, then how did it get swept under the rug?"

She shakes her head. "You know the answer to this, Greg. It's what you do with an inconvenient truth when you're filming. You gloss over it, or don't bother with the facts at all. That may be your answer to why Callaghan and Mallory don't get along."

I feel as if she may be talking about me or about herself, but I can't go down those roads, not right now. "You're saying it's a cover-up. That's crazy! His own son."

She looks at me, flat, emotionless. "I'm saying that it's less of a cover-up, and more of an unspoken acceptance of what it means to be a part of this team."

The implication is staggering, but not exactly surprising. There have always been whispers about just how tough it was to be on the team, but since I've never cared about these assholes I didn't pay attention, or just brushed it off as guys talking shit to make themselves seem invincible.

"But why would Mallory still be involved? His son's dead. What's the point?"

"Maybe Callaghan has something on him. Dirt," Ella says.

That just doesn't sit right with me. Mallory is ex-military. Blackmailing him would be difficult. He knows people, for sure. "I don't know. Maybe he's in the dark. Max played a while ago. Maybe things have changed."

"Does Callaghan seem like the kind of guy who changes?"

"No. Not at all. But it doesn't really matter because it's not like we can say, 'Oh, hey, look what we found hacking into the school. You might want to take a look.' No one is going to take it seriously. We can't fight *that*, this town, the legacy, the 'business' as you call it."

"So what do we fight?"

"What we can. What is happening now. We can expose that, and we can hope that opens it up, gets people looking. But you, me, Ollie, Quinn, we take care of us, we watch out for Kyle and Stephen. We let this play out and do our thing."

"So we make our film and we show the truth. We get it in front of the right audience and the rest will work out?"

Ella's back to life now, all of her seemingly amplified. Her smile is devilish. "Damn straight. But it has to be perfect."

"Ella Bean, what are you up to?"

Ella's dad's voice is in the room with us and I clutch my chest. I don't know why. She's on the bed and I'm in a chair across the room.

He strides over and kisses her head. I never heard him come in the house. Did Ella? Or is he really a ninja-techie hybrid?

"Mischief and mayhem, my usual."

"Greg, right?" Ella's dad examines me, taking in my hand to the chest. I try to be chill.

"Yeah."

"Good to see you again." We shake hands.

"Hey, I'm making tacos for lunch. You're more than welcome to stay."

Ella's not looking for me to say yes, but also not to say no. Wow. "Thanks, but I've got stuff to do at home."

"No problem. The invite's open."

"Thanks," I say and see a shred of disappointment on Ella's face. Her dad turns to go, but she calls to him. "Did you ever check up on that email I asked you about?"

My stomach flutters and the hunger pangs are replaced with pure anxiety.

"I did. Granted you had the correct address, there's no reason it shouldn't have arrived to your intended target. However, you can divert or forward messages to another account. So it's possible it went there and not where you thought it was going." He rocks back on his heels and grins.

"Thanks, Dad."

"Any time. Now you two watch out for the people lurking on Facebook. Creepers, all of them," he says and leaves her room.

We laugh but I have to ask, "You thinking what I'm thinking?"

"Yeah. Callaghan funneled Dr. Philmore's email."

I shake my head and puff my cheeks. The top of the chain is

being kept out of the loop. But we can't fix that. I've tried, twice. It would be nice if once in my life I had success, so I could draw on that knowledge. But I don't. And neither does Ella, or Ollie. Quinn seems to also be in need of *something*. Maybe there's strength in our collective odds. At some point, things have to go our way. Hopefully that time is now.

CHAPTER 20

"SO WHO IS THIS ELLA GIRL?" Mom asks while passing me a bowl of steamed vegetables.

I didn't want to leave Ella's, but it was time and I felt bad that Ella kept pushing back lunch. Her dad came in and asked if he could eat without her. But a look passed between the two of them that said that was clearly not an option.

"She was the girl here the other night." Dad lowers his head and smiles.

"I know that, but who *is she*? Greg, how do you know her?"

"She's in my film class, and we're working on our projects. She needed some help because she broke her finger."

"So why did she need *your* help? Why not someone else?" Mom asks.

"Huh?"

Dad chews his steak. "Yeah, what he said."

Mom gives a little toss of her head, as if she's clearing her thoughts. "It's just that a pretty girl like that always has friends, boys, whatever, to choose from. Why you?"

I bite into my steak just so I have a moment to consider what she's driving at, even though it's pretty obvious: *Son, you're a loser. Why would some hot girl want to hang with you?* I swallow. "We just have a lot in common and she needed help. I'm good at editing, so why shouldn't it be me?"

Mom sighs. She's yet to eat a forkful. "I just don't want you to get used, that's all. You're vulnerable right now, sweetie. Girls, they can sense these things and they take advantage."

I am going to starve to death. "What are you even talking about? How am I vulnerable and how is she taking advantage?"

Dad keeps eating and watching us as if we're on some reality show.

Mom sips her wine. "You're losing weight. Things are changing for you. You're excited and I don't blame you, but you have to watch out. You're getting graded on these portfolios, right?"

I nod.

"Well, I'd rather not have your work become Ella's grade. That's not fair."

I chew on this last piece, eat some vegetables, and wonder just what she sees in me, in Ella. I can't blame her for not knowing everything, but seriously, aren't parents—at least mothers—supposed to have some kind of intuition? "Helping Ella is the least of my concerns," I say and fill my mouth with steak. It's dry and overcooked, but I force it down.

Mom has a question, but I look away and pull my phone from my pocket. I've got a text from Ollie. **Want to swing by tonight?**

I reply before I even know where he lives. **Yes. Time?**

"Hey, no phone at the table," Dad says.

Ollie responds. **7:30?**

Perfect.

I tuck my phone away. "Hey, could one of you bring me to Oliver's in about an hour?" I look directly at Mom. "He just wants to hang. I promise, I won't help him with anything."

Her eyes tighten along with her mouth. Dad offers to drive, and I swallow the rest of my steak.

* * *

Ollie's is a few miles away and Dad jokes that I should walk, but he notices how much I'm struggling to get around. It's not that I'm limping, it's more that my legs don't want to bend at certain angles. I climb out and tell him I'll call later about a ride.

I ring Ollie's doorbell and he answers, looking flushed, eyes bugged.

I step back. "Everything all right?"

He looks over his shoulder and joins me on the porch. "Uh, shit, do you remember how I said my grandfather is sick?"

"Yeah, yeah. Why?"

Ollie takes a second and my stomach twists. He's been crying. "He's not doing well. In the hospital and all that."

"Shit, I'll go. I'm sorry."

Ollie grabs my shoulder. His grip is not only strong, but desperate. "No, don't. He won't let any of us in to see him anyway. Told the staff and all. So we're here, just sitting around waiting by the phone."

"All right." I want to run back to my house so bad, and might if it weren't for my legs. "You don't want to be with just your family?"

Ollie shakes his head. "Come on in. I'll show you."

I wish at this very moment I had some way of recording without him noticing. Because the phrase he used should always be followed by film. Or should it? If I'm going to use other people's lives for my films without permission, then I can't be upset if people think I'm an asshole.

We walk into the house and it's the smell that tips me off. Fried onions and cheese. Grease. Standing in Ollie's living room, I see the mound of food in the kitchen. Sam's sliders, little burgers so good that in two bites one is gone, and then another, and on and on. They're like crack. Around this pile is Ollie's family: mom, dad, and sister. Everyone is Capital F, fat, and elbows deep in hamburgers.

"I only had two. Figured that was all right. But I'll be like them. And Greg, I don't want to."

I feel like an AA sponsor must. I totally understand where he's coming from, yet hate being the one to say no. His grandfather's dying. Why can't he eat some burgers? But I know what will happen. Tomorrow he'll eat two dozen pancakes and a pound of bacon. An hour or two later a giant sub and an entire bag of chips. Then pizza.

"Your room?" I ask.

"Yeah. You can meet them after they've cleaned up."

I follow Ollie up the stairs and down the hall and as soon as he closes his door, Ollie collapses on his bed. I settle into his desk chair—seems to be my place—and let him breathe. A moment later he sits up. "Thanks for not bolting. I know that was gross downstairs, but you have to understand . . ."

I raise my hand. "Don't worry about it. I've eaten eighteen sliders before."

"Damn, I only got to fifteen."

We both laugh. "How you feeling? Your legs, I mean. Shot?"

"Oh, hell yeah," Ollie says. "Dad's been ripping on me all

afternoon, asking what I *really* did with you two."

"That's nasty."

"That's my dad." Ollie looks away. "Anyway, how was Ella? Hand all right?"

"Yeah, she's tough. We, uh, well, she's been doing some research, and I saw some things that got me thinking."

I tell him about Callaghan and Mallory, and about the bros, the hacking, as well as the info from Ella's dad.

"That's just a whole shit-ton of crazy. What are you going to do?"

I chuckle. "It's not *me*, it's *us*. I'll explain. But first, can I borrow this?" I point to his computer.

"Yeah. Hop on. Do your thing."

I go straight to Twitter and kick myself for not thinking of this earlier. I follow @kyle_thompson.

Ollie must sense something because he asks, "What's up?"

"Waiting to see if Kyle's Twitter is safe from the bros." And just like that, Kyle follows me back. "Time to send him a message."

"Balls."

"Balls is right." I type to Kyle basically what I said on Facebook and send. Then I DM @ellafaint. Sent Kyle a message. Will keep you posted.

"Who was that to?" Ollie asks.

"That's Ella's username."

A moment later I have a DM. The message isn't from Ella.

Twitter is safe. I think. We should talk. When? Where?

Ollie reads over my shoulder. "Shit, is that from Kyle?"

"Yeah? What should we do?" I know what I *want* to do, but understand that Ollie's calling the shots here. His grandfather's dying for fuck's sake.

Ollie sighs. "Hold on." He heads out of his room, and I open up a browser and check his favorites. Classic: Epic Meal Time, This is Why You're Fat, Food Porn Daily. I should delete these for him, but that would be cruel.

His door opens, and I close out the screen. "There's the Quick Mart just down the street. If he can meet us there, that's cool."

I send the message to Kyle. A minute later he responds. **Give me 15.**

C u then.

"You don't have to go," I say. "Stay with your family. I'll come back when we're done."

"You remember what happened last time you tried to meet up with Kyle?"

"Yeah."

"Well, I'm not letting that happen twice."

I'm embarrassed and ashamed for dragging him into this, especially with what's going on. "Thanks, Ollie."

"Don't mention it."

We head downstairs and Ollie's family is on the couch, looking bloated, eyes glazed, like every picture I've had taken of me for the past eight years. His dad stands. "Greg, pleased to meet you." We shake hands and he crushes mine. "Real sorry for having to meet you this way, but my father-in-law's touch and go. You understand?"

I don't, really, but I say, "Of course. Nice to meet you." I wave to his mom and sister. "Nice to meet all of you." They don't wave back.

"We're just getting some air, Dad. We'll be back in a little bit."

"No worries. Can't change anything at this point."

We step outside and Ollie says, "Should we text Quinn?"

I laugh because there's no way in hell Q wants any part of this.

"What's so funny?"

"Nothing. I'll check with him now." I text and we walk.

"How long you and Quinn been friends?"

I shuffle along because I can't move much faster. "Long time. First grade? Second grade? Something like that."

"But you two don't hang anymore, do you?"

"No."

"Yeah, that's screwed up. But, well, I guess Quinn's got his own problems, doesn't he? His dad?"

I exhale. "Yup. And there's more to it, I think. I just don't know what."

"There always is."

My phone chirps with a text. Quinn. **Good luck. Keep ur head low.**

I show Ollie the response. "At least that's good advice."

We sit at the picnic table outside the store. It creaks under our weight and Ollie and I look at each other. "We're going to break this thing."

"Wouldn't be the first time," Ollie says.

Kyle appears under the streetlight, circling around on his bike. I'm relieved to see him, but am still tense at the thought of it being another ambush. "Kyle? Hey?"

He spots us and rides over, but looks all around. "No phone, right?"

As much as I'd like to I can't. Not even on the sly. "No. We're just talking."

"Cool." He straddles his bike.

I look around one last time and think about where to begin. "Kyle, I swear, I'm trying to help. What's going on with you guys is terrible, but I hit a snag. What can you tell me about Alva and Gilbey and Callaghan?"

He shakes his head like someone who's seen too much. "Besides what you've seen?"

"I guess," I say. "I haven't seen it all, you know."

"Yeah, I get that. But you know how Stephen got his rib broken and me, my nose. I heard you got the shit-eating recorded, too." He waits for me to answer.

"I did. I'm so sorry."

"You should be, for not doing anything with it."

"I tried to get it to the superintendent."

"Really? And what happened?"

I don't know how much I want to say. He's been terrorized, but I also know from experience that the kids who get it handed to them also become the ones who stick up for those assholes the strongest. Case in point: Alva and Gilbey. "Complications. Something with my email." That's safe.

He nods as if he understands. "I don't know it would have changed anything, anyway."

"Why's that?" Ollie asks.

"Philmore and Callaghan went to school together. Callaghan showed us the picture, early on, before, well, everything. He was talking about how much the school supports the lacrosse program and part of that is because he and Philmore are so tight."

This blows my mind. I guess Callaghan and Philmore could be the same age. It's just that Callaghan seems so downright evil, it's aged him. "Did Philmore play lacrosse?"

Kyle seems to come back from somewhere else. "Uh, no, no. Callaghan didn't say anything about that."

I feel a little better, but not much.

"How much do they talk about Max Mallory?"

Kyle leans back. "An entire presentation dedicated to that dude. He's like everything we're supposed to become. Good student. Went into the military, became a bomb expert or some shit, and volunteered for more tours. We all know he didn't make it back."

"IED," Ollie says. "I remember. The whole town shut down."

We're silent for a moment, and I think back to the day of Max's funeral. They closed school, all the businesses, and everyone in town went. They used the word *hero* so many times. I'm sure I have footage of it saved somewhere.

"Doesn't seem like your captains got the message behind the presentation," I say.

"Yeah, Mallory and Callaghan don't oversee things like you'd think coaches would. It's pretty much Alva and Gilbey running the show. Don't get me wrong, they know their shit about lacrosse. It's just all the rest that's the problem." He looks in my eyes. "So what now? What's your plan?"

"I have some ideas," I say, "but I'm going to need more evidence. And since we got booted from the weight room, I'm not sure how I'm going to get that."

"Yeah, I heard that, too." Kyle seems so hardened, like all of the shit that's happened has become a cast around him. "You want evidence, you should be with us during spring break."

"Why? What's going down?"

Kyle looks over his shoulder and I wonder how long his paranoia will last. A lifetime? "It's the lead up to the big tourney, you know? Hell Week. All sorts of bad shit's supposed to go down. It's all Alva's been talking about. This is where we 'show our strength,'" Kyle says in a voice matching Alva's flat monotone.

I think of the list of injuries and wonder how many bros will have something bruised or cracked or broken.

"I still don't understand why you can't just quit," Ollie says. I thought I made this point clear to him, but he understandably has other shit on his mind.

"I just told you that the principal and super are friends. Who the fuck am I going to talk to?"

"I don't know, the cops?" Even as Ollie says it, I know it's stupid. This town is literally indebted to the bros. You'd have to be an idiot to think the cops would try to shut that much money down.

Kyle laughs a shrill note that makes me look at Ollie. "Do you know who came to talk to us one day, right after the hazing started?"

I don't answer. Neither does Ollie.

"The chief of police." Kyle lets that settle. "Yeah, you think that wasn't on purpose? You think he's going to help us, or all of his officers who used to play here? They *all* come to the games. Who's left, Dun? You think I want to tell my parents about this, huh? I've got nobody."

He's right and he's wrong. There are others—lawyers, state troopers. But I understand his point. Word would trickle back and it would be handled and he would have to pay. "How's Stephen?"

The anger drains from Kyle. "Fucking vegetable. His parents keep asking me why he's so quiet and why his grades are tanking. I tell them I don't know. They scheduled an appointment with guidance. Did you know that Mr. Martell used to go here? Guess what sport he played?"

It doesn't surprise me one bit that the head of guidance is a former bro. "Kyle, thanks for coming. I promise I'll figure something out. I mean it."

He looks at me and in his eyes is a tinge of disgust. It's only a matter of time before he's one of those kids in the hall tormenting everyone else.

For the second time, I actually feel for Alva and Gilbey. I can blame them all I want, and I don't think anyone would argue. But if I do what I'm supposed to, look big picture, then it's impossible to dismiss all that's fucked up in this town. And based on what Ella's found, that begins with Callaghan. And no one's telling that story.

"Just need to figure out a way to get in on your Hell Week," I say.

Kyle's eyes light up as he mounts his bike. "Keep me posted. If you're serious, I'll help you figure out a way. And if you make it there, you don't know me. Understand?" I nod and he pedals away.

"Greg, you're not serious, are you?"

But I am. There are a million reasons why I shouldn't, but there's one very good reason why I should, and sometimes even if the scales are unbalanced, you have to move ahead. "Why not?"

Ollie shakes his head. "Let's get back."

We return to his house and the reality of what has happened hits us both.

"He's dead, Oliver. Gramps is dead."

Ollie sways and falls on his knees at his father's words. His mother and sister are tangled in a knot on the couch, crying. Oliver's father bends down to his son and holds him. Our eyes meet and I mouth, "I'm sorry," and back out the door.

I stand on Oliver's steps and the wailing increases. I walk down the street a bit and begin to call my house. I stop and dial another.

In fifteen minutes, a car rolls up. I climb in and Q starts driving.

"Do you even want to know?" I ask.

"Do you want to tell me?"

"Stop the car."

Q looks at me like I just farted.

"Now!"

He pulls over. "What's the deal? You called, I picked you up and now you're yelling at me?"

I ignore his perfectly reasonable argument. "Why are we still friends?"

Q shakes his head. "G, what the hell?"

"I'm serious. We don't hang out. You drive me to school and

try to kill me in the weight room. You won't talk to me about what's up with your dad or Heather. Fuck! It makes no sense."

Quinn stares out the window for a long moment. "G, I just got my way of doing things, that's all. It's not personal."

"For you, maybe."

"Greg, you're still my friend. I just have a lot of shit going on in my life. . . ."

"And you just don't have time for me."

"The fuck are you talking about? Who's training you and Ollie? Who got you a free membership after we got booted? Who's picking you up right now? And who's *still* helping you with the bros?"

I don't answer.

"You want to know what's up? My dad's an asshole, loves his job and his douche clients more than he does me. And Heather, I don't know. She's older and I don't know if she's interested or not. And I don't know if that's because she works for my dad, or if it's me. Do you want me to answer any other questions?"

If I could feel small, I would. He is a good friend. Maybe *I* haven't been the best. Or maybe it's been both of us. Who knows? Either way, Q's as much a part of my transformation as I am. I need him to help me down this road. And I think he needs it, too.

"You got plans for spring break?"

"G, what?"

"Seriously?"

He laughs. "No, I don't. Why?"

"You do now."

He doesn't laugh again, and he doesn't ask questions. And in the silence between us is our unspoken commitment.

CHAPTER 21

"THAT'S HOW WE DO IT, SON!" One of the bros hops up and down, hanging off another.

"You know it. Fucked that shit up!"

They stare at the kids passing by, daring someone to ask. Because we should all know. The bros won their game on Friday. Woo. Fucking. Hoo.

Quinn and I pass and the bros stare particularly hard.

"Fudgy the Whale, getting packed by Quinn the Queer."

Normally, I'd film and keep on going, but since today Quinn decided not only to talk to me on the ride in, but wait and walk with me, I'll keep filming and return the favor.

"What did you say to me?" Quinn stands real close to both of the bros.

They look at each other, smile, and step even closer. "Get the dick out of your ear and you might hear." The one bro laughs and they pound fists. I don't know their names, can't even tell them apart. With their popped collars and lettuce hair, who can?

Quinn cuts a line across his throat, the universal sign for *stop filming*. I do. He waves his hands to draw the bros in and fits his head directly between them. He whispers, but I can't hear him. I watch the bros' faces. They laugh along at first and then drop and pull tight. Anger? Concern? It's tough to tell.

Quinn stands straight and slaps them both on their shoulders. "Good talk," he says and nods his head, indicating that I should walk with him. The bros eyeball us as we go.

"Did you just dig a deeper hole for us?"

"Please, like you haven't?"

Solid point.

We head to Blint's and he says "hey" to kids in the hall who call out to him. I wouldn't call him popular, but he's known.

Ella's hanging by Blint's door. Fortunately, none of the bros are stacked around Kyle's and Stephen's lockers. "Hey, Greg. Quinn. You still considering your stupid idea?"

"Which one?"

"True, you do have many. Your spring break plans."

"I am. Don't have all the details worked out yet." I follow Ella into class, wondering what she has in store.

Ella says, "I've got your details, and they start with you not being there and us planting hardware on Kyle or Stephen. Because, really, how are *you* going to record them? The *real* them?"

It's the one question I keep coming back to as well. I'll have to make one video, but at the same time, another on a second camera. It's the only way: create a screen and then become a mole.

"You don't know. Shit. Do you want me to start planning your funeral? I promise to have a projector and screen there with classic film highlights. Shit, how is Oliver?"

"Haven't seen him." I could kick myself. The truth is I didn't look for him. I was too busy being all happy that Q was walking with me that I completely forgot.

Taleana walks in the room and looks down to Ella's hand as she passes. "You let me know if you need anything else looked at. All right, sweetie?"

Ella flips her off with her good hand.

"A matching set? Done." Taleana swings into her seat and the bell rings.

"Are you crazy?" I ask Ella.

She nods. "Yes, actually I am."

Blint closes the door. "All right. Now, our next consideration is one that so many students have a difficulty with: time constraints. And no, I don't mean getting to class before the bell." He smiles at his own joke. "Your film must be seven to ten minutes, no more." Then he looks as serious as he can with his birdlike features. "I will stop your film at exactly ten minutes, and will grade you on that." Ella's eyes are fixed on something in the distance and not on Blint. I'm sure her thoughts are tumbling. Yeah, she probably is crazy, which makes me so glad she's on my side.

*   *   *

All day I've been keeping my eyes peeled for Alva and Gilbey, but I haven't seen them. The rest of the bros are still losing their shit up and down the hall. One win? Seriously? But I have heard them adding to it, "This is just what we need before break."

I spy Ollie at our table as Q texts me. Flatbread sandwich, no cheese. Banana. Ollie doesn't have a tray and looks like those abandoned animals on those terrible rescue commercials.

"Ollie, hey . . ." I almost say *how's it going*, but bite my tongue. "Q texted me. You?"

He looks up, eyes ringed in dark circles, face puffy. "What?"

"Lunch, man. You should eat." Or should he? How do I know?

"Yeah. Yeah, I should." He doesn't make any movement like he's going to get up, though.

To be honest, I'm glad. Last thing either of us needs is to be together in the lunch line. "I'll get it for you. Chill."

"Thanks, Greg." His voice is so soft it practically fades out before leaving his lips.

I hop in line and grab two of everything. The lunch lady holds a smirk on her face. I bet she thinks I'm going off the wagon. Well, screw her, the cafeteria slop is way down on my list of Most Desired foods.

When I head back, Ella's with Ollie. They're talking away and Ollie even laughs. I set the tray down and shoot her a confused look.

"Thanks," Ollie says, his voice much stronger.

"No worries. So what are you two talking about?"

Ella perks up. "You know, just how much an idiot you are." She flashes me a big beautiful smile, and I have no doubt that she's sincere.

Ollie bites into his sandwich. "I agree with her."

Ella touches his free hand and I'm jealous.

I take a few bites of the sandwich, which certainly is flat. As in like a tire. "So tomorrow, four to eight?"

Ollie looks up, his eyes glazed again. "Yeah, at MacGregor's. Why?"

Ella coughs and shakes her head. I ignore her.

"I'm going."

Ollie stares for a moment, and I'd like to tell him to shut his mouth because a third of his sandwich is poking out, but the food falling out of his face is the least of his problems.

A tray lands before us and Quinn is here, looking around as if we might bite him, but then he sees Ollie. "Shit." He slides napkins along the table. Ella and I do the same. Ollie grabs them and buries his face. I peer over his now trembling shoulders. Kids are watching, and soon they'll be cracking jokes. Another fun fucking day for Double Stuffed Ollie.

We eat while Ollie regains himself and Ella asks the question I want to. "So, Quinn, to what do we owe this pleasure?"

"I, uh, just figured I should. Okay?" His cheeks are touched with red, his voice unsteady.

Ella answers, "Fine with me."

"We working out today?" I ask Quinn.

He nods and we both look at Ollie. "You should," I say to Ollie. "It'll keep you out of the house."

I see Ella give me a dirty look. She doesn't understand.

"Yeah, I guess. When?"

"After school," Q says. "We don't need to wait for the weight room to be open."

Ollie chews and nods. Ella stays inside her own head, Quinn pops open a milk, and I return to my lunch. We might not understand each other completely, but at least we give each other the space to be who we are. Or who we're trying to be.

CHAPTER 22

I FINALLY SEE ALVA. He's with a mix of bros, all laughing and talking shit to anyone who passes. It's the end of the day, so no one's around to yell at them. Then again, this could be 11 a.m. and no one around here would say shit.

Alva catches me looking at him and he breaks off. "You enjoying the view or recording us? Or both?"

I stare at his eyes and can't help but wonder which socket was cracked. "Neither," I say and hold up my hands. My belly sags.

"Shit, Dun, you need to hit that weight room a little harder." Alva pokes me like I'm the Doughboy. "But you can't do that here anymore. What a shame."

I keep my cool. "It is. But I'm working on a way to get as fit as you."

Alva can't control the laughter that throttles out of him. "You just made my day, shit stain." He claps my shoulder, and I stare at his hand.

"I'm serious," I say and inch a little closer. "You think you've gotten rid of me. But you know I don't just fade away."

Alva's eyes recede into their typical appearance—deadened. "Just what in the fuck is that supposed to mean?"

I laugh. "As if I'd ruin the surprise." I feel him collecting his anger. Now I snag my phone and hit RECORD. When I turn back, he's ready to pounce. "Go ahead. Hit me. Punch me right in the nose. Break it. Like you did to Kyle. Or punch me in the nuts like you did before. Your call," I say.

"Put that away and I will." He swats at my phone, but I tuck it back, out of reach.

"Why? Are you afraid to get in trouble? Who's going to do that? Callaghan? Philmore?" I realize just how stupid this question is as soon as I let it out.

Alva stills. "That's a good point." He slams his fist into my stomach so hard I feel the knuckle on my spine. I double over and Alva stands over me.

"Holy shit. That was like punching a waterbed. You useless fuck. Enjoy watching that." He walks away and soon I hear the rest of the bros laughing and chanting, "Dun the Ton! Dun the Ton!"

· · ·

I don't know if Quinn went extra hard on us today because we won't be here tomorrow due to the wake, or if he's still trying to impress his dad, or if it's because I'm still in pain from that punch, but it doesn't matter. I wouldn't mind one bit being rolled into the casket with Ollie's grandfather. I know that's some morbid shit, but after all the mountain climbers, box jumps, burpees, and push presses we did, everything hurts, not just my belly. And by "hurt" I mean "is broken."

I roll over. Ollie's staring at the ceiling. Quinn is grabbing towels. "You okay?"

Ollie shakes his head. His chest is still heaving as he's sucking air.

"Nice fucking work!" Quinn yells and tosses us our towels. Members look at him and then us and return to their ellipticals or treadmills. The meatheads from last time just chuckle and resume picking up very heavy bars and tossing them on their shoulders. I imagine Alva would enjoy their company.

Quinn's helping up Ollie when his dad walks over. "Hey, rule number three!"

Q turns abruptly and Ollie looks like an enormous ballerina as he spins and somehow manages to keep his feet. "All right, all right," Quinn says to his dad.

His dad's face shrinks down into his neck and darkens. "No! What is rule number three?"

"No swearing." Quinn sounds defeated.

"Exactly! And that goes for you, *especially*." He looks from his son to us and I hide my face in my towel. "Ronnie, Lou, Captain? How's it going?" I peek from beneath the cloth and see him crossing to the meatheads.

They shake hands and talk close and laugh. Quinn's staring at them as if he's about to fly into a roid rage. "Q?" I ask. "Q, stop!" He looks at me and I nod toward his dad. Quinn shakes his head and looks up at the cardio deck.

Heather's running a class, and now that my blood isn't filling my ears, I can hear her sweet voice cheering on the ladies. Even better I can see her bubble butt bouncing as she walks them through the class.

"Are we done?" Ollie sounds like the last kid in class to finish the worksheet. The one who understood none of the material. Q turns back and is all smiles.

"Yeah, man, you did awesome. How you feel?"

"Like dog shit. Sweaty dog shit."

"Let's go shower," I say and he agrees. I ask Quinn as we go, "You all right?"

"Yeah. He's just such a dick. And he shouldn't be in front of those guys. Not to me."

I want to ask what happened, but I doubt I'd get a straight answer.

The shower is heavenly. I consider asking Quinn's dad where he bought the head because if I could get my dad to install this at home I'd be a thousand times happier. I dry off and change in the portion just off the shower. In the locker room, Ollie's nowhere in sight, but one of the meatheads is. A very large and very naked meathead.

"Hey, looky here. One of the boy's blobs."

Two heads peer around a locker. Both smile the same wicked smile, and I could be in PE at this very moment and there would be no difference. The other two meatheads approach, both as naked as the first and all three look me over. The first one speaks.

"It's good you're in here, because, damn, you fucking need it. How old are you, son?"

I don't want to answer, not only because these guys are naked and this is insanely uncomfortable, but clearly these guys have some kind of relationship with Quinn's dad, and Quinn hates them, and out of solidarity with Q, I want to tell them to fuck off. But Quinn's dad owns the place. I understand that they can mess with me and I cannot complain.

"Sixteen," I say.

"Jesus H. Sixteen with bitch tits and a belly so large all three of us could fuck it."

I'm sweating again and starting to really understand why Quinn dislikes these assholes.

"Tell me," another of the meatheads asks, "can you even see your dick when you look down?"

All three laugh, but not just because the insult is funny, but because they know the truth.

The first one grabs my shoulder. "Hey, look, we're just busting balls, it's what we do. No harm, right?"

I nod because I can't speak.

"You're working with Quinn and that's great. You and the other whale. Awesome. But listen." He pulls me close to him. "Don't let him turn you into a pussy. He knows his way around here, but thinks he's better than us. Especially us." He pats one of the guys across his chest and the wet slap reminds me that they're naked.

The other two nod and so do I.

"Hey, I never got your name." He sticks out his hand for me to shake.

"Greg." I shake and feel so anxious to leave the room I'm eye-balling the exits.

"Good to meet you, Greg. I'm Ronnie and this is Lou and Captain."

I shake hands with the other two. Normally I'd ask why this guy's name is Captain, but I want as little to do with these men as possible.

"See you around," I manage to say as I go.

"Same here. Although it'll be hard to miss your fat ass."

The laughter dies out when the door closes behind me. Q's standing in the hall. He doesn't meet my eyes. "G, I'll explain."

And as much as I want him to, I don't need it. Pieces are falling into place already. His "way of dealing with things" isn't a result of randomness. Just like Ollie's fighting the environment he was brought up in, so is Quinn. Ella is right. We're all a mess on the inside.

CHAPTER 23

THE ONLY OTHER WAKE I've been to was for my great aunt Jeanine. She was eighty-nine. The service was horrid, all these old people shuffling around like at the deli counter, picking up their slip and waiting for their number to be called. Some of them sat in the front row, just off from where I was standing in the receiving line, and they stared at the casket like they were jealous of Jeanine. I stood and sweated under those pink-colored lights and looked forward to the reception after. I knew there would be food, and a shit-ton of it.

All these cousins I didn't know watched me like I was a carnival show. They just kept stuffing me. My stomach hurt, my eyes watered, but I kept going. I'm sure it was because I felt like

I fit in. Their little seven- and eight-year-old awe felt good, like praise.

I look around the funeral home now, and I'm happy not to see many kids. There are the same old people, padding over the carpet with canes and walkers, and there's the receiving line, and in it, Ollie. I file in behind the few who haven't already paid their respects and breathe. The smell got me last time. I don't know if it's the flowers or what they're trying to mask. I remember that from Jeanine, the way she smelled like death. Like makeup, flowers, and chemicals. I think I want to be cremated.

There's no one else from school here, not that I expected anyone. Well, maybe Ella or Quinn. But they didn't see what I saw, so I understand.

I reach the receiving line and shake hands with some uncles and aunts, I guess. They all look like Ollie, or more specifically, Ollie's mom. They're round, squish-faced, and doughy. The flowers aren't doing anything to mask the stench coming off them. But, in fairness, those pink lights are hot as hell.

"Greg," Ollie says.

I shake his hand and it feels weirdly formal. "You hanging in there?"

"Trying to." He looks down the line at his family. "They're falling to pieces, so it's not easy. Like a ripple effect, you know?"

I nod, but I don't know.

"Hey, Dad, you remember Greg?"

His mountain of a father turns to me and shakes my hand. "Greg? Yeah, of course. You were, uh, at the house."

I hop in so that he doesn't have to continue. "Right. I'm sorry for your loss."

He says nothing, just sucks his bottom lip under his teeth.

I say to Ollie, "I'll stick around for a bit. Let me know if you need anything."

"Thanks."

I move down the line and the only people left are Ollie's mother, sister, and a woman I assume is his grandmother. They are all in black, no makeup. Just blank, surprisingly tearless faces.

I reach Ollie's sister, and she looks up but doesn't speak. His mother turns to me like some mechanical mannequin. "I'm sorry for your loss," I say.

"Yes, thank you," she responds, as if I've just complimented her drapes. We shake and her hand is cold and clammy. I wonder if she's on something.

It's the same with Ollie's grandmother. She's so vacant I move away quickly, which leaves me directly in front of the casket. I watch the two people before me. They cross themselves and kneel at the casket, say a prayer, and cross again and move to the side where collages of the family are set up. My legs feel weak. It may be the workout yesterday, or it may be the emotion. Either way, I'm happy for the pew thing-a-majig to become available so I can kneel.

That is until I'm kneeling. And then what has occurred, what I'm doing, washes over me. *This* is Ollie's grandfather. This is the man that knew he was dying and told his grandson that he needed company. That Ollie needed to find me. I am grateful to this man, because Ollie came along just when I needed him. And it sucks that I won't have the opportunity to ever say so. Not that I would have.

I sink down onto my heels and look like I'm praying. I don't know any words, and I don't know if there's a God or not. It's not as if my family goes to church. But I can ask whatever powers that be to just give me a second of their time to listen.

I need a shot, an opportunity to make right on all that I'm trying to do, not just because I'm fat and don't want to be, but because I want to help Ollie and Quinn and Ella and Kyle and Stephen, and for some reason the only way I believe that will ever be done is through film, by exposing the bros, by setting something right in this world. God? Gods? Isn't that what we're supposed to do while you're up there tinkering? Aren't we supposed to gather our strength and emulate you? Or have I, again, seen too many goddamn movies? Either way, help, please. I'm a fat, loser kid, but that doesn't mean I'm useless. Don't you write me off, too. If not for me, do it for Ollie's grandfather. He wanted better for his grandson. What's the harm in that?

I cross myself and stagger over to the pictures. My head's swimming, but I manage to focus. It's a patchwork of family events from three quarters of a century. Old black-and-whites and glossy Polaroids and faded Kodaks to more current digital prints. Regardless of the age of the film, the images are all the same: happy, fat people. Every one of them is smiling. A lot like Ollie.

I press closer and look into their eyes and try to sense the pain and desperation I see in my own. It's not there. I turn back, and sure enough, a couple of the uncles are laughing with some old fart who's just come in. Ollie and his dad join in, and it's as beautiful as it is tragic.

A few minutes, or maybe a half hour later, Ollie is at my side. He says, "Hey," and I say the same back but he doesn't continue and that's fine.

I ask Ollie the question I hoped I'd have the courage to. "I know this isn't the best time, but can I ask you something?"

"Sure, Greg." Ollie's voice is vacant.

I clear my throat. "I'll be straight; I'm worried about you. Something this big, emotionally, that can be devastating for your goal."

"What? I don't know. . . ."

"Please, hear me out." I cut Ollie off and feel bad for it, but I have to say this, here, now.

He nods.

"You know I plan on filming the bros over break. I want you to join me."

"What? How?"

"Don't worry about all the details. Right now, it's coming with me, tomorrow, to a meeting with Philmore."

"And after?"

"We'll see."

Ollie's face wrinkles. "Greg, I'm not real clearheaded right now, so could you be a little more specific?"

I can't. Because if I tell him, he won't agree. Shit, I'm not even sure Philmore will agree. But if the super does, I need Ollie. "All I can say is that I have a plan that will help you honor your grandfather, and in the end may do some real good at our school."

Ollie swallows and stares at his grandfather. His eyes widen. "Okay. What time?"

"After school. I know you have the funeral. I can get Quinn to pick you up."

"No worries. Somebody here can take me." Ollie now has tears in his eyes. "Thanks, Greg. I don't know what we're doing, but I trust you. And I'm glad that he . . ." His voice wavers. "I'm glad that he'll get to look down and see me, not like this." He holds up his arms to display himself, and I say one last prayer that I've made the right move.

CHAPTER 24

ALL DAY I'VE SHUFFLED THROUGH, not even recording, just playing in my head, over and over, the loop of how I want to phrase this pitch. The one to Philmore, at the meeting I managed to arrange before I went to the wake. So much hinges on this, and I'm only going to get this one chance.

The last bell rings and I head to the parking lot. Quinn's waiting at his car. But so is Ella. And I do *not* want to have this conversation right now.

"Greg, so what is this?" she asks.

"Putting things in place for spring break," I say. It's not a lie.

"What, exactly, does that mean? You don't know what you're doing."

I ignore Ella and ask Quinn, "You couldn't wait? You had to tell her?"

He holds up his hands. "It's not like that, G. She's like psychic or some shit, just knew and has been harassing me for answers all day."

"I don't have time to get into all of it right now. I don't want to be late. But here's the short version. I spoke with Philmore about my plans for spring break, and I also suggested that he speak to Callaghan about an email I sent, and that Philmore didn't receive."

"Are you crazy?" Ella's eyes are enormous and her mouth hangs open.

"Maybe you're rubbing off on me." I smile, but she does not seem amused.

"We gotta go." Quinn gets behind the wheel.

"Shotgun." Ella jumps into the passenger seat. "We can talk on the ride over."

I climb in back and hope that Ollie shows.

He's there when we roll up, leaning against a car with a cousin or uncle or some random logger that he found. This guy is grizzled: full beard, plaid shirt, work boots. I wonder if he went to the funeral that way.

Quinn parks and I say, "Both of you, stay. This shouldn't take long."

"Famous last words," Ella says through a half smile, half frown.

I walk over to Ollie and the woodsman. Ollie looks plenty

sad, dark circles under his eyes, pasty skin, but it's made worse in contrast to his companion, who looks downright ruddy.

"Greg, hey. This is my cousin, Whitman."

Whitman reaches out an enormous mitt. "Pleasure, Greg." We shake and my hand, forearm, and practically my elbow disappear. "Glad to hear you're helping out O Ring. It's what Gramps would have wanted."

I force myself not to laugh at "O Ring" and say, "You're welcome." Then I look at them both. "Was it a nice service?"

Ollie looks down. Whitman answers. "It's what he would have wanted, so yeah, it was nice." He stands and the car rocks behind him as his weight shifts off it. "See you back at the house, O Ring."

Whitman climbs into his car, which seems physically impossible. We watch him leave.

"He got the good genes," Ollie says.

"What?"

"He's not just fat, but big all over. And strong. We talked a little about working out. He's got a seven hundred–pound deadlift."

I whistle. "We should bring him to meet Captain and the rest."

Ollie laughs. "Yeah, that would go over well."

I size him up for a second. He looks like he's doing all right. Enough so that he should be able to handle this. We head inside and I hope Ella is not recording the two of us taking up the entire span of the walkway.

The secretary is much nicer this time around. Probably because we have an appointment. She lets us right in and has us sit around a conference table twice the size of my dining room's. "They'll be with you shortly."

Ollie turns to me when she's gone. "They?"

"Philmore, Mallory, and I'm betting Callaghan."

"You said Philmore, that's it."

"I spoke to him and asked for Mallory to come along. Then I told Philmore that Callaghan had an email from me meant for him. So who knows what's going down?"

Ollie looks at me as if he'd like to cry or fight. The door opens and I guess now's the time for him to figure it out.

All three stride in, Philmore, dignified in a tweed coat; Mallory sleek and crisp in a button-down; and Callaghan, pressed as always, but looking very disheveled in the eyes. Philmore shakes hands with us while the other two sit.

He looks at Ollie. "I am sorry for your loss, Oliver." He waits for Ollie's response, which is barely a nod. "I buried my father at the same funeral home, and it was one of the saddest days of my life. But I was fortunate, like the two of you seem to be, in that I found a friend." He looks over at Callaghan.

Callaghan smiles and my insides shrivel.

Philmore sits and crosses one leg over the other. "So when Mr. Callaghan comes to me with issues, I listen as a professional, but also as a friend. After our conversation, Greg, I spoke with Mr.

Callaghan about that email. I don't know why it never reached me, unless you had the wrong address. But that's beside the point."

I don't buy that for one second.

Philmore continues, "When he told me that you recorded our lacrosse team, I was confused because you had just called and asked about an opportunity to do more of the same."

I feel Ollie shift next to me, but I refuse to look at him.

"Therefore, I'm glad we are all here, including Mr. Mallory, because I am still perplexed over all of this. So, please, explain."

This is why I enjoy film. I don't have to do anything *on the fly*. I can record, edit, and arrange my thoughts and ideas in a coherent manner. Even though I've practiced what I intend to say, the pressure I feel right now, from all sides of the room is enough to unravel me. But I clear my throat and begin.

"It's true that I recorded the lacrosse team. But that was accidental. However, I think—and Mr. Mallory, I believe your son's past attests to this—that these accidents are sometimes really creative gifts."

Holy shit am I sweating. But so far, so good, even though I can tell that Mallory does not like that I've brought his son into this.

"And as you may have heard, I am seeking some of that same discipline in my life. The very element that Max attributed his success to."

Mallory's nodding now.

"Lies. These are all damn lies. This boy has done one thing: try to incriminate my boys. Period." Callaghan lifts out of his chair when he speaks.

Philmore raises his chin. Mallory's eyes darken.

"I understand that you may think that, Mr. Callaghan, but I assure you I look up to the boys' hard work, in spite of what you may have heard," I say.

That last part felt like ripping out a part of my soul.

"Therefore I would like the opportunity to be a part of their environment, and I can think of no better time than during the build-up to the tournament. I remember when I was young, I'd see the team around town, and they were superstars. I was in awe. Then the tournament began, and the entire town came out in support. It was no surprise that we won State that year, and every year since then. The tournament, it's almost magical in the way it affects everyone." I know I sound like every pathetic cheerleader or useless teacher or business owner, but I have to push on and seal this deal. *This* can be my sacrifice.

"I ask that you please give me that opportunity. I know I'll learn more about all the things your son valued and reflected in his life—the same things I seek—in one week with the team than I will searching for a lifetime on my own." Fuck, it's as if my insides have been pulled out and I'm being forced to eat them.

The men all look at one another and then Mallory speaks. "You want to play, son?" His voice is like smoke, wisping out, with a surprising potency.

"No, thank you, sir. That would be an embarrassment." I turn to Philmore. "What I'm proposing is twofold. One, I *would* like to join the team for conditioning purposes." Ollie looks at me as if I've just revealed that I'm female. "Actually, I'd like both of us to join."

This doesn't help his appearance, but I know that if I go through this without Ollie, he'll fall back into his old habits. Plus, I need him.

The men grumble and Mallory sits back in his chair, shaking his head. Philmore sits up. "Greg, you said this was twofold. What's the second part?"

Yup, it's go time.

"To return to your son, Mr. Mallory, he is what gave me this inspiration. I do not expect to be given a handout. I know that this part of the season is the most brutal, but also the most reward-ing. I want to highlight this for the booster club. I want to use my talents to create a PR piece that you can use to demonstrate just why the donations and support are so vital. You can show them exactly how your son's memory lives on."

Mallory sits back, and I swear there's a touch of a smile on his face.

"You can't honestly be considering this?" Callaghan directs his question at both men. "I'll be damned if I have to let a couple of fat boys join the ranks just so they can lose weight and make a pretty video—excuse my description, Matthew." Callaghan turns to Mallory. "Especially since the one who is making it is renowned for his lying."

Philmore nods at this and stares me down. I knew this was the one area where my plan could fall apart. He says to Callaghan, "Jeremiah, you do not need me to remind you of the importance of the booster club. And there's something here in his suggestion. It smacks of brilliance."

My skin prickles at the suggestion. *Brilliance?*

"Shouldn't we have Blint in here for *that* conversation?" Callaghan fires back.

Mallory leans forward. "Watch yourself."

Philmore snaps his head around toward Ollie and me. "Gentlemen, our company. Let's not forget ourselves."

Callaghan closes his eyes and rubs them. Mallory nods and sits more upright. There is so much tension between them it's insane. I wonder how Ollie is holding up, but it's as if he's not here. He's staring, and I can imagine what he's seeing.

"So, what do you say?" Philmore asks.

"I like the idea, and so would Max. If these boys can trim down *and* give me something fresh to show our supporters, I see it as a win/win," Mallory says.

"As do I." Philmore extends his hand to me. I glance at Callaghan before reaching out to the superintendent. Callaghan seems as if he's lost a fight, and if that's the case, I've got a pretty good guess who he's going to take that out on.

Philmore's grip is firm. "Excellent. I look forward to the results of this project. Thank you, Greg, and you, Oliver." He looks back at the men. "Now, if you'll excuse us, we need to iron out some things."

I nod. I don't say thank you, or anything else for that matter. All my words are depleted.

We leave the office, sign out, and head through the front doors. I jog to catch up with Ollie.

"Ollie, hey, we should talk. I know that was a lot to process. You want to go somewhere?"

He keeps going, head down, arms swinging. I know the look. Fuck, I've lost him.

I walk to the car, just after Ollie has passed it, and Ella and Quinn climb out.

"G, where's Ollie going?"

"He's got to burn off that conversation. I think it was too much to swallow."

"Not funny, Greg. What did you do?" Ella steps within inches of me.

"It's not something I want to get into here. Let's go elsewhere."

"No!" Ella turns away. "Ollie, I'm going to kick his ass for you, right now," she yells.

Ollie raises his hand and does a fist pump.

"Shit, G," Quinn says. Exactly what I was thinking.

Ella kicks my shin and I cry out. "What did you do?" she seethes.

"Hold up! I'll tell you."

"You had better, Greg Dunsmore, and it better not be bullshit. Tell me *exactly* what you did."

I rub my shin and feel the egg building. "All right. Shit. Chill." When I'm done explaining, Ella sighs.

"Is that it, all of it, the truth?"

"Yes."

She smacks me so hard I fall back against the car. "You're an asshole! Who sells out their friend like that, without warning, especially after all he's been through?"

My ears ring and my face throbs, but her words hurt more.

"And this plan of yours, it's terrible. You *are* going to give them a good film, I don't doubt that. But how will that be useful to you? And at what cost? We didn't dig into this just so you could keep going and make your own grave. That was stupid, Greg. Plain. Fucking. Stupid."

Quinn steps in. "All right, all right, ease up."

Ella spins on him. "No, I won't. You're no better. You'll do what he asks when it's convenient for you, but you don't consider the consequences."

"What are you talking about? I don't step and fetch for G. But I am his friend, and that's what friends do. Help."

"Really? They don't steer you away from your own destruction?" She tilts her head, reappraising him. "And really, who are you to talk about being his friend? You're more like a copilot in his misadventures. Grow the fuck up, Quinn. Stand up to your dad—yeah, I've heard—and decide who you really are."

"Why? Is that what *you've* done? You're so awesome that I should listen to you? Great, you were called a slut and bullied and tried to kill yourself. Then your dad helped you run from your problems—I heard, too. *I've* never had that option."

He turns away and balls his fists. "Fuck!" His scream echoes off the walls and I worry someone—Callaghan—is going to come out for us.

"Yup, turn away and scream like a baby. Don't face it. No wonder you two work. Greg likes to look at everyone else's problems but his own, and you—"

"Shut up! Shut the fuck up! *You* do not know me."

Ella smirks, as if this is what she expected, possibly what she wanted. "Let me take a stab. Mom and Dad run a business. That business is health and fitness, but really it's mostly narcissism. You sell the latter, not the former, and you as the son are expected to tow the line."

Quinn's shaking and I know for a fact that so far, Ella is spot on.

"But something, or someone, has made that very difficult for you, and you can't stand it. You don't feel good about yourself. You don't fulfill the image. So you bust your ass working out. That doesn't solve the problem. You fight with your dad. That doesn't work. You meet a girl, but she's connected to your dad, so no point in pursuing that. You take on a project with your fat friend, whatever, and so far, that's going well, but in the back of your head is that question: *When am I gonna fuck this up?*" She takes a breath. "How am I doing so far?"

Ella looks down and breathes deep. I prepare for whatever's next. She looks up, at me.

"So you heard my dad say to stay away from Facebook. It has a little more to do with him working with retired cops and regurgitating what they say. My past isn't pretty, and my online existence was even uglier." She looks over at Quinn. "I know you're pissed, but this is the part you should listen to. I'm not judging you, just spelling it out."

My heart quickens and this anticipation feels worse than any prior to a workout.

"The day I tried to kill myself . . . I posted on Facebook. I left a note on my nightstand for my dad, but I wrote a final message for *them* to read. I don't know, I thought it would hurt." Ella's voice wavers and I expect tears, but she coughs and starts in again, her voice strong. "Yeah, well, I was wrong. There was one comment, like immediately after. Four words. That's it, but that was everything. You want to know what they were?"

No. Yes. Shit.

"Greg, do you want to know?" Almost a whisper.

I shake my head, but she grabs my hand and laces her fingers into it. I'm too upset to enjoy this, and that fact strikes me enough to look at her.

"Greg?"

"No," I say, even though part of me does.

"Come on. Just four words."

"What were they?" Quinn asks.

Ella wheels around but still holds my hand.

I don't know what Quinn sees in her face, but he says, "Ella, it's okay, some other time. I'm sorry for what I said."

"No, you're not. And that's okay. You wanted to compare stories. Are you ready now?"

He starts talking. To me.

"Those meatheads, Captain and the others?"

I nod. Ella looks between us.

"Yeah, well, there was this one time. Really there were a lot of times, but once that went too far. All four of them cornered me one day in the locker room. They'd said shit before about how they liked the way I looked. Grabbed my ass a few times. But this day, my dad wasn't there. He was out buying equipment, I think. Well, we were all in the locker room and they saw me with the towels and one of them said, 'We'll give you something to clean up.'"

Ella squeezes my hand tighter. I can feel my heart pounding away beneath my layers of fat. Quinn, skinny Q, is pouring out his heart in front of us, and I feel as if he's someone I've never met.

"So they crowded in, all naked, like they always are, and they started to, you know, play with themselves. I . . . I didn't know what to do. I wanted to run, but they're massive. I knew it would get worse if I tried, so I just stood there. I kept waiting for someone to show up, but it was only around three, the place was empty. And the four of them, they just kept doing what they were doing and saying shit to me like, 'Look, he likes it.'"

"And that's when I started to hate. Them, my dad, me. I'd been angry, but this took it to a whole new level."

I know he's not done. It's in his eyes. Like the look that came over Ella. These are his *four little words*.

"As soon as they were gone I decided to ramp up my working out. To use it like a suit of armor against them. I haven't stopped. And when I go to my dad's gym, they're there, and he has no idea."

The quiet that follows is so sharp I can feel its edge pressing against me. Holy. Fucking. Hell. "Quinn?" I say, but I don't know how to continue.

Ella does. She lets go of me and walks over to him. "I'm sorry, Quinn."

He nods and, amazingly, she doesn't push. She does grab his arm. "You deserve better, and your dad deserves the truth." She looks at me. "We all do."

I get it. Nothing under the radar from this point forward. Just the truth. I've got so much to learn, and none of it has anything to do with losing weight.

CHAPTER 25

I HAVE TRIED TO MAKE CONTACT with Ollie for more than a week. He won't return my texts or calls. I don't know where he goes for lunch and he sure as shit hasn't worked out with us. I'm down to 295, but it's a hollow victory. Because the meatheads are there and Quinn hasn't said a word since the other night.

If Ollie's not with us, he's probably stuffing his face and gaining back all the weight he's lost. Even more, spring break begins tomorrow, and Hell Week on Monday. *We* need to be there.

Ella and I walk to Blint's. She's prepared for this upcoming week. Both she and Q. I don't know how she processed all that she did and then said, "All right, so here's what we need to do," but we have a plan because of her.

Ella never told us those four words, but I hope she tells me. I think even a part of her still needs some truth.

"Greg?"

I ignore the voice.

"Yo, Greg?"

Kyle and Stephen are waving us over. We cross to them.

"Hey, so, you ready?" Kyle is oddly happy. Maybe he's on meds.

"No, not even close," I say. I have no clue how Alva explained this opportunity to have me under his control, but bros have been rolling up to me all week and whispering, "Hell Week," a lot like Danny Torrance with his "Redrum." It's unnerving.

"There's no way you can be," Stephen says, and his voice is terrifying. Ella and I both take a step back. This is the most I've heard him speak in weeks.

"He's right." Kyle pats him on the back and exchanges a look with me that is a mix of pleading and confusion. "What about Ollie?"

I shake my head. "Wouldn't know. Haven't seen him."

"He's in the bathroom during lunch," Stephen says.

"Yeah, it's where we go. Eating with those guys just isn't an option, but we can't be seen elsewhere, you know," Kyle adds.

The bell rings and Ella and I go into class. Taleana's there with her friends. "There's my little slut," she says. "I've got plans for you, sweetie. Gonna be your pimp."

Ella says, "You just try."

"Oh, I will."

Blint taps on the board to get our attention and writes in his neat print: *Rough drafts are due 5/2.* "I know this is in your packet, but I always feel it's necessary to remind you of important dates. This one is worth twenty-five percent of the project." If anyone has a shred of panic, it's not evident. "Good. Now today we're going to have a discussion on safety for the filmmaker. Take out your notebooks."

Blint cues up the screen. Possibly today I'll learn something very worthwhile.

"I want you to write down anything you see within this documentary that demonstrates the filmmaker's safety is at risk." Blint darkens the room and hits PLAY.

We watch a film about rebel fighters in Sudan and I scribble notes about the environment. There are guns everywhere. The filmmaker's living with his subjects and barely speaks their language. And he discusses how his satellite phone was stolen. The last scene shows the rebels around a campfire. There's joking and drinking and then nothing. Blint cuts it off.

"Okay, now you'll get into groups and I want a consensus on what the safety issues were."

"But nothing happened? He's fine," some kid says.

"You don't know the end of the story," Blint replies and has us count off and move into groups.

Lucky me, I'm with Taleana, two of her friends, and a couple of burnouts. I am the only one with notes. We sit and stare at each other, or rather, I feel them staring at me.

"Dun the Ton, you know you've got answers, just fork 'em over."

I don't look to see who said this.

"I can see them from here, fat ass." Taleana.

"They're probably all about how there wasn't enough food." One of Taleana's friends.

There's laughter and the kid next to me pulls my notebook out from beneath my arm.

"Two more minutes," Blint says, and the kid reads my notes aloud.

The laughter stops, because there's nothing about food, only reasonable answers. The kid tosses my notes back. "We'll just use his answers," he says, and the rest start shooting the shit about their plans. Except for Taleana. She stares at me.

I'm used to being stared at, it comes with the territory, but Taleana brings an intensity I haven't felt. Not in a while.

"So, Dun, you got plans for over break?"

Right, like she doesn't know. As if her evil boyfriend didn't tell her the first second he had a chance. I just shrug.

Her eyes smolder. "You think you can handle it?"

My skin tingles, and I shrug again.

"Can't wait to see the video. How fucking awesome will that be?"

Great. I swallow and notice that the side conversations have stopped. Of course they're listening to Taleana. Why wouldn't they? I shouldn't say what I'm about to, but what does it matter?

"No better than what I've already seen."

The group watches Taleana to see if this is an insult. Her eyes bug for a second, but she leans forward. "You haven't seen anything yet."

· · ·

Of course Ella wanted to know what Taleana said to me, but I just told her it didn't matter, that it was more of the same. But I know it wasn't, just like I knew there was more to the Sudan rebel documentary. Well, there was no more footage, just the film-maker's dead and mutilated body. It was found, along with his phone, after no one had heard from him in six weeks. Then some-how—Blint didn't even know—other rebels found the body and the phone and returned the film with a letter to the family. The rebels he'd been with had been ambushed. All of them had been tortured and mutilated, made into a warning sign.

I told Ella not to look for me at lunch and she understood.

My phone chirps with a text. Taco salad. Don't eat the shell. 1% milk. I pocket Quinn's message and head into the bathroom. It's empty. I peek under the stalls for feet and almost pitch onto my face when the bathroom door opens behind me. It's Ollie, holding a brown paper bag and a water. He's confused for a second, but the door opens behind him and in walk Kyle and Stephen.

They must sense the friction because they stop and wait, watching the two of us.

"Ollie, hey, don't go. I just want to talk."

I can only see one side of his face, but it's red and he's breathing heavy. "If I wanted to talk to you I would have returned your calls."

I lean against a stall. "I know, but—"

"But nothing!" Ollie yells. "We have nothing to say to each other. Not after what you did."

I put up my hands. "I understand. But I can't go through this without you."

"How is that my problem? Why should I risk myself for you and another stupid project? I don't even understand why you're doing this. You want to *help* them?"

His words echo around the tiled room, at Kyle and Stephen. They haven't moved and aren't eating.

"Ollie, there's a lot I haven't been able to tell you because of your grandfather. I was going to explain after the meeting, but you stormed off."

Ollie looks at me as if he's going to bash my head in, and for a moment, I believe he could. Then he folds in on himself.

"I had every right to. I felt used."

"That's because I used you."

He looks, I think, to see if I'm making a joke. I'm not.

"I admit to it, Ollie. That was a total dick move, even if I was going to fill you in. This is my problem. It's how I fuck everything up. Like me filming people in the halls without them knowing. It's not right. But with you, it's so much more. Please don't let me have messed this up." I point between the two of us and Ollie nods.

"I know you mean well, Greg. I do. It's just, Hell Week? The tournament? What are you thinking?"

Kyle and Stephen have opened their lunches. I think it over and realize it can't hurt to have someone on the inside know the truth. Especially them. They probably want this even more than I do. I explain about the spy cam Ella has, the system in place to capture the video onto the Cloud, and the *real* video we intend to make, not the one I pitched to Philmore, Callaghan, and Mallory.

"Greg, you're sure about all of this?" Ollie says.

"It's Ella's plan and she's the most legit person I know."

He smiles. "Did she kick your ass like she said?"

I smile. "Kicked me in the shin." I pull up my pant leg and show him the bruise. "Then she smacked me so hard my ear rang for an hour."

"Good," he says. "She's awesome."

"Can't argue about that," I say, and I take a good look at Ollie now. He's not nearly as pudgy as I figured he'd be. Without working out, I figured he'd start to swell. "Just tell me one thing, huh?"

"What?"

"Your lunch? What is it?"

He eyes his bag. I see him squeeze the water bottle. "It's a turkey wrap, no mayo, mustard."

"Anything else?"

"An apple."

"Hmm." I don't mean to sound like a grandmother, but I know I do.

"The hell's that supposed to mean?"

"You still give a shit, or you'd be eating like a pig again."

Ollie doesn't speak. I think he's just waiting for me to go. So I step away.

"For what it's worth, Ollie," Kyle says, "I think you should do it."

Ollie looks at him. "Why?"

"You'll get a good workout." He laughs, but Ollie doesn't. I take another step.

"If you hate them now, you'll come away wanting them to burn in hell." Stephen's voice is direct, no waver. He pins us both with his glare.

"But I don't hate them. I never wanted to. That's Greg's thing, and your thing, not mine."

"Bullshit! Those guys torture everyone, and if you don't hate them for that, then fuck you!" Stephen's voice rises. "We're part of this thing that's been huge for years, that the town loves, that is the most successful business going. Did you know that these fucks get the most scholarship money over every team in the country?

I did, and I wanted some of that. But I didn't know they were a success because they run the team like they're in the military. One falls, they all fall. That weakest link shit. And how do they make you stronger? You already know. We agree at the beginning, as freshman, to accept it all or to walk away. I thought I could handle it. And I wanted people to look up to me. It's pathetic, but it's all I have. And if you two don't succeed, then when I'm a senior this had all better be worth it, or I'll find you and fuck you up for failing!"

Ollie sighs. "All I wanted to do was make a friend, and lose some weight. Why do we have to fight the bros?"

"Why *not* us? Give me one good reason why it shouldn't be us, the two fattest fools in this school," I say.

"Because we won't win."

I think of the medical info, all the injuries. And there's a good case not to fight them. Yet, we can handle *this*. "They will already have won if we don't fight."

Ollie nods, tucks his shoulders, and shoves his way past Kyle and Stephen and out the door.

. . .

I'm in the computer lab for no good reason. Everyone else has gone home. Spring break is underway. But I thought maybe I'd see Ollie and he'd tell me he was going to join us at Peak Fitness, or even better, that he's in on the plan and we're all good. None of that has happened, and it's about time for me to meet Q.

I pack up, and while I'm zipping my bag, feel his presence.

"Mr. Dunsmore."

I sit up and look at Callaghan. He's filling the doorway, arms folded across his chest.

"Are you ready for tomorrow?"

"Absolutely," I lie.

"And Mr. Leonard?"

"He's all set." Why not keep lying? I think I get a pass with this asshole.

Callaghan sits down next to me. "Greg, listen close."

I do because I know I have to, not because I want to.

"You *will* create something powerful for Mr. Mallory. And maybe, just maybe, we can look past your previous indiscretions and let you move on with your life. Help you with that scholarship."

My breath catches and I hate myself. But Callaghan hears it and smiles.

"Exactly, Greg. That's what you want from the audience. Something *that* good." He leans close, closer than I'd ever want him to, and I can't help but think of Quinn and the meatheads. "Think of the future you could have. *If* you truly know how to put your skills to work."

Thankfully, he doesn't wait for me to respond, just gets up and clacks out of the lab. Getting out of this town, away from these assholes, shit, that's been the dream ever since I figured out how to edit. Now that it's a potential, here I am planning a film that will destroy it all. But isn't that Ella's point? Facing my fears, not running. I'm putting my faith in her, and I'm scared. I'm worried that her plan is perfect and that I'm going to fuck it up. I think that even more than a scholarship, even more than weight loss, I have to figure out how to fight. Not like the bros, but in my own way.

I duck out of the lab and head to Q's car. "Ready?"

He's leaning against the side, getting sun. "Yeah. No Ollie?"

I let the silence speak for itself.

Quinn climbs in and we roll. When we are within a few blocks of the gym, we both stare at the sight on the sidewalk: Ollie, lumbering with purpose. Quinn pulls over while I roll down my window. "Ollie?"

He keeps trucking. Quinn has to move back out onto the street and then dart over. "Ollie, where the hell are you going?"

He doesn't slow down. "I don't know yet."

A car crawls up our ass.

"G, I gotta move," Quinn says.

Ollie's looking ahead as if he's about to murder someone. "Yeah, go," I say.

We pull into the parking lot and get out and lean against the trunk. A few minutes later, Ollie rumbles toward us and throws his bag down at our feet. "Listen, because I'm only saying this once. We are doing this shit only so I can lose weight. I don't give a shit what the bros do to each other. If they lay a hand on me, I'll knock 'em the fuck out."

I've never heard Ollie talk this way. I love it.

"When we get back, we'll keep coming here. But that's it. I don't know if we're friends or enemies. I'll know after, I guess."

Ollie should be out of breath between the pace of his walk and the speech he just gave, but he's not.

"Deal." Q offers Ollie his hand and they shake.

Ollie and I do the same, but I say, "Thank you." Ollie's done talking though, so we head inside.

Of course the meatheads are here, and of course Q's dad gives him a dirty look, as well as us. And of course I want to beat the hell out of all of them, but I'm saving my energy. One fight at a time.

We head into the locker room and change.

"You guys are going to get run into the ground. There won't be any weights. The bros are all about speed and explosiveness."

I wish Quinn weren't right, but I'm sure he is.

"So today we're going to find the point where you break down and find a pace to keep you from going there."

"But if we break down, then we don't have to do any more," I say.

Quinn shakes his head. "If you break down, there's nothing you can do to stop them."

The sound of weights banging off the floor and deep,

guttural screams seep through the door. I understand exactly what Quinn means.

Ollie and I follow him outside to the field adjacent to the gym. It's muddy, but the grass has turned green, no snow. Q walks long strides and drops orange cones every ten yards, for fifty yards. He returns to us and pulls a stopwatch from his pocket and tugs at the whistle around his neck. "It's real simple, we're doing suicides. Seemed appropriate."

Neither Ollie nor I laugh with Quinn.

"Anyway, we'll do five sets after you've warmed up. The first will be easy, too easy for the bros. The second will be faster and the third will be at a pace that should make you drop. For the fourth and fifth, I want you to come just under the pace of the third. You should be able to tell by how your lungs burn and how fast your heart is pounding if you're there. At least that's what I hope." He looks at us. "Questions?" We shake our heads. "Go run the perimeter four times." Q blows his whistle and we take off.

It's fifteen minutes of pure hell, and then we're down to the last sprint.

"In five, four, three . . ." Quinn counts down and I hold my breath, trying to slow my breathing. I fell to the ground after the third set, as did Ollie, and finding a pace during the last set was almost impossible. But Quinn yelled and motivated and we finished alongside each other.

Ollie's covered in mud splatter, like we've been playing rugby, and his hands are red and raw. He's as exhausted as me, has to be, but there's a fire in his eyes that I know I don't possess. At least not here, like this. Maybe behind the lens, or at my computer. Shit, I need him more than I thought. The whistle blows and we're off again.

I follow Ollie's lead and bend and touch at the cone with him. We move back to the start and bend and touch and are off to the twenty. We're in a rhythm, and I feel what Quinn said, a certain burn. Manageable, not life sucking. I pay attention to my heart as we move from cone to cone. It's in my throat, but not beyond. I can swallow and still hear over the thudding.

We touch at the fifty and Quinn screams, "Sprint!" For the first time today, Ollie smiles. I tuck my head and we take off.

Mud is sailing behind us and I'm pumping my arms so hard I can feel the rub just beneath my armpit. But we fly for fat boys and crash through the finish. We do not fall over. We keep moving so we don't cramp and Quinn is all smiles.

"Simple as that, boys. Keep your pace. You'll never catch the bros, but that's not the point. You've just got to run with them."

When he has enough air to speak, Ollie says, "We'll keep up." He claps my back.

"And maybe beat them at their own game," I say and we head inside, knowing that our words are more prayer than confidence.

* * *

"So you and Ollie are good?" Ella asks and I cradle the phone against my neck while I fold my clothes. I could put her on speaker, but I don't want my parents to hear what she might say.

"I think. He's still angry, but I don't blame him."

"Yeah." She sighs. "He's in a shitty spot. His grandfather, now this. I'm amazed he's not at IHOP right now."

"Or Taco Bell."

"Or the Cheesecake Factory."

This shit isn't healthy, but what can we do? "Are you ready?" I ask.

"Sure. My dad's used to me spending vacations holed up in my room in front of the computer."

This image makes me sad because Ella is so cool, and I know she's not in front of her computer only because she's into it, but because she has no other options. Her past is a pure example of why I have to succeed. The *assholes* can't always get their way. Someone needs to be there for us.

"All right. But I'm going to owe you for this. Big time."

"Yes, you are. Because if we pull this off . . ."

I look over at all the gear Ella snagged, either from her dad or that she bought with her own money: a GoPro for the film I'll need for Mallory; a mini wireless camera that feeds directly into my phone; and this recovery stick that pulls everything off my phone and onto the computer. There are some apps, too, that she found and kicked my way. She has literally thought of everything. I just need to make it happen.

"Hey, if I haven't said it, thanks. Without you . . ." This truth stuff has so many consequences.

"Without me, what? I didn't catch that last part."

I can't tell if she's being honest or egging me on. "Without you, I don't know. I just think things would be very different."

There's a pause and I replay what I've just said. That was cool, right? Honest but not overboard?

"Thanks, Greg. I guess I feel the same. We're not out of the woods, but thank you for realizing we have to try. I can't live through this shit again. And those poor boys. No one deserves that."

I don't know if it's because we left it unresolved, or if it's because I'm so into this moment and how it looks in my mind, the two of us, split-screen conversation, but I ask, "What were those four words on your wall?"

Another pause. This one longer, and I know I've gone too far. "Ella, I'm sorry. I—"

"Do you remember how I tried to kill myself?"

How could I forget? It's not as if I have any other friends who've told me they tried. "Sleeping pills."

"Right. And I posted right before I was about to go through with it. A last ditch plea, I guess." I hear her door creak and close. I imagine her shutting her eyes and steeling herself for what she's about to say.

I close my door and do the same. "Right, so those four words, they came after you posted what you were going to do?"

"Exactly." Her voice wavers.

"What were they?"

She clears her throat. "Swallow the whole bottle."

My heart slams around as if it is lost and searching for its home. "Goddamn," I say.

"Exactly."

And because I have to know. "Did you?"

"What do you think?"

I'm fat and, therefore, because of the way people have treated me, understand desperation and how it creates this void, this gaping hole inside. For me, there's never enough food, never enough nice comments to make up for the rude, and barely enough hope to get me through the stretches of depression.

Fortunately those pills weren't enough to allow Ella's void to swallow her.

"I'm happy you're here."

She sniffs and I hope she's not crying. "Me, too," she says. "Me, too."

CHAPTER 26

"YOU READY?" OLLIE ASKS as we climb out of Quinn's car. He has the same fire in his eyes as he did on Friday.

"No. You?"

He laughs. "How could we be?"

Quinn takes our bags out of the trunk and sets them on the ground.

"Did Ella tell you to be like our chauffeur or something?" I ask.

"Or something," he says. We grab our bags. "Just be careful. Both of you." The bros are everywhere, and Quinn shakes his head and climbs back into his car. "I'll be back at three." He pulls away and it feels as if my stomach's attached to his bumper.

"Just remember why we're doing this," Ollie says.

I want to talk to him more about this, review our emergency strategy, but there's no time.

"Well, well. I was worried we'd have to go drag your fat asses out of bed." Alva rolls up. "Even though it would have been hysterical to watch. Let me see your gear."

I hand over my bag. "Front pouch. Nothing fancy, just a GoPro and my phone." He unzips and looks in while I touch the spy cam attached to the inside of my shirt. It's the beauty of being big. I have fabric to work with, so cutting the hole and applying the Velcro strips was kind of easy.

Alva hands it back. "Make sure it all works. You can't afford to fuck this up." He turns away and lets out a shrill whistle, using his finger and thumb. "Inside. Now."

The bros stop, midsentence, and walk into the gym. Ollie and I file in with them, and my heart is galloping, spinning, doing flips.

We enter from the opposite side and this, in itself, feels very unnatural. I eye the tunnel of the bleachers, where all this started. What if I'd just ignored what I'd heard?

We put our bags down in the corner and Alva and Gilbey take the center. Callaghan and Mallory are on the far side.

"Gather round and take a knee." Alva waves his hands like a welcoming uncle and the bros converge. I find Kyle and Stephen and it's impossible to detect their hesitation. My throat tightens and Ollie and I move forward. "Not you two. Stand." We stop moving. "No, over here, with me." Alva's all smiles and this makes me want to run from the room more than anything.

We move to Alva's side. Ollie stares at the floor, and I decide to do the same.

"Boys, I'm sure you're wondering why we decided to bring along guests during this week when we must be our must focused, our fiercest." Alva pauses. "It's simple: motivation." There's murmuring but he continues. "As lacrosse players, we're not just fast and powerful, we're fit and healthy. As is obvious, these two do not share these traits."

My head is surging, trying to make sense of the thesis he's about to defend. Because these guys are anything but *healthy*. They're downright sick. Then again, they know nothing else.

"So while we tighten up our own skills, we will help them with theirs." Alva laughs. "Don't worry, I will run you into the ground, too. But if Dun the Ton and Double Stuffed Ollie can hang, then you'd better be able to."

The bros look at us like specimens, something to size up and critique. Their distaste is obvious.

"And while we do this, we will showcase just what it means to be a Warrior. Dun will film, because Mr. Mallory has asked him to do so. In Max's honor, we will show how good it can feel to be in shape, how important it is to allow your will to bend to a power much greater than your own, and as with fire, be turned to ash. And then, like the phoenix, rise."

Alva's voice takes on a minister quality and I have a tough time keeping my laughter down because of his mixed metaphor and his stupid notion that bending over and taking it is somehow noble. But it all makes sense. These kids are more brainwashed than I thought. I glance over at Callaghan, and he's downright beaming. I'm sure he penned this speech.

"So let us recite our motto."

The boys all bow their heads, and in unison, begin: *Our allegiance is to the Warriors, our bodies are weapons, ready for sacrifice . . .*

Ollie is paper-white. Kyle and Stephen are chanting, but it seems as if it's being pulled from them, rather than flowing as steadily as the rest. They finish:

We will dominate at whatever cost to our opponent or to ourselves.

I've heard these words too many times by now. But this time they feel new, like a threat.

"Let's get to it." Gilbey claps his hands, and as one, the boys rise and form five lines. "Hop in," Gilbey says to us, and because there is no other choice, we do.

* * *

Thank God Q had us run those suicides, because that's all we did. We warmed up with a few slow ones, picked up the pace, and then I lost track of how many sets. But I listened to my body and didn't break. It was tough with the GoPro bobbing on my head, but whatever, I'll deal. Ollie was solid, too. And not that anyone said anything positive to us, but at least we didn't hear any shit.

Alva and Gilbey lead a pack of bros out of the back room with Med balls.

"Fuck, I hate these, Greg." Ollie shifts from foot to foot.

"Who knows, maybe we'll do something else with them?" I don't know why I try to stay upbeat.

"Five lines," Alva yells, and we all fall in.

The drill is simple. Throw the ball into the wall and roll out so the guy behind you can scoop it up and toss it. Repeat. The guys all toss, scoop, and sprint. I wait for my turn, scoop, plant my foot and toss, and roll out. A whistle blows and I know it's for me. I look back and there's the ball, a few inches from the wall. I must not have thrown it hard enough.

Gilbey trots over. "Dun, what kind of a bitch-ass toss was that? The ball weighs twenty pounds, not two. Throw that piece of shit like you mean it!" He's in my face, and in my mind I can already see the footage. *Keep going.*

"Gilbey!" Alva snaps, and Gilbey looks to him. Alva's pointing at his own head, but Gilbey doesn't get it. "What the fuck's wrong with you?"

Alva bounds over, grabs Gilbey under the armpit, and spins him away from me, away from the camera. The bros look at their captains. Kyle nods at me, but I can't judge the meaning.

Gilbey returns. "Dun. Throw it harder next time." He walks

away. I get into the end of the line and wonder if I should just roll it like a bowling ball instead. But the lines resume and Ollie's up, and he slams that ball. Alva actually cheers for him, and insanely, it seems genuine. I find myself staring, knowing full well that by doing so, I'm providing just the footage Mallory wants. But that's the plan, isn't it? Shit.

Twenty minutes later, covered in more sweat than if I'd been swimming, a whistle blows and Alva announces a water break. Ollie and I meet at our bags.

"How you feel?" I ask.

"Not bad," he says and swigs. "Happy you have the camera, though."

I drink and agree. The GoPro could just save us, especially now that Gilbey is rolling out a bucket of sticks.

Once we're all gathered around, Gilbey points at three guys at a time. Each wordlessly grabs a stick, and all the guys form five lines with each stick wielder spaced out about ten feet from the next. I look over at Kyle and he doesn't see me, but his face reveals all I need to know. This is going to hurt.

But it can't be that bad, not if it's on film.

"Greg, let me see what you have there." Mr. Mallory's voice catches me off guard. I jump. He laughs. "Easy." He extends a hand and I know what to do. I pull off the GoPro and give it to him. "Very nice. Top of the line, Greg. You'll make some excellent film with this."

"Thank you, sir," I say, adding on the formality, hoping it might help.

Mallory smiles, waves at Callaghan, and leaves. Callaghan watches the door close and crosses to me. Without a word, he takes the GoPro from my hands. My legs almost give out.

"Remember, if you don't react fast enough, that's your problem," Alva says.

The first bros go at the whistle and the drill is simple: the first guy with a stick swings at your head, the second your belly, and the third, your feet. It's so predictable that everyone moves before the stick comes their way. I feel much better.

Then it's my turn and the whistle sounds and I duck low to avoid the hit, but it comes at my feet and feels as if it's taken off a piece of my shin. The next strikes my ear before I know what's happened and I roll into the third, like a lance to the gut. I fall to the floor and hold on to everywhere that hurts. The whistle blows and I cringe, thinking they're coming for me, but when I look up, it's just the next row, and in it, Ollie. I brace for him, but he flies through, unscathed. He shoots me a bewildered look and then I'm being lifted.

The one bro puts a stick in my hand and says, "Your turn."

"But I can't. I won't swing like that," I say as they're moving me.

"Yes, you will, Greg." Alva grabs my shoulder. "You will and you will make it hurt, or you'll wish you had."

I look past him, to Callaghan, who has the camera in front of him, the red light confirming that it's recording. I reach into my shirt and turn on the mini camera.

"Get set!" Alva screams. I grip the stick, last in line.

The whistle blows and out flies one of the bros. He ducks, dodges, and gets to me, waiting to jump. But I don't swing and he runs past.

"Dun, you have to swing," Alva says.

"No, I don't." The room quiets after I've spoken.

"Yes, you do." Callaghan steps forward, the camera no longer recording.

"Then give me the camera, and I'll record the rest of this."

He lets the GoPro dangle at his side. "You see, Greg, this is the sort of discipline you talked about needing. The ability to shut up and take orders."

"I never said I needed that." My throat is dry and I know there's not enough water for it.

"It was implied," Callaghan answers and looks at me like I'm already dead.

"If that's the case, then give me my camera and I'm gone. I never agreed to hurt people, and I can't see how you having that on film is going to help with the booster club."

"Do you really want to cut and run?" Alva asks, joining us. "Do you really want to find out what will happen to you if you don't keep up your end of the bargain?" He doesn't even bother to look at Callaghan to see if this is all right. Because of course it is.

"Yes, let that sink in," Callaghan says. "There are very real consequences here. You're not going to fail some project. I'm going to make your life very . . . difficult."

I consider how this must look, how his words sound. The mini camera is rolling, so I need him to answer a question. "What exactly do you mean? Is this a threat?"

"Yes, yes it is. You agreed with Dr. Philmore to proceed with this. If you do not, you'll have to pay the price. Is that something you want?"

Shit. I know what he means. No scholarship. Ever. "No, sir."

"Then get back in line," Alva says, and it might as well have been Callaghan speaking.

I do, and I understand what he's doing. I've done it for years. Gathering evidence.

I grip the stick. And I swing. The head of the stick hits the kid in the ankle, throwing him off balance. He lands awkwardly, tries to right himself, but falls to the court, smacking his face. Alva and Gilbey scream happily. Callaghan smiles and keeps recording.

*   *   *

When we break for lunch, Mallory returns from whatever errand Callaghan sent him on.

Ollie sits next to me on the floor, where I'm leaning against the bleachers. He opens his lunch bag and his food selection is the same as mine. Apparently Quinn delivered the same instructions.

"That was weird, huh?" he asks.

"Yeah. I'm not sure what to make of it beyond them trying to put me in my place."

Ollie chews his sandwich. "Wasn't that effective, though, was it?" He points to his chest, where, on me, the camera is hidden.

"No, not really." I catch Alva looking over at us. He nudges Gilbey, who nods, but they return to their meals.

"Three more hours, Greg, and day one is over."

I sip my water, my sandwich lodging in my throat. Once it's clear, my eyes sting, but I say, "Don't jinx it."

And Ollie doesn't seem to do so. We do shuffling drills and resisted sprinting drills, which is near impossible tethered to Ollie. We do squat jumps and lunges and hops and fast feet. I try not to be impressed, but watching the bros as I suffer, I can't believe how agile these guys are. The GoPro bobs and I stare at feet that move three times as fast as mine and never once stumble. Mallory's film will come together easily.

The whistle blows and Mallory and Callaghan make their way to center court. The bros take a knee. Ollie and I lean on each other as we go down. I'm not certain that even with his help, I'll be able to get back up.

"Excellent first day, gentlemen. I'm proud of the shape you are all in. It will get progressively harder, but you older boys know this. Help the freshmen through."

I look at Kyle and Stephen, who have managed to stick with one another all day. They look beat, but neither seems concerned by what Mallory just said.

"Rest up, ice, and eat. This sacrifice you offer over spring break will provide you with the tools to deliver an excellent performance this season. Now, say it with me . . ."

The bros all bow their heads and say their chant and I close my eyes. I envision how I will edit Mallory's piece, and I wonder if I'll get anything valuable for the other.

"Let me just take that from you."

I feel the GoPro lifted from my head and look up at Callaghan. "What?" I sound so stupid.

"I'm just going to hold on to this for now. Make a copy in case something happens to yours."

"But that's my camera."

"Your point?"

The bros are done with their words and are all looking at me. There's nothing I can say. He's taking the GoPro. He'll make a copy of what I recorded today. It doesn't really make a difference, but still, he's just *taking it*. And I have to accept that. "Okay," I say.

"You're learning already." Callaghan stands and looks over everyone. "Boys." He and Mallory walk away and I keep my eyes on the floor.

"Ollie, give me a hand."

"I can't, Greg."

Ollie's still kneeling and his face is upturned, eyes bugged. Then I see what he sees. The bros all have socks, and in the end of each is a lacrosse ball. They're wrapping them around their hands, and I know exactly what they intend to do.

Gilbey steps forward. "Stand up." Neither of us move. Gilbey points at a group of bros, who advance on us and lift us to our feet. Alva joins.

"Hand it over, Greg."

"Mallory took my GoPro," I say to Alva and he shakes his head.

"Your other camera, asshole."

My legs seize and out of the corner of my eye I see Ollie look at me. It's like the kiss of death. The same bros who lifted me, now grab my arms and Gilbey reaches under my shirt, finds the mini camera and pulls it out. He hands it over to Alva, but not before wiping off my sweat on his shorts.

"Him, too." Alva points at Ollie, who begins to protest, but ends up just staying quiet. He's learning as well. Gilbey comes away with nothing.

Alva nods and holds up the mini camera to the bros. "This is what we need to beat out of Dun the Ton. He wants to make us look bad, even though he's been given this opportunity to train with us and lose that coat of disgusting. Can you imagine how he could twist every drill we do in here? Can you see how he would try to make us look?"

"Probably as bad as we looked in the film that bitch he hangs with is making," Gilbey says, and it's clear that Taleana has done her reporting.

"Or worse," Alva answers.

I know how this is going to feel. I've been struck by so many objects over the years that this is actually not new. But the amount is. I hope the bros are limited in the swings they get. Baseballs hurt, but lacrosse balls are the worst because they're so dense.

There's a commotion, and Stephen emerges, carrying an iPhone. My heart sinks. The case has a film lens on the back, eclipsing the lens of the phone. My phone. Stephen hands it over and does not look at me.

Alva holds it up. "This is your first lesson." He removes the case and sets my phone on the ground. "Stop filming and instead look in the mirror. The picture's much worse there." He swings his sock like a mace, and it whips forward, shattering my screen. Two more flicks of the wrist and Alva has turned my phone into fragments on the floor. He steps on them and the crunch is dampened by the anger pumping through my ears.

"Second lesson. Same as the first." He sets the mini camera next to the remains of my phone and Gilbey smashes it with his heel.

Even though I should be afraid, I'm not. I'm pissed. I have so few things in my life that I love, and to see them crush one doesn't diminish me as they hope it will.

Gilbey smiles his devilish smile when he's finished and I look right into his eyes. "Should I applaud or something?"

Gilbey twitches, as if he'd like to lunge, but Alva steps forward. "No, hold the applause, we're not done. We're going to drill the last lesson into *you*."

The bros move in a swarm, encircling Ollie and me, slamming the lacrosse balls into us. The hits come in a volley up and down my body, but not into my head or face. I refuse to cry out, but do hear Ollie scream, "Stop! Please!"

And they do, at the whistle. And then, like monks, they silently stalk off to their bags, where they each place their weapons. They leave and after the last exits, Alva calls, "See you tomorrow. Hell Week has only just begun."

CHAPTER 27

QUINN KNOWS WITHOUT US SAYING a word. He rushes out of the car and opens the doors. Bros laugh as we make our way into his ride, but we ignore them. Q takes off and I turn to Ollie. "You okay?"

He just stares out the window.

Shit, I hope they didn't break him. I hurt everywhere, but am still so pissed, I don't care about the pain. "How'd you guess, Q?"

"Huh?"

"How'd you know we'd be busted up?"

"I think I could have guessed, but Ella texted."

"What?" If the spy cam was busted *before* the beating, how would she have a clue?

"I'm gonna let her explain." Quinn shoots me a look that's half grin, half what-the-fuck.

I settle back into the seat and feel the bruises ripple beneath me. What the hell are we in for now?

Ella is pacing in her driveway when we roll up. "Are you all right?" she asks.

"How? How did you know?" I say.

I expect a sarcastic answer like the one Q gave, but instead, she grabs my bag from my shoulder and twists it around. "You see it?"

"See what?" My body hurts and I'm tired and I'm in no mood for riddles.

She points at the label on my bag, and it's shiny in the middle. Then she unzips it and pulls a camera from the smaller front pouch.

"This is connected to *my* phone. I watched it all, recorded it all."

"Even the beating?" Ollie asks, and I don't know if it's worse to hear the word out loud or to know that Ella watched.

"We'll talk about that. First, let's take care of you two."

We follow her to the side of the house, to her hot tub. Ollie looks at me, and he offers the faintest of smiles.

Ella lifts the lid. The water's not bubbling. Then I see the bags of ice lined up next to the tub. Shit. "Even five minutes in there will help so much, but let's go for ten."

"Damn, I'd so like to, but I forgot my bathing suit."

Ollie nods at my words.

"No worries," Quinn says. "I dropped by your house, Dun, and picked up a change of clothes for both of you."

"What?"

"Come on, you never lock your back door."

I don't know if I'm more upset that he snuck into my house or that he knows how easy it is yet never comes over when I'm there.

"Let's just get this recorded, too," Ella says.

"What?" I ask.

"Your bodies."

I wait for the joke. It doesn't come. "Fine. Not that it will help. But Quinn will do it, not you."

Ella hands the phone to Q. "Let me know once they're in." She heads into the house.

"Do we really have to do this?" I ask, looking back at the ice tub.

"It was my idea. You have any clue what you're going to look like?"

In fact, I do. I once saw a documentary about Olympic weightlifters, and in it they showed part of their recovery, getting beaten by a rubber mallet. Not really, but close enough. The trainer pounded out muscles, whacking out the knots and shit. The lifters left the table bruised but loose. I'm sure the bruises will be similar, but I'll feel like a piece of meat under a tenderizer.

And I'm right. Ollie and I take off our shirts and we're dotted like the Spotted Elephant from *Rudolph*.

"Just get in," Quinn says after he's paused the recording, his voice gentler than usual.

My balls climb into my throat and I legitimately feel as if I'm going to have a heart attack. Ollie's breathing as if he's only got one lung, and our skin, where it's not discolored from our bruises, is bright red. This so better be worth it.

"Okay, so here's the deal," Ella says, rolling up to us as if we don't look like dying marine animals. "Good news, I saw the beating because of that camera. Bad news, with where it was and how they circled you, the video's not clear. Greg, you'll need to get your bag closer tomorrow."

"T . . . tomorrow? We can't g . . . go back," Ollie says, his teeth chattering like I've only seen in movies.

And this is all my fault. Him. Me. Sure, *I* didn't beat us, but there's a hefty responsibility on my end. In more ways than one. "We do, though. Because if we don't, it's going to be worse," I say.

Ollie shakes his head. "You don't know for sure."

"I do," Quinn says. "You walk away, they've won. And besides, I don't know if you can walk away. Not if you're going to see this plan through."

Ollie punches the water and stands, looking like an angry blister, his stretch marks purple, matching the bruises. "Just what is this fucking plan? Give me all the details. Greg gave me what he thought were all of them, but clearly you kept him in the dark about some things."

It's a good point, and maybe one I should be pissed about. But I believe in Ella. If she didn't want me to know about the third camera, it was for good reason.

"You sure?" Ella asks, her voice sweet, not snarky. And I notice that she's not looking away from Ollie. She's taking him in, all of him, and doesn't seem repulsed.

"As sure as I am that I want to get out of this tub." He grabs the edge and Ella snags a towel. Ollie climbs out and sits on the bench on the edge of Ella's lawn. It can't be more than fifty-five degrees out, but he is already losing the red tinge.

I hesitate, because I worry that she may not look at me the same way she looked at Ollie. I'm afraid to see the disgust in her eyes. But Quinn says, "It's time, G," and I have no choice.

I step out and Ella hands me a towel. Before I can get it around my shoulders, she grabs my arm. I stand there, stupidly trying to figure out what to do. She holds me at a distance and examines me, turns me around like someone might a piece of artwork or a dress. When she looks back into my face, she's crying. I hand the towel back. "Take care of yourself first," I say. She wipes her face, and I give her a moment, joining Ollie on the bench.

He looks at me. "We're in it now, aren't we?"

"We are, but when haven't we been?"

Ella crosses to us, her face dry of tears. "All right, so let me spell out what I have planned. Feel free to chime in if it sounds stupid. First, I get all the video from your iCloud account, Greg.

If it didn't get there, we'll use that stick. It'll pull everything off your phone, no problem, even if it is in shards in your bag. Okay?"

"Sure," I say.

"Good. Now, second, you'll position your bag a little better. We'll talk and figure that out. Make some excuse about needing an inhaler nearby. You have one, right?"

"What fat kid doesn't?"

"So this means we're going back?" Ollie asks, as if this was the furthest possibility.

Ella looks at me. "Are you going back, Greg?"

"Absolutely." I slap Ollie's back. "We have to. You know that. We show a brave face tomorrow, and they'll think we can take it."

"But can we? What if this was just the beginning? What if it gets worse? What is *too much* in your book?"

Defining *too much* has always been a problem for me. Couple that with what I know these boys are capable of, and I only have one answer. "I don't know. But I'm willing to bet we're not going to find out."

"Why? Because Callaghan and Mallory are there? Remember, Callaghan took your camera away. Then they left us with them. You think they didn't know what was going down?"

"He's right, G. From the sounds of it, you were set up."

"But you said we needed to go back and face them."

Quinn looks up for a second. "I did, and you do, but I'm not saying it's going to be easy. Ollie's right. You need to know when to walk away."

My body's heating up, but not in the way I want. "All right, we'll figure that out. Let's just have Ella finish her plan. All right?"

Ella slaps her forehead. "Shit, I got lost thinking about how to use this footage."

I love her for this.

"All right, so you'll make it through the week, I'm sure. Really." She smiles at Ollie. "Then I'll create an awesome film for Mallory. I'll make it so good it will be the next lax bros pride montage. Right, Greg?"

"If you think you can."

"Challenge accepted. And at the same time, I'll make the video we need. And then you know what I'll do with it?"

I know what she's going to say before she does, and I want to stop her, but I know that's impossible.

"I'll sneak it in for the film contest."

I feel my face fall. I thought she was going to leak the video, not do this, sacrifice herself. I know we need an audience, but *I* should be the one to make this offer, not her. But I also understand where she's coming from. There's no guarantee that my project will get selected. Hers will. It's awesome, like her. And mine's just struggling to survive, like me.

"Trust me," Ella says.

"I already do, but let me use it for my entry."

Ella scowls. "Everything you film is tainted. You know that. It won't work. It has to be me."

I look her straight in the eye. "I *might* be good enough to get looked at by the film schools, but you *will* be. If you do this, you kill that. Haven't you been a victim enough?"

Ella rears back, eyes wide, and I'm prepared for her to slap me. But she just backs farther away, retreating into herself. Q shoots me a look. Ollie stares into space, and once again, I've ruined everything. Because that's what *I* do.

•   •   •

My parents aren't home yet, which is awesome. Mom's on break, too, but she spends the days with her teacher friends, shopping and going out to lunch. Dad works, like usual.

Even though I took the ice bath, I feel the need to shower. Mostly because I don't want to do so later and have Mom catch the bruises as I'm leaving the bathroom.

I turn the heat way down and scrub. I'm sore and exhausted, my mind scrambled from the day and the conversation at Ella's. What I said came out all wrong. I just don't want her to go too far. She's like me, still hurting from eighth grade, hurting from now, and wants revenge, at any cost. But not this way. She deserves better.

I towel off, head to my bedroom. It figures that Gilbey has already posted on Facebook, thanking everyone for an "awesome day 1" and adding that the "last exercise was the best." Douche.

Other bros chime in with agreement and speculation about tomorrow. And what happens then will decide it all. If they break Ollie and me, there will be no video. And who knows what the fallout of that will be with the administration? Whether Callaghan will follow through with his threat. Even worse, the bros will have won, have free reign, and I can only imagine that freedom will cost dearly. I pull up my iCloud.

I scroll through for today's video. Nothing. Before I left Ella's I handed over my phone—what was left of it. She didn't say anything, and I don't know if I crossed the line with her, but now I have to reach out. On my old phone, I text, Nothing on iCloud. Let me know what you find with that stick.

I wait. No reply.

Downstairs, I hear the door open, and Mom call for me. We'll have dinner and I'll bullshit about how the day went. I can see it all, just like I always do, this version of my life that I plot and script. Am I ever going to be able to just let my real life unfold?

CHAPTER 28

QUINN PULLS UP OUTSIDE Ollie's house and honks. "You hear from him since yesterday?" he asks.

"No, but it's not like reached out. I suck."

"Good point."

We both look out the window and wait. No Ollie.

"Want me to honk again?"

I know there's no point, but say yes.

The honk bleats into the morning and the door doesn't open. I think I knew yesterday that Ollie wasn't coming. He's had enough. I don't blame him.

Quinn pulls up to the school. "You want me to wait? You know, in case they ambush you from the start?"

"No," I say, "I'm not afraid." I open the door.

"Yes, you are." Q's voice is gentle, like yesterday. "I'm just saying. I'd be scared, too. This is no joke."

"I know. But I have to."

"You really don't. I don't know that the bros deserve your help, as shitty as things are. And consider what Ella's going to do to herself because of this."

I look at Q's profile, all lean, telling me what I don't need to do. "Think on this. Besides me being fat, what's my biggest problem?"

Quinn shrugs.

"You really don't know?"

"What do you want me to say, Dun?"

"Just be honest."

Quinn looks down. "No one believes you because you've always been a liar."

Good. He nailed it. "And if I'd been more honest things might be different. They might not. But answer this: Would you be closer friends with me if I didn't have such a rep?"

Quinn stares out the windshield. "That's not fair, G."

Bros are exiting cars, heading inside, probably getting ready to mess me up, and I'm grilling Quinn about honesty. Fucked up.

"No, it's not," I say. "But when has fair ever existed?"

"It would be easier."

"*That's* why I'm going in. See you at three." I close the door before he can say anything else.

I walk into the gym, shoulders pinned back. The bros watch me, whisper and huddle, but nothing happens. I set my bag separate from the rest and look around. No Callaghan or Mallory. Just Alva, Gilbey, and most of the team, including Kyle and Stephen.

"Where's your butt buddy?" Alva asks.

"Don't have one. But if you mean Ollie, he's not coming."

Gilbey laughs. "One down, one to go."

His words crawl over me, but I dismiss them and watch Alva. He calls the shots, and he either didn't hear Gilbey or is ignoring him. "That's too bad," Alva says. "I think he's actually bigger than you." Alva looks at my bag. "Why'd you put your shit over here?"

"Inhaler. Now that I know what to expect, I think I should have it close by."

"Oh, so one day with us and you know what to expect, is that it?"

My mouth's dry but I make myself answer. I have a feeling I'm going to be doing a lot of that the rest of the week—embracing the pain. "More or less."

"Guess we'll find out which it is." Alva blows his whistle and the bros line up. The ones just arriving drop their shit and fall in. I swallow and feel my heart in my throat.

"Warm it up with two miles around the field," Alva says, and the lines head out the doors. He looks at me. "Need your inhaler, Dun?"

"No, I'm still breathing." I take off and join the back of the line, where I stay for all eight laps.

We head back inside and Mallory and Callaghan have arrived. Mallory brings me the GoPro. "Hey, Greg! Mr. Callaghan told me about what you got. Keep it up. Love what you're doing so far. You really have a head for this." He laughs at his joke and I thank him and strap on the camera. I can only imagine how this must feel, to talk film again, maybe like he did with Max. I'm about to hit RECORD when Callaghan comes to me.

"Not yet." He looks at the camera.

"It's not on," I say.

"Good. I'm also happy to hear that Oliver couldn't hack it. This sport, it's not for everyone. It's a good lesson to learn."

"You make sure of that don't you?" I lean in, matching Callaghan, and he steps back. Then he gets his demonic look of happiness and claps his hands.

"Bring it in, gentlemen." The team converges and takes a knee around their coach and our principal. "You should record this, Gregory."

I turn on the GoPro and take a knee with the rest.

"I just wanted a moment of your time so that I could remind you about the roots of our game. Some of you need a refresher on what you symbolize."

I know that Callaghan used to play, and I've been in his office enough to know how deeply obsessed he is, but this sounds like the beginning of fanboy material, or a sermon.

"The Natives created this game. Not the way we play it, but the essence is the same. For them it was a ritual, something used as a means to an end. To settle problems, to prepare for war, to celebrate the gods." Callaghan's voice is slow and steady. Like he's savoring every detail. "*I* used to focus on *that* element before I played, always remembering what this game is about. Not the points or the tricks or the stick handling. No, the way that this is an act to serve a much higher purpose, to help prepare for the world."

Lacrosse as religion? Is that where he's going? Or is it all a metaphor for life? Either way, it's a frightening thought.

"I hope you can focus on the same, boys. Consider the tradition. Consider the honor and discipline. We are trying to instill that sense of purpose, not just through *some game*, but through ritual."

His little speech solidifies for me why our school is the way it is, with the cliques and the bullying and the bullshit. Why he has his evil minions. This asshole believes that pain is the answer to enlightenment. That if we suffer enough we'll know the world better and become better people. I've suffered a lifetime and the world still makes no sense to me. I make films about it, and still it's murky. At this point, I should be a prophet and Ollie an oracle. And I feel sorry for the bros, especially Alva and Gilbey. If all this has forced them to believe that torturing people is an indicator of success, there may be no hope for them.

Alva takes the middle after Callaghan. "Five lines, let's get to it."

I move into place and look at my bag. It's perfect. Whatever ritual they dish up, I'll get it on film, and then we'll put it out for the world to decide whether it's character building, or just crazy.

. . .

We bring it in for the end of the day and Alva gives a little speech about resting up. I tense from head to toe. Every bruise has nagged me, but I've ignored the pain because I knew I had to make it to this point. But when Alva finishes, the bros grab their bags and start taking off. Gilbey looks at me as if he'd like to pounce, but he checks Callaghan and Mallory off in the corner and turns away as Philmore walks in.

Our superintendent joins Callaghan and Mallory and they immediately start talking. I take my time at my bag, glancing over every few seconds, the GoPro still recording. The men do not seem happy. Whatever Philmore has said isn't sitting well. They all turn and look at me.

I'm used to being the object of attention, and I know when things are about to get ugly. I hold my breath, and pull the camera from my head. The shiny center of my bag winks at me and I turn away from it, so this conversation will be directly in its path.

Philmore has broken away and is heading toward me.

"How are you, Gregory? It's good to see you."

"Fine, sir. Thanks. Good to see you, too." My voice is at once both too loud and too choppy to pass as anything but nervous.

Philmore frowns. "Relax, Greg. I just wanted to check in, and see what happened to your friend. You made such a compelling speech about needing one another. And now?"

He leaves the question hanging or I don't hear the rest because I'm too busy focused on the fact that Philmore's in the loop. He knows exactly what is going on here. But why? What is at stake?

"I think he's sick. Ollie's not the kind of guy to just ditch."

"Sick? How?" Philmore sounds like a skeptical school nurse.

"I don't know. I haven't heard from him since yesterday, so I can only guess."

Philmore eyes me. "It's interesting that you haven't had any contact, when it seems all you do is use that phone of yours."

Is he trying to make it clear to me that he knows *everything* or is he just being an asshole?

"I've reached out, but he hasn't replied."

Philmore cuts me off by waving his hands. "Yes, yes, yes. That's besides the point, Greg. Just tell me, will Oliver be joining us again, or will it be just you?"

His tone, combined with every other element of this conversation, has me creeped out. But I can pull this off. Like Quinn implied, I'm a good liar.

"If he's well enough, Ollie will be back. We've got a bet going on who can lose the most this week, so he'll do whatever it takes."

Philmore smiles, and it's so like Callaghan I'm confused for a second. Then he says, "Whatever it takes," repeating my words to me, like it's some kind of incantation.

I nod because I just want him gone.

"All right. It's been a pleasure, Gregory. I hope you win that bet." Philmore doesn't say a word to either Mallory or Callaghan as he passes by them and heads out the door. The two look at each other and Mallory walks to me.

"Why don't you take the camera with you tonight? You can get started on the editing. I've heard that's the most difficult part." He winks and I feel better. He's so different from Callaghan that I have trouble understanding why. But with his convenient absences when shit goes down and Philmore showing up, it's become more clear: whatever's going on, Mallory's just a pawn.

"All right," I say and stuff the GoPro into my bag.

"Tell Ollie I hope he feels better." Mallory claps my shoulder and heads back across the gym. I watch him go and see that Callaghan has already left. I feel a pang of guilt for what we are doing. Because, now, if we mess this up, we're pissing on Max's memory. I didn't get it until now. But seeing even this much of his dad, in person, I feel as if his accolades are deserved.

I head out, spot Quinn's car, and hop in. "Ella's," I say, and he takes off.

Ella's dad answers the door. "Hey, Greg." He looks over my shoulder. "Good to see you, Quinn." I feel stung by their familiarity, but push it down.

"Is Ella home?" I ask.

"Yeah, she's editing away on that project you guys have. By the way, good luck." I feel saddened by the fact that he's so involved with his daughter's life. My parents have no clue about the contest—about anything, really. But maybe this is what happens when your daughter tries to kill herself?

In Ella's room, I don't know where we should stand, so I wait. "He still here?" she asks.

"See you, Bean!" her dad calls and the door closes.

"Answered." Ella shakes her head. "Ugh! Greg! Philmore!"

I move to the chair and Quinn leans against the wall. "I know. What do you think?"

"Too many things. But mostly, what Philmore said was weird, but nothing really substantial. Right?"

"Exactly. He knows what's up, and I'm sure it's Callaghan who's telling him. But why does he give a shit?" I lean forward and realize how sweaty I still am, but also how much smaller my gut is.

"I don't know." Ella looks at her computer. "It has to be something with the booster and the money. Shit always goes south when money's involved. But, hey, at least no beating today."

"Yeah, at least there's that. Hey, are we cool after yesterday?

You didn't reply to my messages."

"That's because I didn't like what you said. I needed to chill." She stares at me. "I am not a willing victim, Greg. I don't know if there is such a thing. Is that how you see yourself?"

"What? I don't . . ."

She holds up her hand, the one with the splinted finger. "Exactly. It's a pretty messed up idea, right? So don't use that logic ever again. Now, I get you're trying to protect me. It's nice. But I'm making my own damn choices, so cut the shit. We're too close to seeing this through for that."

There is nothing for me to say to this besides, "Okay."

"Good. I watched that conversation between you and Mallory, twice. He seems cool, but *something's* going on. I think he's caught in the middle."

"I was thinking the same thing."

Quinn laughs. Ella and I turn to him.

"I don't get you two. Mallory's a monster like Callaghan. Mallory's cool. Now Philmore's the one to watch. You want me to keep going?"

"No, it's pretty clear that you just feel like being an asshole, so shut the fuck up." Ella's calm in spite of her words. "Greg, I'll edit the best I can. But the bros, they need to slip up."

"Agreed. Hopefully they do it to one another and not me." I give her the GoPro so she can upload all the footage while Q paces in and out of the bedroom.

"Check with me later," Ella says, "I've got everything from your phone, too. The stick nabbed it. And make sure you check on Ollie." She clears her throat and yells, "Unless that's too much trouble for you, Quinn. Don't want to mess up your OCD work-out schedule."

He walks out and I grab my bag. "Thanks, Ella." I hope she understands on how many levels I mean this.

"Anytime, Greg. Us film geeks need to stick together."

And I know I felt it before, that she'll be fine with or without our school's tech, but damn if her confidence, her resolve, doesn't reinforce it.

Quinn's in his car, gripping the wheel when I get in. "She's a bitch."

I hold up my hands. "Relax. Just because she called you out doesn't mean she isn't right."

"What?" he says, but it seems more automatic than anything he truly feels.

"Quinn, we know you work out like a triathlete to put up a wall between you and those meatheads. And we know your dad's oblivious. It's not your fault that he wants to be a dumb-jock of a gym owner and let his customers shit on you. Just don't take it out on us."

"G, remember when I said it'd be easier being friends with you if you weren't such a liar?"

"Uh, yeah."

"I take that back. You being honest is even worse." He peels out and I don't know if I should take that as a compliment.

*   *   *

I stand on Ollie's front porch and wait. I rang the doorbell but didn't hear any reaction. The yard's overgrown and weeds are popping up alongside the newly green bushes. Someone needs to take care of this.

Then the door flies open and out comes Ollie's dad. "Get the fuck out of here before I call the cops!"

I hold up my hands for the second time in fifteen minutes. "Mr. Leonard, it's me, Greg! It's all right!"

He stops and looks at me, eyes wild.

"Is everything okay? I just wanted to see how Ollie's doing."

"What's that supposed to mean?" His anger has fired back up and he's in my face. "Did you come back for round two?"

I'm so thoroughly confused, but then Ollie's dad looks past me. "Two of you, huh? I'll fuck both of you up." He grabs the front of my shirt, squeezing hard.

I'm tossed to the ground and hear Quinn yell, "Take it easy," before a louder yell comes from the house.

"Stop!" Ollie's voice cuts through the commotion and his dad reels back. I pull myself to my feet and notice that Q has a stick in his hands, not that it would have helped much against Mr. Leonard. I turn to the house, and there is Ollie. His face is purple, an eye swollen shut, lips cracked, dried blood on his shirt.

I don't need to ask, because I know who did this and how. It only took one punch for Alva to knock me out. By the looks of it, it took much more for Ollie.

Fuck the tech program and the hope of a scholarship. Fuck all the stupid films I made because I was hurt. Fuck all the lies. Fuck who I used to be. It's time for the fucking truth.

CHAPTER 29

BY THE TIME I GET HOME, my parents have already returned, dinner is almost ready, and they want to talk.

"There he is," Dad says. "How was today? You look exhausted."

I smile limply and don't know if I want to sit down or collapse on my bed. Ollie's story keeps repeating in my head. *I thought it was you at the door.*

Mom pops out of the kitchen. "Sweetie, you do look beat. I've got a nice meatloaf for you." She squeezes my arm and I wince. She looks at me and I can smell the wine on her breath.

"Thanks. How was your lunch today?" I ask.

"Fabulous! You wouldn't believe what these women are up to . . ."

And she rambles on and on, slightly drunk, about the various "crazy" things all her teacher friends are into. I act like I'm paying attention to her, but it's only Ollie I can see and hear: *When I came out, I didn't know what was up because Gilbey and Alva seemed like they were really checking on me. Then I took the first hit.*

"Greg? You with us?" Dad asks and I come back to the living room. "Ha! Your stories are putting him in a coma."

Mom frowns. "Are you sure you're okay?"

"Fine. I said I'm fine. Shit, just let it go."

"Whoa, whoa. Watch the way you're talking." Dad's voice is still calm but edging up, and this infuriates me.

"Why? What have I said? *Just let it go?* Is that too much? Or was it *shit*? What a terrible word. How about *fuck*? Is that all right? Because I've had a terrible *fucking* day! So, please, just give me some *fucking* space!"

They sit back, stung, and look at me wide-eyed for a second, before Dad unleashes. "You will not talk to us that way! You listen to me. You can be upset as much as you want, but you control yourself!"

"Ha!" It's a genuine laugh because he's such an idiot right now. "'Control myself'? You think yelling at me while I feel like shit to control myself is the answer?" I laugh again. "Fuck you."

Mom steps in front of my father. "Gregory Francis, I have no idea what's gotten into you." Her words are slow because she's been drinking, and I don't feel like waiting for her to finish.

"Food, Mom. Tons of *your* food. That's what's gotten into me. And that's why I feel this way."

She plants a hand over her mouth like she's slapping herself. Dad steadies her. "Just go to your room until you are ready to act civilized! And you had better come down with an apology," Dad says.

I stand. I feel like I could fight or cry. I don't want to do either, but I'm at that point of no return. "Here, let me say it now, so that I don't have to come back down. I apologize for being such a fuck-up. I'm working on it, in more ways than you'll ever understand. So do me a favor, have my back no matter what. Be prepared to fight for me. I deserve that. I've deserved that all of these years."

They speak, but their words are meaningless, because the storm in my head drowns them out. I head upstairs.

In the bathroom, I pump the hot water and strip down. The polka-dot bruises pop in the mirror, but I know that Ollie has a matching coat, and much more.

There was nothing I could do, Greg. They're so strong, and I don't know how to fight. The only thing that saved me was Dad getting home from work. They left when he pulled in, but he saw them, and it wasn't hard to put two and two together. He demanded to know who they were. That's why he bugged on you and Quinn. I told him they were old friends who were assholes now. He got confused. I lied, Greg. I didn't tell him they were lax bros. I couldn't. I knew you needed the time.

I make a fist and bite on it. It helps muffle the scream, as does the running water. But nothing can dampen what I've seen, what I know, and what I have to do.

. . .

In my room, in complete dark, I lie on my bed and hear our fight being rehashed by my mother. She's talking to her sister and crying and drinking wine. I hear the glass clink every time she sets it down. I'm sure my dad's pacing. But they're not going to come up here. That was too much for them to handle, but just exactly what I needed to say. They're going to need to digest that for a while.

The phone chimes and I have a text from Ella. **Here's the rough cut of what I have so far.**

I click on the link, and it brings me to Ella's YouTube channel. She has more videos than I do. How have I not checked her out before? I mean, her work.

Of course it's excellent. It captures this undeniable camaraderie that the bros have and puts Mallory at the center.

I reply, **That is AWESOME! But, hey, I need to tell you what happened to Ollie.**

Already know. Quinn texted me.

"What?" I say aloud, then type, **???????**

What, because I told him to fuck off, u think we don't communicate?

I feel like reaching through the screen and shaking the shit out of her. Not to hurt her, but to break loose some of her awesomeness so I can have some for my own.

Thanks. I don't know what else to type.

Will do. You let me know how things go tomorrow. U ok?

Now I know what to type, the truth. **No.**

• • •

Bros slide out of cars and watch me from beneath their hoodies. I feel their eyes and hear them talking. Shit.

Inside, it's worse. They openly point and laugh. It's like I'm the prized pig at some roast. I think they forget I'm human and can understand body language.

I set my bag down and Gilbey struts over. I pull the GoPro out of my bag, because if it's going to start this way, the least I can do is try to protect myself.

Gilbey reaches across me and puts his hand on top of the camera. "Not yet, chubs."

I look at his hand and keep my eyes on it when I speak. "Why? You have something in mind? Like what you did to Ollie?"

I expect him to show some emotion, even amusement, but his face is a mask. "Just leave the camera be, for now."

"For now? As in I can have it later? *After*, you mean?" I turn to Gilbey and remember butting him into the locker room wall with my gut. That's not an option now.

"It's the same thing, Dun," Alva says, appearing as if on cue, from the shadows.

The rest of the bros move as well, as if to some silent signal. They form a half circle, penning me in. I hear Ollie's words and I ignore the camera.

"So this is how you have to do it? Two-on-one, like with Ollie. Or the strong versus the weak, like with Kyle and Stephen." Both draw up short when I say their names. I look at them and wonder why I thought they offered a shred of hope.

"You see, Dun, that's the way the world is. We live in our world, and it's the only thing that matters. Our results speak for themselves, and if we have to fight for them, so be it."

"More like imprison people in it." I'm saying this as much to get at him as I am to let Stephen know I understand. "You take people's choices away and make them believe what you tell them. You only provide your way. That's not real life."

Alva narrows his eyes. "Sounds like you're talking about your little movies, Dun."

That hurt, and I don't have a quick comeback. Instead, I watch Alva pick up the GoPro and walk over to Kyle. He straps it to his head, and Kyle doesn't resist, just lets him do as he pleases. Alva turns the camera on, the red light glowing against the early morning dimness. He raises his arms and the bros tighten up, the half circle impenetrable.

Gilbey walks to the middle and bounces on his toes. Alva moves to the opposite side and swings his arms and neck. It's two-on-one, again, and I know I'm going to end up like Ollie. But now they'll have it on film, and who knows what they'll do with it, how they'll edit this to make it seem like I started this fight.

"Fine!" I scream, "You want this? You two want to kick my ass, go ahead. I'm not afraid. Ollie survived. I will, too."

Gilbey laughs and advances. "I wouldn't bet on it."

And right before his punch lands square in my nose, I look at Kyle and see the red light isn't on. He's not recording. I am thoroughly fucked.

I go blind from the hit but feel the explosion of blood as it gushes down my face. One of them laughs, and I'm punched in the jaw. Something cracks but I can see again. Not that it does much good. Alva and Gilbey trade off with each other.

"This is why you're pathetic, Dun. You can't even fight back." Alva doubles me over with a shot to the gut. He's right, but he's also wrong. I have to live through this to prove that, though.

"Lights out, bitch!" Gilbey elbows me in the back of the head and I fall to the floor, no hands to stop myself, just my forehead on wood.

"Yeah!" Alva screams, and in his voice is everything I hate. So even though the blood running down my throat is choking me out, my head feels caved in, and all of me is a crumpled, useless mass, I smile. I roll to the side and I turn to him and I smile as wide as I can.

They attack. The kicks are nonstop, and I can feel skin hanging loose at my cheek where it's been ripped away. They bark insults and I will my body to pass out so I don't have to endure any more, but, like usual, it doesn't respond.

And then all at once, the fighting stops. There's a noise, something loud, vibrating the air, but I can't make out what it is. Then hands grab my face and I'm pulled upright. My vision is cloudy and I have no sense of what's about to happen, beyond being certain that it will hurt.

"Greg? Greg, can you hear me?"

I can hear, but *who* is this?

"All right, I've got you." Mallory lifts me as if I weigh half of what I do. He seats me in the bleachers and yells, "Get me some water! Now!" A bottle appears, and I realize I can see again, still fuzzy, but better. "And a towel. Jesus Christ!" Mallory tips the bottle into my mouth. "Don't drink, spit."

I do, and the spray is pink. I repeat the process and Mallory dabs at my face. I'm beyond the pain. I feel almost sedated.

"That cheek needs stitches." Mallory speaks close to my ear, and I wonder if he spoke this way to his son. "Hold this, right there." He leaves the towel at my cheek and I pin it in place, but I'm not sure I have the strength to maintain the pressure.

"What is going on here, Mr. Mallory?" Callaghan's voice is clear through my busted head.

"Was just about to ask that same question, Mr. Callaghan. Looks like a fight with Greg, here, and our captains."

I can't see Callaghan, but I'm sure he's thrilled with this. "Let's get to the root of this. Alva. Gilbey. Who began this skirmish?"

"I wouldn't call it that. Look at Greg," Mallory says.

"Thank you, but let me handle my boys first." Callaghan clears his throat and I look up. He's in the center of the half circle. The bros haven't moved. Mallory shakes his head. "So?" Callaghan looks at Alva and Gilbey, whose hands are covered in my blood.

"Greg started it. It's recorded, sir," Gilbey says. Alva shoots him a dirty look and I wonder when they planned this, and whether Gilbey's fucking up his lines.

Callaghan looks around and sees Kyle. "Who put this on him?" he asks.

"Greg demanded we do it, sir. He was crazy, so we did. You'll see," Alva says.

Callaghan takes the GoPro and looks at the screen. He frowns, hits a button, and frowns again. "There's nothing here. You can't view it."

Mallory moves away from me. "Of course you can't. That's not how they work. You have to upload it."

Callaghan looks up and it seems as if he'd like to square off in the circle with Mallory. "Fine," he says.

"What were you expecting to see?" Mallory asks.

"Obviously I was expecting to see what our captains told me I would." Callaghan shoots Alva and Gilbey a look so dark they bow their heads.

"But do you really need the film to see what went on here? *I* walked in on this. *I* saw what they were doing. And just look at their hands. Is there really a question?"

"Yes, there is." Callaghan shoves the camera back into Kyle's hands and turns to Mallory. "If these boys were defending themselves against a crazed student, that changes everything."

"Greg? You're calling Greg *crazed*? Are you kidding me? Him against these two? Please. Remember, I am the father of a former captain. I know what it takes to achieve that position. So don't you try and pass that bullshit over on me. These two beat the shit out of him. Period. There's nothing more to it."

Callaghan clenches his jaw. I should look away, but I don't. His eyes alight and I'm still not afraid.

"You of all people should know when to hold your tongue, Mr. Mallory." Callaghan gives his assistant coach and the booster president his full and intense attention.

"What did you just say?" Mallory says.

"Apparently your ears are going the way of your mouth, so let me make this clear, do not speak about these matters. They are not yours to meddle with."

Mallory's back straightens and when he takes another step toward Callaghan, it is very obvious that his military physique has not withered. "Not mine to *meddle* with? Interesting choice of words coming from you."

"Watch it!" Callaghan barks, lifting a finger to Mallory.

"Point that finger at me again and I'll take it off your hand. I am not your servant. You do *not* give me orders. We have an arrangement, yes, but you will listen to what I have to say about what I have seen with my own eyes."

Callaghan does not drop his finger. "You do not hold the upper hand in this arrangement, so I would think about where you want to go from here, because we both know how this will end."

I, along with every bro, am as confused as transfixed. What the fuck are they talking about? I wish I had the GoPro, so I could have the right angle for this. I need to watch this again, and I don't know if my bag will pick up this conversation from so far away.

I look past the men to Kyle, imagining what it would look like in his shoes, and I see the light cradled in his arms. The red record button is on.

Mallory yells something inarticulate, a frustrated growl.

Alva calls out, "You should leave, Mr. Mallory. We have unfinished business, and you aren't part of it."

It's like slow-mo, watching Mallory size up Alva, as if he's looking at a child or small, yapping dog. There is no fear in Mallory's eyes, but there is disgust. "Who do you think you are talking to, Andrew? Huh? You think I'm one of these boys, who is afraid that if he steps out of line he'll get messed up?"

"No, sir. I know who you are," Alva says.

"Who am I?"

Alva shifts his weight. "Master Sergeant Mallory, father of Corporal Max Mallory, booster club president and assistant coach."

"And which of those is the most important title?" Mallory asks.

"Master Sergeant, sir," Alva says, but it sounds hollow.

"You are wrong, Andrew. Father. That's the answer."

Callaghan sighs. "Can we get on with this, please?"

Mallory looks like he'd love to hang Callaghan with his own tie, but he stays calm and focused on Alva. "Father is the answer because he was everything to me and to this town and to this team. *He* was a warrior. And he didn't become that way by torturing the weak. He guided, he taught, he motivated. That's what leaders do. You," he steps closer to Alva, "you are weak. You rule with fear. You and this team and your behavior are a poor legacy for my son. This is not what Max would have wanted. Were he here . . ." Mallory cannot finish. His chin falls to his chest.

Alva smiles and now Callaghan steps forward. "But he's not. So let us carry on." Callaghan claps. "All right boys, two miles. Go." And they file out, Alva and Gilbey included. Except Kyle. He hangs back, holding the GoPro. "Give me that." Callaghan reaches for the camera, but Mallory whips around.

"No. That's not yours; it's Greg's."

Callaghan takes it from Kyle and tosses it toward me. It falls to the floor with a crack. "Oops," Callaghan says. "Your filming is done, Greg. We do not need you anymore." He walks away.

Mallory crosses to the camera and picks it up and hands it to me. "Idiot. Doesn't he know these things are indestructible?"

I know I'm supposed to laugh. He just called my principal an idiot. But there's nothing amusing in this moment. I'm still in pain, still confused, and know I've lost.

"Thanks," I say, "for sticking up for me. It's how you said."

"It always is, Greg."

I hope I don't have to ask. It hurts to speak.

"My son was captain for Callaghan, and let's just say there's a lot he had to do, a lot behind the scenes. You're like he was, Greg. You've got that inquisitive nature, so strong it'll get you killed."

I know it's a compliment, but still, *get me killed*?

"You should keep filming, keep investigating, you'll find more than you've ever hoped for." Mallory grabs my shoulder to get a good look at me. "In the meantime, let's get you to the hospital."

I shake my head because I don't want to open my mouth, but this makes me nauseous. "No. It's all right."

"Greg, no need to be tough here. You're hurt."

It's the smart move to let him help, but no, I want to stick to our plan.

"Already have a ride outside."

Mallory squints. "Were you expecting this?"

I shrug.

"Greg, is there more I should know?"

I can't. Even though he may be so in the dark that he deserves to know more than anyone else in this town. Not yet. Soon.

My face pounds from the little I've already said, but I force myself to answer. "I'll have that film for you next week."

"Greg, what? No. That's crazy. You don't . . ."

"Don't make a liar out of me. I told you I would make it." I grab my jaw, unable to say more.

"That's the last thing I want to do, Greg." He sighs. "You go ahead and make that film. I don't know why you'd want to, but I'll be honest, I'd like to see what you can put together."

That makes two of us.

CHAPTER 30

"HOSPITAL OR HOME?"

I shake my head at Q. "Ollie's."

"If you say so." We take off and Quinn keeps glancing over at me, probably hoping I don't get blood all over everything. My cheek's bleeding again. I'll need those stitches. At some point.

Quinn checks his phone. "Shit. I missed her text. Ella was yelling at me to get you."

I shrug and ten minutes later Ella's in the backseat.

"Greg, seriously, the hospital, not Ollie's."

I hold up the GoPro. "I'm not going anywhere until I see what's on this."

"But I have the other camera's footage."

I wait for Ella to say more, but she doesn't. If she watched, then she knows that if the GoPro was on, it has everything.

We pull into Ollie's, and his sister is peering out the window. I wave but she just stares. We pile out of the car and Ollie's front door opens. His banged-up face watches us, then clearly sees me. "Greg, no, not you, too?"

I look past him, to his sister, now on the front porch. What must she think? That this is just the inevitable next step to what she's already experiencing? I hold up the GoPro and Ollie says, "What?"

"He's not going to get treatment until we see what he has." Ella pauses. "Even though I've already seen it."

My anger boils over. "No, you haven't."

Ella's eyes pop. "Okay, Greg. Let's go."

We do. Up to Ollie's room where Ella hooks up the camera while we sit on the bed. She joins us and we all witness the conversation between Callaghan and Mallory and Alva.

The recording ends and Ella turns to me. "This is the conversation they had after what those fucks did to you?"

Both Ollie and Quinn are confused. "Why does what they say matter?" Quinn asks.

"Because this, right here, is what we need," Ella says, pointing at the screen.

Ollie chimes in. "There's a reason for all this, Quinn. It's not *just* that the bros are psychos. Something bigger is going on. This shows that how the bros are, that's just a consequence."

Ollie's words cling to each of us for very different reasons. We are all quiet until Quinn asks, "Hospital or home, G?"

"Hospital," Ella answers for me. "Give me your mom's number and I'll call."

I hesitate. My parents aren't exactly happy with me right now, so maybe they won't pick up. But if I don't call, I take away their opportunity to have my back, to do as I asked. I hand the phone to Ella.

* * *

I don't know exactly what Ella said, because she ducked into the hall to speak to my parents while Quinn and Ollie found some gauze. All I know is that when Mom showed up, she knew I'd been jumped and that the kids had stolen my phone. She was a mess, but she also kept asking me about Ella, as if she were some silver lining in all of this.

After the doc glued my face together, I had to talk to the police. I told them I hadn't seen much, no faces, remarkable clothing. I gave them nothing and they sent me home. And I know I should feel like shit for lying, but what could I tell them? I've seen both at games. They would have stepped out for a second and then Callaghan would have appeared. I couldn't accept that. Not after going this far. I may have to eat this lie when I get the truth out. But that's all right. It's not deception to hurt anyone but me. So I'll pay that price if that's what it takes.

And during the ride to the hospital, I came to terms with this. I also tried to understand Mom's sense of everything. I agreed with her about how amazing Ella is, but I also felt she missed how equally important both Ollie and Quinn are to me.

That was solidified by how much they dropped in to check on me throughout the rest of break. Mom almost shit when she saw Ollie's busted face, but he reassured her it was pure coincidence, that he'd gotten into an accident moving some of his grandfather's things into storage. At least the second half was true.

Quinn came by between workouts and we shot the shit, watched TV, and talked about what Ella was up to when Mom wasn't hovering.

Ella only dropped in once, on Saturday. She looked fried and said she was done, just needed to finalize everything. But she'd succeeded. I turned on a movie and Mom and Dad smiled goofily at us. But within a half hour, Ella was asleep, and she barely woke up enough to say good-bye when her dad picked her up.

My parents and I have reached an almost comfortable state. I think maybe they understand me, but until this is all over, I can't really know. If I could bring myself to apologize, I would. But I'm too wrapped up in this tunnel, trying to see it all through to make amends with them. Maybe they'll forgive me without it, once they see.

The tournament begins this Friday with an enormous pep rally.

Signs went up all over town this weekend. Everyone's offering a special for people attending the tournament, and the three hotels in town already have NO VACANCY on their signs. But in spite of the madness that's about to ensue, Callaghan wants to get the vote for the film trailers on. Or maybe he's doing it now to be a dick because kids can barely focus at the moment.

Mrs. Olmstead hands me a slip of paper when I walk into history. It's very simple, just a list of the eight projects up for review with our names and a box next to each for ranking. I don't even need to see the trailers to know how to vote. I rank Ella first and Taleana last. Which means I have to put myself seventh. At least I rank the other projects based on what I know.

I stand and hear kids whispering my name. Could be about the film. Could be a couple of bros whispering about break. Could be the same old shit I'm used to. Mrs. Olmstead frowns as I approach. "Gregory?"

I hand her my slip. "I need to use the bathroom."

She looks at the paper. "How could you have voted? They haven't played the videos yet."

"Mine's one of them. I'm in the class, so I already know."

"Hmm. It's foolish to be so arrogant."

I want to smoosh her face almost as much as I want to run and hide. "Yeah, me, *so* arrogant. Just put that with the rest. I guarantee the results are rigged anyway."

I step out of the classroom as the announcement for teachers to turn on their TVs booms over the PA. The bathroom is around the corner, cool and dark when I enter. I sit in a stall, crack out my phone, and text Ella. You okay?

Fine. You?

In the bathroom.

Eww. Gross. Or are you hiding?

What do you think?

Meet me before Blint's. The videos are starting now.

K. Good luck.

I open up Facebook and watch the "voting" play out in real time, as someone has created a post critiquing the videos as they go up. The girl Anna in our class gets shredded, as does this kid, Jared, and another girl, Erin. Taleana's goes up and it's one line: You know how to vote on hers. I shake my head and wait for the rest. Ella's goes up and I cringe. Some of Taleana's crew post variations of, Slut trying to fuck everyone over, but other kids post, That wasn't half bad. I want to see the rest.

Then I read my name. Dun the Ton! Sweet! This is going to be epic! I wait and in a minute the results are in.

No shit? I thought he looked smaller. I mean, for him.

Bet he like Photoshopped himself. He ain't lost shit.

What's this one really going to be about? Did Dun set up a spy cam in the girls' locker room?

Only way he's losing any weight is if he cuts off a limb. Anyone got a saw?

I stop reading and close my eyes. I'm not surprised, but that doesn't help. What Quinn, Ollie, and I have done is no small feat. But it doesn't matter. All my anger, all my desire for revenge and to remake myself is for shit. Nothing I do will ever matter because it's me and the even bigger shadow of my past looms over everything.

•   •   •

It seems as if the bros have been ordered to add insult to injury—or just more injury. They've been slapping the bruises on my back and saying, "Great video. Hope ours is better, though." And, of course, "Fat fuck."

Surprisingly, none ask about Ollie, who said he just couldn't come in today. Not that I blame him. I wish I'd stayed home. But I figured they'd at least slip a little and say shit. But Callaghan's orders to keep zipped lips must have been strict.

I meet Ella and we walk to Blint's.

"That was rough, huh?"

"Understatement," I say. "But they seemed to like yours."

"Who gives a shit what *they* like. I only care about our other project."

I grunt. "Me, too."

"How's Ollie?"

"He's down and out." My cheek pulls uncomfortably when I speak, but at least I'm healing.

A kid walks past and looks at me. "Holy fuck, if you looked any more like a cow I'd milk you. Dun, your video was all wrong. You're turning into a farm animal."

"Why don't you go fuck your . . ."

I put a hand over Ella's mouth. She rips it away and the kid says, "Thought that was your job," before walking away.

"Why'd you do that?" she asks.

"Shit, Ella. Low profile. Remember?"

She balls her hands into fists and holds them up around her face. "Gah, I just want to kill something."

"Oh, you just wanna *fuck* something? Shocking." Taleana walks slowly toward us, a pack of cheerleaders behind her.

[327]

I know Ella is close to breaking. She's worked so hard the past few days. Now this?

"I think it's time we got this shit between us straight," Ella says.

"It's pretty clear to me. You're my bitch." Taleana pushes Ella's forehead.

Ella is unfazed. "And it's pretty clear to me that you're a dumb, clueless bitch, whose world's about to get rocked."

The cheerleaders squeal. I think I do, too.

Taleana steps to Ella, so close. "You? Gonna rock my world? How's that?"

Ella smiles in the face of this.

"You see, Taleana, you only know one way to be ruthless. And I can go to the hospital to get that fixed." Ella holds up her splint. "I'm capable of so much more, and there isn't anywhere for you to go to get healed."

Taleana presses Ella into the locker and grabs her injured hand, putting her weight into it. "Unless I break all of you. Then what?"

Ella looks her straight in the eyes. "It won't matter. I can hurt you even if I'm dead."

Taleana backs away. "Guess we'll find out."

The bell rings and the pack laughs its way into Blint's.

"Are you okay?" I ask. "We can cut."

Ella straightens herself. "I'm fine, Greg. Remember, I'm not a victim."

My words tossed back at me hurt, but I hope like hell she's right, and I was wrong.

Blint tries to settle us and makes a joke about having a spring break hangover. We all stare and just wait for him to move on and get to the results.

"So the votes are in," Blint says, and the class actually comes to life.

"Now, remember, just because your film wasn't nominated doesn't mean that your film isn't good or that you will receive a poor grade."

"Just get on with it," a kid up front yells. I agree with him.

"Well, yes. Fine. In no particular order, the top three are as follows: Taleana Malberry." Her friends go bananas and Blint can only stand in front of the room and wait. Taleana blushes and feigns embarrassment.

"Second, Ella Jenner." Blint waits for applause, but none comes. Not even Ella is smiling. But I offer a golf clap.

"Low profile, Dun," she says.

Blint sighs. "And third, Greg Dunsmore."

There's more silence, except for the roaring, *What?* in my head. I read the comments and have heard more all morning. How can this possibly be legit? Unless it's not. Unless what I said to Mrs. Olmstead was true. But why? What do the bros have to gain through this? And Ella's? Was hers picked the same as mine, or did the school actually understand how good her work is? Shit, at least she doesn't have to sacrifice her entry now. We'll just use our other film in place of my entry.

"So congratulations are in order. Next week we will have an assembly for viewing the three documentaries. I am dedicating the rest of class time this week for preparation." Blint directs us to the lab. "Please, get to work."

"Yay for us, right?" Ella says.

"Woo hoo."

"What is this all about, Greg?"

"They're keeping us in line. Just like they always do."

CHAPTER 31

THE DOOR OPENS AND OLLIE PEERS OUT. His clothes are wrinkled and he seems as if he's just woken up, but he forces a smile. "Hey, Greg."

"Hey. You ready?"

"Yeah."

I wait for him to walk out but he just stands there. "Come on." I wave and step down a stair and he nods like I've just solved all his problems.

We walk to the car and he shuffles along. Before we get to Q, I ask, "You gonna be all right? Cause if not, we don't have to do this. We can all just chill here. No big deal."

He looks away at Quinn's car. "We're still trying to lose weight, right?"

"Sure," I answer, and am not happy with the weakness of my voice. I pray I'm not letting this all fall to shit just because it no longer matters for my project.

"I still want to, you know, *improve*, in spite of . . . everything."

"I wish that was the same for everyone. You know?"

"Story of our lives, Greg."

"Truth right there. You okay, though, with everything that's happened?"

"No, but you can't be either."

"That's not my point. You lost your grandfather and then I pulled you into all of this. It can't be easy."

"It isn't." He digs the ground with his toe. "My grandfather always had a way of making me feel better. One talk with him and I didn't care about what the kids at school were saying."

"He's right. They don't matter."

Ollie tilts his head. "You know, I've been thinking about that, and I don't know. They do matter, don't they? Look at Callaghan. He's just a grown-up lax bro, and he's doing the same shit. I know my mom and dad deal with crap all the time for being big and so does my sister. So, yeah, I get it, *fuck 'em*, but at the same time, we can't. Isn't that why you started this whole transformation?"

"It is. But I think it's pretty obvious that I'm still fat. Not like I'm going to lose a hundred pounds in the next week."

"So because you can't have it now, it's not worth it ever?"

Ollie's question makes me want to sit down. I feel like he's beat me upside the head. And I'm not sure why. "No, I mean, yeah, it is worth it."

"That's why I'm still in this, Greg. I know it's worth it. Long haul. That's what my grandfather wanted for me. That's why we're going to keep at this in spite of the bros. Because there will always be bros."

I reach out and hug Ollie. I don't care who drives by and sees us or what Q might think. Our two enormous bodies are wrapped up and it's good.

*   *   *

In spite of the bruising, the workout feels right. It's nice to have weights back again, and Q directing us. Ollie and I front squat because the bar hurts too much on our backs and we do box jumps and push-ups. And for most of the jumps I do just that, jump. Half of the push-ups aren't from my knees. I'm getting stronger.

Q checks to make sure I haven't busted a stitch and throws us towels. We drink from our water bottles and Heather appears.

"Hey, Quinn, how was your break?" She bumps his hip with her ass. "I've barely seen you all week." She's all sweaty from having taught a class, and how Quinn doesn't just suggest they go in the back room is beyond me.

"It was good. Were you busy here?"

"You know, same ol' same ol' with my ladies." She smiles and leans in. She is so into him, but he's kind of standoffish.

Weights clang to the floor. Captain yells, "Fuck, yeah!" We all look over.

Ronnie, Lou, and Captain all have maniacal faces, challenging Q. His dad pops out of the office and stares at the back of his son's head. Everyone here knows what's supposed to happen, and we're all waiting on Quinn to take care of it. Which is really unfair, but what can we do? He turns to Heather, but I catch his eye. I pop a thumb over my shoulder at the meatheads and Q just shakes his own. I turn around.

"Hey, rule number three. Remember?" I say to the meatheads.

The three meatheads look at each other and laugh. "Whatever, Pudge. You lift this kind of weight and then you can talk. Until then, you and your busted face can suck it."

"You'd like that, wouldn't you?" The words leave my mouth and I picture what is about to happen to me. Do body bags come in my size?

Captain steps over the bar without looking down. He keeps his eyes pinned on mine and approaches. When he's fully in my face he's bigger than I remember, and more fierce. "The fuck did you just say to me?"

My heart is up in my eyeballs, pounding, pounding. I'm weak from the workout and scared. I lick my lips to apologize but Quinn says, "You heard him."

Captain looks at Quinn and back at me. "Guess you didn't listen to my advice. Turned all pussy on us, huh? Just like Q, here."

Ollie moves forward. "Why would anyone listen to *your* advice? Look at you."

The pounding moves up into my temples as Lou and Ronnie join the confrontation at Ollie's words.

Captain laughs. "Look at *me*? You *should* look at me. I'm a fucking work of art and you're not even a rough draft."

I have to give him credit for the analogy. Not bad.

"What's going on?" Quinn's dad's voice cuts through. I step aside.

"Frank, your son here just insulted us. Could you do something about it?" Captain smirks at me.

"Quinlan. Apologize. Now!" Quinn's dad is twitching. His muscles are popping along his shoulders like the bones are trying to come out.

Quinn looks at him, at Heather, at us, but not at the meatheads. "No."

"What do you mean, 'No'? That wasn't a question. Apologize."

Captain chuckles. I so want to jump in and help Quinn, but there's nothing I can do. Quinn sighs and I know what's coming. He's going to give in and probably work out the rest of the night and straight through tomorrow. "I'm sorry, Dad. I'm sorry that I didn't tell you this sooner. But a few years ago, Captain and Ronnie and Lou . . ."

"Whoa, whoa, whoa! Hold up just a minute. Let's not get ahead of ourselves. Your dad asked for an apology, not story-time." Captain nods at Quinn's dad, who nods back.

"Quinn, I said . . ."

"Mr. Casey, let Quinn finish." Heather's voice is so soft, as if it's coming from someone's earbuds. But we all hear her. "Please?"

"Heather, this doesn't concern you."

"Yes, it does, Dad. And if you would for once just shut up and listen you might understand." Quinn stares at his father.

Quinn's dad locks his jaw and crosses his arms over his chest. The meatheads do the same. I silently root for Q, and he opens his mouth, and this time, lets out exactly what he's been trying to say for all these years.

* * *

Quinn's dad didn't want to let him leave to bring us home, but Quinn told him that he'd come back and they could keep talking. Because once Quinn started, he didn't stop, and his dad didn't make him. Captain and Ronnie and Lou tried to, but Quinn's dad held up a hand and we all listened to story after story of what they'd done. None of them tried to defend themselves. They just said "bullshit" a few dozen times and started racking their weights. Then Quinn's dad yelled at them to stop and to get out of his gym.

Q pulls up to my house and I say, "Uh, Q, I don't even know what to say."

"Then don't say anything. You don't have to."

Fair enough. I open the door. "I'm proud of you, man. That took guts."

"Thanks, G. You, too. But neither of us are done yet, huh?"

I climb out. "Not even close." I close the door and he pulls away and I'm bursting to tell Ella what happened.

I bolt up to my room and bring up FaceTime and call. She answers and I tuck away how much I still hate my image on this phone. Her face searches mine. "News? I can tell. Hold on. Me first."

I say, "Okay," high-fiving myself because there's no way she can top what I just experienced.

"So, in our desperate attempt to do whatever the hell we're doing, I can claim success."

"What? How?"

"Our film. The real one. I know we need it for tomorrow, but I've figured out a way to make it even more awesome."

"What do you mean?" I sit down, slowly.

Ella's always sarcastic and a little abrasive, but all of that is evened out by how open and positive she appears. Not now. She's morphed into the girl who still lurks inside, the one capable of swallowing a bottle of sleeping pills. My neck and arms tingle. "Wait and see," she says, "wait and see."

For the first time, that phrase scares the hell out of me.

CHAPTER 32

QUINN PICKS ME UP and doesn't say anything. Not new for him, but I can tell he *wants* to speak. He keeps looking at me and nodding and then back at the road.

"Just say it, man."

He screws up his face like he doesn't know what I'm talking about.

"Really? You're going to pretend there's *nothing* you'd like to get off your chest right now?"

He works his jaw. "True. But that's not what I was thinking about."

"All right. What then?"

"You look good, G. For real. Like I said, we ain't done, but so far, so good."

Q doesn't look at me when he says this, and that's fine with me. When I feel like my voice is strong enough I say, "Thank you."

We pull into the parking lot and there are signs and banners and Warrior images covering every possible spot along our front entrance. This continues throughout the school, around the field, and all over town. We are all a part of this Warrior homage, and I have to wonder if one little film is enough to tear it all down.

"What about Ollie? He coming back?" Q asks.

"Don't think so. He's going to spend the rest of the year at home. Least that's what he said."

"He's going to keep working out, though?"

"Even if we have to move the program to his house."

We pass by Alva and Gilbey and a handful of minions. "Warrior tournament, Dun! Aren't you glad to have seen what we're capable of?" Alva shouts.

"Yeah, I just can't wait until everyone else gets to see it, too."

He gives me his dead eyes as an answer.

"Was that a good idea?" Quinn says.

"Part of the plan."

"If you say so."

We head into school and Callaghan's at the front door. "Mr. Dunsmore. Just the man I wanted to see."

"Good luck, G," Quinn whispers as Callaghan directs me toward his office.

"Sit," Callaghan says as he and I enter his office. I sit, and he proceeds to stare at me for a solid thirty seconds. I scan for anything else to look at, but all he has are the damn lacrosse pictures. They don't help.

"I understand that in spite of everything you went ahead and created that video for Mr. Mallory."

"I keep my promises," I say.

"Hmm." Callaghan sits on the edge of his desk. "Not that it matters. We won't be showing it today."

My mouth goes dry. "Why's that?"

"I'm pretty sure you know the answer to that question. Your track record makes me wary of whatever you touch. You've handed off one video, but who's to say you haven't altered things so that you show another? A little sleight of hand?"

I will myself to stay calm. "I understand your point, sir, but I worked hard on that project, and Mr. Mallory is thrilled with it." Those were his exact words when we watched it together on Wednesday, *thrilled*. And Ella agreed, after much protesting, to leave her name out of this. One casualty is enough.

"Yes, but you'll have a chance to show off your, *talents*, next week with your documentary. I think any more would be overexposure. Don't you?"

I know I have to agree, but that doesn't make it any easier. He called our bluff, but we knew he would. "I guess."

Callaghan stands. "That will be all, Mr. Dunsmore. I have an extremely busy day ahead."

"Yes, sir, but may I ask one question?"

He doesn't look at me when he says, "If you must," having already turned his attention to his computer.

"Why the hazing?"

He clicks his mouse and doesn't respond.

"Because I have a theory, but it could be just some stupid story I've concocted."

Callaghan turns and his face is his mask of evil. "That wouldn't surprise me. That's the way it is with your films. All the little lies you weave. It's a lazy man's storytelling. You're too busy with making it fit your premise to see that the details that get you there matter just as much as the whole."

This is it. I've got him engaged. Now or never. "Then tell me if I've got my details straight. Mallory is the money maker. His devotion to the programs is second to none because of his son. To both lacrosse and to tech. He brings it in and then Dr. Philmore directs it. And as long as you keep winning, it's all good."

Callaghan stares at me and I brace for the impact. "You can't let this go, can you, in spite of what I just said?"

"You just told me I was a lazy storyteller, not getting my facts straight, and here I am asking for them and you're telling me to let it go?"

Callaghan stills, no doubt measuring what he intends to say. "In a different context I may have had respect for you, Mr. Dunsmore. You've got a solid mind. But in this one, the only one that matters, I feel nothing but disgust at your inabilities. You cannot seem to rein yourself in. You are a slave to your own desires. You have no ability to serve a power higher than you. Your rituals are all self-serving."

He's right, I admit it. I have for so long served my wants, my desires. But not anymore. "Thank you," I say, and walk out of his office.

*　*　*

"If you can eat, the chicken salad is a good idea."

I turn to Q, who's standing behind me. "Yeah. Thanks." It's all I can manage.

We get our lunches and sit with Ella, who looks as strung out as I feel.

"You okay?" I ask.

"I think we're past the point where you get to ask that question." She stabs a cinnamon-covered apple slice with her fork and bites it in half.

Quinn eats his salad and looks at us, but says nothing.

We've kept him in the dark because it's just easier. The less anyone knows the better. But it now feels like Ella and I are sharing this enormous burden, and we both want to just be done.

"Could it get any more pathetic than this?" Gilbey sits down with us, followed by Alva.

"I hear we're not going to get to see the film you made for Mallory." Alva stares at me, a grin emerging.

"What?" Ella asks.

"Callaghan's decision," I say, and look away.

"I bet it would have been stupid, anyway. You didn't even get us kicking your ass," Gilbey says and laughs.

Alva clears his throat and shoots him a look. Gilbey ducks his head.

"There's still time. The documentary contest is next week." I bite my salad, even though my face feels numb.

Alva considers this. "You really are that stupid, aren't you? Handing me all the ammo I need ahead of time."

"My God, you're so much better than us. I should bow down or some shit. Or is that *eat* shit?" Ella says.

Alva looks at her like he might an opponent. "Who the fuck asked you to open your mouth?"

Gilbey laughs, Alva glares, and Ella glows red. I pray she doesn't lose it.

"I'll speak whenever I feel like it. Thanks. Use that line on your bitch girlfriend, but don't try that shit with me."

Alva smiles so wide and his eyes grow so cold he could be Callaghan's child. "I'll let her know you said that."

Ella fades to pink, but says, "Don't worry, she already knows."

Alva loses his grin, smart enough to know there's something to what Ella's said. He turns his attention to me, though. "As soon as this tournament is over, I'm coming after you. Mallory came in too early. I didn't get to finish. Not with you or Double Stuffed. Thought you would have understood that message. Shows how stupid you really are." He turns to Ella. "And don't think for one second we don't have things in store for you. Once a slut, always a slut." Alva and Gilbey stand and then walk away.

Quinn's shaking he's so mad, and Ella's staring into space, possibly plotting a murder. My salad is not even a third eaten, but there's no way I can get through another piece. I already feel like I've bitten off more than I can chew.

* * *

The auditorium is bubbling with noise. The entire school's piled in for the last hour of today. Instead of wanting them to all shut up, I'd be fine if we kept on like this for the rest of the hour. *Nervous* is as pathetic a description for my state as *dick* is for Alva.

Callaghan stands at the mic and raises his hand. The crowd settles. "Let me remind you that this is still the school day and that you are being held to our code of conduct." He scans the crowd. "Now, Mr. Mallory has a few words."

Ella and I both take a breath before the booster club president takes the mic. "Today marks the beginning of a long-standing tradition at our school, the Warrior tournament."

The school erupts with applause and Mallory smiles. "And

this year, we have something special for you."

I watch Callaghan, who leans just so slightly forward at this.

"Many of you know that my son, Max Mallory, was a star lacrosse player here. He died serving our country, but attributed his successful military career to the discipline and work ethic he received through lacrosse under Mr. Callaghan." Mallory extends a hand to our principal, who attempts to arrange his face into a smile.

The room booms with applause.

Mallory adjusts the mic and looks down. "Recently, a fellow student, after having spent time with our lacrosse team, asked if he could create a film to honor Max's memory and to serve as inspiration going into our tournament." Mallory pauses. "That student is Greg Dunsmore."

All heads turn to find me, and because of my size, most find their target, especially Callaghan, whose face is now ablaze.

Behind me, Quinn squeezes my shoulder. "Don't know what's going down, G, but keep breathing."

"I have seen the video, and it is simply a stunning tribute. We owe Greg a round of applause for his impressive ability." The school claps but then chants, "Dun the Ton!" over and over. Mallory waves them to stop and I search for Alva. He looks as if he's ready to bolt from his seat. Probably right for my face.

Ella reaches out and grabs my hand. She squeezes and doesn't let go.

"Well then, could we dim the lights?" Mallory asks, looking

up to the booth. As the lights dim, he steps away from the podium and Callaghan rushes to him.

Their exchange is tight, but it's obvious that our principal is unhappy. He says something and Mallory shakes his head. Mallory ignores Callaghan, and he speaks into the mic. "For the town. For our school. For Max. For all of us Warriors." He steps back and sits amid cheers.

Ella and I knew it would come to this, that we'd have to go to Mallory, that Callaghan would never let my work be shown. But once Mallory saw it, I knew the plan would work. And when I explained to him that I figured Callaghan would stop him, he said, "I'd like to see him try." Because there is no one in this town that would deny Mr. Mallory a chance to showcase our most beloved hero. I'm just sorry that no one here will get to see that video.

The lights go off and just as the film begins I say to Ella, "Whatever happens, I'm proud of you."

Her title pops: *Film This*. No one understands. But they will.

In the movie *Fight Club*, the main character works the camera at a movie theater. While there, he splices brief shots of porn into children's movies. The images are subtle, yet not subtle at all. They're jarring because of what they show, but also because the audience has to ask itself, *Did I really see what I think I did?* It's a brilliant tactic, and Ella has used it effectively.

The first image is the bros dropping from the balls striking them in the faces and guts. Then it's right to the drills I filmed with the GoPro. The school shrugs but no more. The bros surround Callaghan, and his sermon about ritual fills the auditorium. I see Mallory's confusion and hope that he doesn't interrupt this, because this is not the film he saw. He's rooted in place, and seems intrigued rather than upset.

On screen, following Callaghan's speech, there's a brief clip of a boy in compression shorts and a full nelson. Callaghan's voice is just audible, "What's going on here?"

Sure, it could have been part of the film, his voice, just background noise, but that image, no way. Heads turn now.

Back to drills for a minute and all is settled. I squeeze Ella's hand. She's placid, watching her film as if it's someone else's.

The next scene is of the bros, Alva talking about the strength of the team and the sport at the school and then it cuts away to two boys being force fed, and the contents on the spoon are very brown.

Someone in the audience yells, "Hold the fuck up!" but the film keeps going. More shots, extolling the camaraderie of the team, and then the screen darkens and I'm glad the lights are off because there's just the perfect amount of saturation in order to see the outline of our gym, a wall of bros wrapping around, and me in the middle, facing Alva and Gilbey. I watch the first punch but have to look away. Ella puts her arm around my shoulders. I've watched this enough to be desensitized, but not here, not now.

The next scene, though, is the clincher and I pull myself together for it.

Callaghan stands with a loaded lacrosse stick, ready to fire, as the underclassmen chant: *Our allegiance is to the Warriors, our bodies are weapons . . .*

"Watch and learn, boys," Callaghan says, and fires the first ball into a lax bro.

As it was in the gym when I recorded this, it is the same now—stunned silence.

Callaghan whips the ball at the next bro's head and he goes down.

"The words. Let me *hear* them! Your tournament is right around the corner. Without discipline, you will disappoint. If you disappoint, this will only get worse."

The drill continues, and around us, the audience flinches and cries out until it's over and just our principal is on the screen, and he speaks his truth.

"Put away your fear of being hurt and replace it with your desire to inflict pain. Then, and only then, will you ever succeed."

Next, Ella has filled a black screen with simple white text:

PAIN IS THE MOST EFFICIENT OF TEACHERS, ITS LESSONS NEVER LOST, EVEN WHEN WE ARE.

There is silence. There is Ella's hand holding mine. There is my heart pounding. And there are three sensations. One, elation over having pulled it off. Two, guilt because of how Mr. Mallory must feel. Three, fear of whatever's next.

Callaghan strides to the center of the stage and screams

into the mic. "Turn it off!" But the film has already ended and Callaghan stands against the dark screen with the title of the film burning over his shoulder. "Lights!" They pop on and he surveys the crowd, who are all talking and pointing and looking confused and angry. Mallory is stupefied.

"Silence! I said, silence!" Callaghan's voice booms from the speakers and the school obeys. I can only see his profile, but it's enough to notice how hard he's gripping the mic and how much he's grinding his teeth.

"We should go," I whisper to Ella.

"It's too late, Greg, there's nowhere to go." She doesn't sound upset at this, just matter of fact. And she's right. We keep our seats.

"What you all just saw is a betrayal. That film was obviously peppered with a misguided attempt to cast our lacrosse team in a negative light. We all know about Greg's past films, his *lies*! Therefore, all of this is circumspect." Callaghan seethes while staring across the sea of students.

Someone yells, "Bullshit!" Another, "Show it again!"

There's a resounding swell of agreement and then a chant begins, "Show it again! Show it again!"

My heart swells. The one pumping the blood through me so that I can appreciate what is happening, so that I can appreciate the girl whose hand I'm holding. I feel swollen with pride in our work, and what it has done. Because these kids know. I'm sure comments are already on Facebook, Twitter, and wherever else. As much as I hate these kids for all the bullshit they've put me through. It's not all of them, only a fraction. The majority is rising up now. And holy hell, I helped make this happen.

Callaghan stupidly calls for silence again. It's not happening. He looks around for assistance, but there's no one around, only the bros, who look equally pissed and confused. "Goddamn you, Dunsmore!" he screams and slams the mic onto the stage.

That does it. The room is quiet once more.

Callaghan stands at the edge and finds me in the crowd.

"Don't you think for one second that you'll get away with this! I will have you expelled from this school. You can kiss any thought of film school good-bye. You fat, conniving little shit. You will not undermine all I have created," he snaps, and Alva and Gilbey pounce.

Callaghan's not really saying and doing what he seems to be? Right? But he is. And that must mean he just doesn't care anymore. I know that feeling all too well. With this realization comes fear greater than any I've felt before. Callaghan, unwound, is capable of anything.

"These boys are going to carry you out of here, and they will tear you from limb to limb. I hope you're satisfied."

His words trail as Alva and Gilbey approach. I release Ella's hand and stand. If this is what it's going to come down to, so be it.

Alva punches me in the gut and I double over. Gilbey follows with an uppercut to my nose. Blood sprays. They back away at this, and I'm able to stand. Quinn jumps in.

"All right, G. Let's do this."

I grab him before he can throw. "No. Not this way. Let me do my thing."

"What?"

"Trust me."

Quinn gives the slightest of nods, but I know he's going to break his hand on one of their faces if this doesn't work.

Alva's smiling and Gilbey's bouncing on his toes.

"Go ahead. Keep throwing your punches. Knock me out again. Tea bag me, again. Beat me until I'm unconscious and keep at it until I'm dead." I step closer. "Because you're only doing what you're told. It's not really your fault."

Alva works his jaw. "The fuck are you talking about?"

"He did this. Callaghan. I know all about it. All about you. What's been done. You are a warrior, Andrew. You've done your job. You've paid the price to get here. You have lived by the code. But none of that matters now. The higher order you serve is gone."

Alva's eyes glisten, and it must be from anger, from the restraint it's taking him to listen to me. But something tells me it's not. "How, Dun? How *doesn't* it matter? How is it all *gone*? Your stupid film has done nothing. Like always. The tournament's here. We are going to win State. We will be champions, again."

"No. No, you won't." I turn and I see what I knew I would: a school that figured out the instructions behind Ella's film title, because we knew it would come to this, too.

Almost everyone has a phone in hand, recording.

I turn back to Alva. "Because we've just filmed this."

CHAPTER 33

ELLA'S HOME SMELLS LIKE FLOWERS and something sweet. Not sugar or syrup, but something more potent.

It's been a little over a month since the pep rally and so much has gone down. Callaghan has been suspended, pending an investigation. Dr. Philmore's still working, but he's under the microscope as well. The bro's season was canceled, which devastated the town, and is the reason Ella, Quinn, and I joined Ollie for tutoring for the rest of the year. Our lawyers agreed we would receive too much unwanted attention. Which really meant we wouldn't be safe, not with angry bros prowling, as well as some in the community still supporting them. But there are signs that things are changing. People are starting to accept the truth.

That's because the team is willing to talk. The cops have everything I recorded and they use it to interview the bros. So Kyle and Stephen tell me. There will be a trial, or multiple ones, really, and we'll have to testify. I'm sure it will get ugly, but that's the price, and I know I'm willing to pay it.

"Ready, Greg?" Ella smiles and my insides feel light, but I don't have to tell myself to be cool anymore. She accepts me, and that helps me from getting all sorts of awkward.

We head out to work on settings and capturing transitions for our work. Ella's enrolled in some online film course, and I'm doing the lessons with her. Really, I'm just trying to keep up.

We shoot kids driving by in cars. Some flip us off. Others honk and swear. I find something dead and crawling with insects and Ella records the ants carrying the pieces away. A house is being built and so we shoot roofers flipping sections of plywood to a guy perched on the frame, shirtless, smoking a cigarette without touching it, placing every piece perfectly. We're getting the hang of it.

"Break?" she asks.

I'm already a swampy mess so it's a no-brainer. "Yeah. Under the tree."

We sit and drink from our water bottles and the breeze feels good.

"Are you going away this summer?" Ella asks and wipes her mouth on her wrist.

"I don't think so. You know, the trials and all. My parents think it best to stick around. Maybe after?"

She nods. "Yeah, I think we might be doing the same. It sucks, though, we'll be stuck around here, caged up."

"We already are." I laugh.

"How do you think it will be next year, when we go back?"

"Quinn says he's only going to work out once a day, and Ollie's going to be homecoming king."

"What about you, Greg?" Ella's tone's light, but I know she wants me to give her a real answer.

I've thought a lot about this, and it's weird, because I've hated school for so long that looking forward to it seems impossible. Yet, it's more than that.

"I don't think I ever told you my story, the reason, I think, for why I ended up like I did."

Ella doesn't speak, just looks at me and waits.

"It was at the end of fifth grade, I had this teacher, Mr. Tanner. He was a cool guy, always made a big deal out of everyone's birthdays. He held a party at the end of the year for all the kids whose birthdays were over the summer, like me." I can see the classroom, our little desks in clusters, the sun pouring in, everyone smiling. "So he brought in all this food—cupcakes, cookies, ice cream, and on and on. Well, surprise, surprise, I stuffed myself. Seriously, I ate six cupcakes, I don't know how many cookies, and a heaping bowl of ice cream. The kids laughed because it was crazy how much I was packing away."

"That wasn't your first time, though, was it?"

"What, eating that much?"

She nods.

"No, it wasn't. And maybe Mr. Tanner guessed that. I don't know. Or maybe he was just nervous I was going to puke every-where, because he pulled me aside and said, 'Greg, fat kids eat like that. You don't want to be a fat kid, do you?'"

Ella sighs.

"Yeah, it was uncomfortable, and then it stayed with me, that question. And of course I didn't. Who does? But something inside kept telling me I already was a fat kid, so I should just go with it, keep eating." I look up at the clouds. "And I did."

"That is some kind of crazy self-fulfilling prophecy," Ella says.

"I know. Talk about saying the wrong thing at the perfect time."

"I hear you. So, how does that relate to school next year? Are you going to hunt down Mr. Tanner and kick his ass?" She laughs, but I think she's halfway serious.

"No, no, that's not it. I'm not blaming anyone. It may sound that way, but I've been thinking about this, now that I'm not wor-ried about getting killed by the bros. I think I could legitimately point the finger at teachers, or my parents, the kids at school, and certainly at myself. But where does that get me?"

"I don't know."

"Exactly. So the hell with it. School next year is going to be like the first time that I can go in with a fresh start."

"How so? You're going to have all of this shit behind you."

"Right. But that's not what matters."

"How? Look at what happened to me. Certain things follow you, whether you like it or not."

"You're right, and I have to learn to be okay with that. I know I'm never going to escape my past. My 'fresh start' is being able to roll with that. To let things happen and not feel compelled to manipulate anything. To trust in the truth of things and embrace that." I lean back and feel the breeze lift my shirt. I don't immediately pull it down over my belly.

"Damn, Greg. That's deep. You have been thinking. Good."

"Glad you think so." I sip my water. "So are you coming over tonight?"

"As if you even needed to ask me."

*   *   *

Quinn is the last to arrive, but he has good reason, he had to wait for his dad, who hangs behind us with my dad, while Ollie, Ella, and I take up the couch, and Quinn and Mom bookend us on the chairs.

"Everyone ready?" I ask, and my stomach is spinning in circles. I've edited and reedited this piece countless times. It's not completely finished, because I'm not completely finished. Neither is Ollie, and I'm guessing the same is true for Ella and Quinn. But that's the point.

This weight loss transformation video was supposed to be the crowning jewel for Blint's class, my middle finger to the school. But it has morphed into something much greater. Here we all are, which means so much to me, I can't put it into words. And so I try to swallow the enormous lump in my throat. I stare at the TV. I feel amazing, and Ella's hand finds mine as I press PLAY.

ACKNOWLEDGMENTS

I spent close to two years as a personal trainer, and I have spent over twelve as an educator. The only times I have ever witnessed authentic change is when the client or student was willing to leave the past behind, but not to escape from it, rather to learn from it. Those who were able to maintain the trajectory were the ones who made the change for themselves, not for anyone else. It is my sincerest hope that Greg's transformation is as authentic as those I have had the privilege to see.

I am fortunate to have such amazing professionals to work with, people who watch my own transformation and cheer. My agent, Kate McKean, is as staunch an advocate for my writing as any author could hope for. She, again, provided me with her incredible insight on *Press Play*, and can claim a win for selecting the title. Thank you, Kate, for all your diligence, patience, and guidance.

This is the third project of mine Lisa Cheng has edited, and her vision, as always, was superb. She manages to see both the forest and the trees and helped me navigate with deft suggestions and spot-on questions. Thank you, Lisa, for your steadfast belief in all that I am capable of.

Carrie, my wife. You alone are witness to my personal growth. And you alone have always been the catalyst. Thank you for your unwavering love and support.

My daughters, Grace and Kaygan. I am anxious for you to read my books, but not just yet. I don't want you to grow up too fast, because I love you both, just how you are.

To my family, who is so often in the dark until they get a final copy, my constant thanks for understanding that these stories are so worth the wait.

Mark Ayotte. This has been one transformative year for you, and you have weathered the storm with such strength. Thank you for finding the time to read my work, while your own story has been so tumultuous.

To my friends, who enjoy this crazy road I'm on, but who would still be there for me if I weren't, thank you for accepting who I am.

And thanks to my fellow authors and booksellers and bloggers and everyone else in this community. All of life is a story. Thank you for helping to foster mine.